SKIN TOUR
BY R.W. CLINGER

Herndon, VA

Herndon, VA

Special thanks to Stephanie Ciummo for all her help and support.

We make an awesome team, Baby Bunny!

When my computer crashed, Mary Arnold was there to pick up the debris. A big thanks.

I'd like to give a great big man-hug of thanks to those at STARbooks Press for their invaluable assistance, teamwork and believing in my work

For Kenito, always.

CONTENTS

Part One – Bring on the Men

Chapter 1 – Ogling Mr. Chaz

I should be hard for Mr. Chaz's high school jock son, but I'm not. Instead, I have an interest in Mr. Chaz, or Daddy, as I often call him: forty-one years old, shoulders of a linebacker, eyes of grey-steel, narrow lips, thick stubble on his chin, a ladder-like chest covered in thin black hair, smooth as butter between his legs and under his arms. He's been divorced from Margaret Chaz for the past six months. Corey, his seventeen-year-old son, comes to visit his father every other weekend; Corey's cute, but not hot like his daddy.

I know why the Chaz marriage didn't work out. And, maybe other tenants in the apartment building in Flamingo Cove, Florida, know, too. Mr. Chaz obviously could not keep his eight inches of hard cock in his chinos while married to his accountant wife. He liked blond errand boys with sculpted tummies and taut bottoms. One adorable blond boy after the next ripped their unhappy marriage apart; this is why he lives in apartment 4-E, forced to move out of his Tudor because of his extracurricular activities with men. I even know some of the blonds' names: Colin, Tyler and Rocket. I must admit he has good taste in errand boys, especially if they're twenty-four, fit and horny – just like me.

We play a game, which is just between men. Something just for kicks. Boy Flirting with Daddy/Boy Needing Daddy. His body language says to me: Come and play with me, Derek. Eat me up. Do something dirty with me. Use me the way you want to use me. If you want me ... now is the time. Don't be shy. I'm here for all of your naughty needs. Ogle my goods, and let me shake my ass in your face. Go ahead and sniff my balls. You know I like that. I always like that.

So I ogle and sniff the architect and continue to play our game. I become naughty and on the brink of falling in love, lust ... something with him. Truth is I just want to be close to his skin, surrendering to my greed for his professional flesh to touch my flesh. Mr. Chaz is my obsession and likeness, someone I sort of crave and desire more than anything.

I don't give him gifts: a paperback novel by Peter Cameron, a box of chocolates with caramel centers, a blue-and-gold striped tie. Nor do I follow him to 2838 Rossner Street where he sometimes works on the fifth floor. I don't know his friends: Ivan Mercer, Raub Spenston and Leo Hough. I never watch him eat lunch at Pyro's Deli, enjoying a Rueben with a small scoop of potato salad and a diet iced tea. I don't look through his mail: electric bill, flyers for local grocery stores and the latest issue of *Money*. And never – absolutely never! – do I break into his apartment when he's not at home and use his soap and shampoo in his shower, take a whiff of his boxer-briefs from a hamper, and climb into his sheets on his queen-sized bed and take a nap.

I'm not this type of man.

Honestly.

Did I mention that sometimes I lie?

"Good morning, Mr. Chaz," I say with an ear-to-ear smile. I stand at his apartment door, holding a cardboard tube filled with blueprints. Of course I already have a boner in my jeans, knowing exactly what is about to happen between us.

Mr. Chaz smiles back from his foyer, eyeing up my blond curls and pretty boy face, thin eyebrows, sharp nose and medium-sized shoulders. He studies my five-eleven frame, rippled stomach and biceps, and possibly drools with affection. "As usual, you're right on time, Derek," he says, looking delicious this morning in his gold tie and snug jeans, edible in all the right areas. "I'm glad you caught me. I was just getting ready to head into the office and accomplish some work."

"You can do some work on me," I suggest, heavily flirting with him, grabbing my junk with an open palm and tugging it with a gentle pull.

I hand him the cardboard tube and collect a check as my payment. Is the money for sex today? Is it ever for sex? I'm never really sure. But, if he wants to pay me for sex, pumping my rump with his hearty dick, then I will be glad to accommodate my homoerotic nature to his needs. The offer will be accepted without question. I will become a hustler and take his money, plus a tip, whatever he has to offer. This doesn't happen today, though. Mr. Chaz merely thanks me for my services, and I turn away, ready to carry out the rest of my day.

"Derek," he clears his throat. "Do you have a moment?"

I maybe have the rest of my life for him. I stop dead in my tracks and spin around like a go-go dancer. "As a matter of fact, I do."

Pink flamingo boys! The man is far too handsome for my sexual hunger. Daddy-perfect for my queer needs in all the right ways. He is a six-two structure of beefy muscle and Hollywood face. Everything about him is to die for. Think George Clooney with a splash of rugged gay.

I want to touch him with my fingers, tongue and cock. I want to rip his clothes off, baring his bottom and tools. I want to be pounded by the architect: on the hardwood floor, over the couch, against the wall – anywhere. I want him to squirt his manly seed into my ass as he applies bite marks to my corded neck. I want him to spank me and call me the nastiest names. I want him to ...

"Come in. We need to talk business."

Whatever he wants. I step inside his apartment. Everything is brown and masculine. It looks like an office at a bank instead of a middle-aged man's place of residence. I take a seat on a brown leather sofa, and he sits across from me in a matching chair. His legs are spread wide open, and he shows off his private goods to me: a denim covered treat to fulfill my hunger; something that I have been craving since our last encounter, which was just two days ago.

"Derek, how long have you worked for me?"

"Since you moved in. Six months."

"It's been a progressive six months."

"I hope so."

He reaches between his spread legs and adjusts himself; it's enough to make me go mad, wetting my thirst for his skin and our bodies to connect. Mr. Chaz says, "You've obviously established yourself in a professional manner during this short period of time."

3

"I try to do my best."

"Of course you do."

I'm edgy in his presence. Our meetings are always so short and direct: deliver these documents to The Borman Agency on Cuba Street; copy these blueprints; don't forget to pick up my dry cleaning. This is what I do. This is how I make my living.

"I need you for something simple, Derek."

I hope it's to climb between his legs and rip off his stylish denim with my teeth again, growling like a dog. I nod my head, hungry for his skin. Maybe he wants me to accomplish this. Maybe not. I'm not sure. Will he let me bite him? Does he want to be bitten? Or, am I to be gentle with his flesh, like most times, submissive to his man-handling and rough play.

"I need your opinion regarding these jeans." He stands and shows off the denim. He turns around and wiggles his ass like a naughty supermodel. This is just part of our little game. A teasing and pleasing act between men. Perhaps foreplay before some heavy-duty, rock-my-rump sex.

He has a nice ass: compact, bulbous and trim. No, it's a beautiful ass: perfectly squeezable, kissable and lickable. My cock jumps a little in my own jeans at the sight of it. Droplets of thick cream leak out of my hose and decorate the cotton cup of my boxer briefs. I begin to sweat under my arms, and my heart races with a chaotic tempo.

The sex game continues. He's very good at his character today. I'm weak in the knees. Hungry for him. Honry as hell. Ready to strip him out of his clothes with my fingers and mouth. We deserve Academy Awards; this is how much we've mastered our shared game.

"So, what do you think?" He runs a palm along his right buttock, spins around, shakes his goods, and says, "I was meant to tease men."

The magic of this game always prompts questions, and this is why it never becomes old. Is he semi-hard? What has he been feeding his dick? Is his cock really that big? I swallow saliva down the back of my throat and blink a few times. I'm not even drinking and feel intoxicated, numb because of the architect's wicked performance.

He steps around the coffee table that temporarily separates our bodies. Mr. Chaz moves up to me and says, "Go ahead and touch it. Something tells me you want to."

Let the game continue. Amen! I have more questions on my end: How does he know that I want to fondle his goods? Is he clairvoyant? What kind of other superhuman powers does he have that I don't know about?

"You've been sleeping in my bed when I'm not here," he confronts me, making me feel like a very bad, bad boy. "You've been using my shower and eating my food."

I'm not surprised by his accusations. Some days I can't stay away from Mr. Chaz, overly fixated with him and everything in his singlehood world. Helplessly, I utter, "I didn't mean to. Honestly, I didn't."

"Some of my clothes are missing. Do you have them?"

"I do," I whisper. It's no lie. I'm not keen on lying – sometimes. I keep his clothes in a meticulous pile next to my bed: dress shirts and shorts, underwear, cotton socks, a jacket and belt. Someday I will give them all back; then again, maybe not.

"You've used my toothbrush and deodorant."

"I have," I admit.

I also take things from his apartment, which I guess he knows about: his remote controls, pictures, glasses, ties, blueprints, pens, an umbrella, statuettes, linen napkins, his razor, and a couple paperback novels. Keepsakes. Things to remind me of Mr. Chaz. His belongings that I can now call my own. My secret stash.

"Shame on me. I should be spanked. Are you going to spank me, Mr. Chaz?"

A smile rises on his face: helplessly greedy, sexually animated, without any inhibitions whatsoever. "I just may do that, Derek."

"And, you'll make it hurt?"

5

"Only if you want it to, of course."

I do want it to hurt; this is why I visit him on the fourth floor. Young men need spanked for using an architect's toothbrush and deodorant. What other punishment is there?

"I'll have to slap your mouth with my cock."

"I like when you do that."

"You sound eager."

"I'm always eager to be your boy. It's why you like me. You do like me, Mr. Chaz, right?"

"Of course I do ... naked and prepared to be fucked. I like you over the arm of the living room sofa the best. Is that how you want it today?"

"I do ... yes. Sooner than later." I'm ready to reach out for his extension of man-goods when his cell phone buzzes on the coffee table. Mr. Chaz breaks off his proposal when he looks down at the cellular and sees that it's Corey, his son, calling.

He says something disheartening like: "I really must get this."

Fuck! I'm ignored. He walks out of the living room with his son against his left ear. I don't know what they talk about. Nor do I care. I'm over the cock-tease and decide to leave, sneaking out of his apartment, unheard.

If Mr. Chaz asked me to marry him tomorrow, I would. Honestly, I wouldn't even have to think about; this is how much I like him. Is it love? I'm not sure. Do I want to be in love with him? Perhaps; again, I'm not sure.

I dream of owning a house in Virginia with the architect, something palatial and uppity with giant white columns and floor-to-ceiling windows. Maybe Tara from *Gone With the Wind*. A plantation just for men and boys. I want a staff of ten: groundskeepers, butler, cook, chauffer and maid; bare-chested young men who are fresh out of high school that I can ogle and crave, but never touch. And, I want to own this plantation with Mr. Chaz. Acres after acres of land that is planted with tobacco or cotton and ...

I want him to be my boyfriend, if nothing else. Someone I can watch movies with on a Saturday night and cuddle against his bare skin. A person I can tell my secrets to and not worry about being judged for them. A significant other I can wake up to every morning, stare into his shadowy eyes, and be the happiest man in the world, knowing I have someone to love next to me.

Until this dream happens, I still have our game. Mr. Chaz will let me be his pet, and I will only bite him if he asks me to. He will welcome me into his apartment, and I will comfortably fall on my knees with an open mouth. Cordially, I will suck his rod or apply smooth and long strokes to his tight bottom. If he wants me to pinch his quarter-sized nipples, I will. If he asks me to run my fingertips up and along his hairy chest, pressing them into his flesh, I will. If he begs to have his drooping balls to be lapped and sucked, I will. This is what our game entails. This is our relationship ... until the next level, when he finally asks me to be his boyfriend/lover/husband – someone of a privileged position in his life.

We can build things together as a couple: a life, romance, erections.

Too bad I like him more than he likes me.

His loss, I guess.

Our game is over now, but only temporarily. Mr. Chaz will call me again. I'll run up to his apartment, and he'll beg me to ogle his skin. He'll call me a very bad boy, pat me on my head, and if I'm good, he may just feed me a treat.

For now, I back away. I find my apartment and watch some *Oprah*. I read a few chapters of Michael Cunningham's *The Hours*. I bathe in bubbles. Awaiting his call is half the fun.

Chapter 2 – One's Private Affair

The apartment building at 2711 Flamingo Cove doesn't have a name; its tenants merely call it "the building." The structure is eight floors high, has over forty apartments inside, a laundry area in the basement, and a screened-in gym and pool in the rear. Approximately sixty residents live in the building. Sinese Management owns the building, one among three properties along Florida's Gulf coast. Oliver South is the maintenance guy. Chase Belldin is the lawn and pool boy. Mr. Tummie is the mailman. Carla Withers does Avon and Tupperware. Joey Morelli can set up a fitness program for just about anybody. Robb Wentworth does nails and hair in apartment 2-C. And Fisk Deveraux grows pot on the eighth floor.

In truth, we are one happy family. Flamingo Cove is quiet, relaxed and super queer. Republicans tend to stay away – thank God! European boys are always welcome. And, the pool area doesn't require suits, only if you're considered hot by a majority of tenants.

Felicia Horodowski, the forty-something lesbian in 1-B, has stomach cancer and requires a fresh dose of marijuana for her pain. This is where Fisk Deveraux comes in handy.

Let me explain: I run errands for over thirty-five tenants in the building; this is how I pay my rent and purchase provisions. I obtain my daily exercise by running the stairs instead of using the two elevators. So after leaving *Oprah*, Cunningham and my bubble bath, I climb to the top of the building and hook up with Fisk in apartment 8-F.

Fisk is the building's likable and accommodating drug dealer; every apartment complex has one. The guy is a sexy twenty-year-old Italian, hung like a fucking horse, over-the-top hunk with narrow shoulders, a comfortable lisp, capable looks that men and boys drool over, and has an appetite for redheads. Fisk flunked out of Flamingo Cove College in his sophomore year because of too much drug use; his major was business management, which was no surprise. Now, he makes money from dealing, has never been busted, and continues to sell whatever is needed and cheap on the drug market.

I knock three times on his apartment door, but he doesn't answer. Fisk is probably blitzed on a green pill called Smooth, unable to answer his door, which has happened a number of times before. Like most of my employers' apartments, I have a key to find my way inside. Fisk's key is marked with a green marijuana leaf, which doesn't need any further explanation.

The marijuana key is on a ring in my front pocket. I dig it out, slip it into his door, turn the knob on the door, walk inside and ...

Holy fucking Tinkerbell! Fisk is buck-naked on the middle of his living room floor. Two orange-satin pillows rest under his head. His legs are in mid-air and spread wide open. The guy man-handles a black dildo in his tight asshole and watches two firemen fucking on a massive LG screen in front of him.

To my surprise, he doesn't know I've entered his apartment, witnessing his solo playtime. I stand next to the door, decide to quietly close it behind me, and keep watching him in motion.

The dealer lets out a grunt and pushes the tool inside his hairless ass. His cock is nine inches of cement, lying flat against his lower torso. Bubbles of man-sap drip out of its untouched cap. He sweats from head to toe as the firemen on the flat screen share some heavy barebacking. Fisk whimpers with delight at the sight of the hot and steamy action. Another inch of black plastic is shoved into his bottom and he murmurs, "Fuck me ... Fuck me hard." He pulls the dildo out of his middle, pushes it in, pulls it out, in, out, in and ...

I must leave, but decide to stay – shame on me. Intruding on one's private affair with a plastic tool can be a favorite hobby for an errand boy, right? The horny voyeur in me decides this is true, so I stay and study the young man at work.

The firemen on the LG continue to rock each other's worlds with some heavy-duty cock-in-ass motion. Fisk is wide-eyed and pushes another inch of plastic into his pink core. He lets out a masculine whine and spreads his legs wider.

I am still unseen at the door, armor-hard between my legs. I think about whipping my goods out and man-handling them, totally turned-on by Fisk's motion. I'm a good boy, though, keep zipped up, and continue to watch his dildo-ride.

With his left hand occupying the tool in his rear, Fisk begins to play with his cock by using his right hand. Fingers and palm start to rub the nine inches up and down. Sweat rolls off the bridge of his nose and firm tummy. The dildo enters his bottom yet another inch, this time staying there. He grumbles with delight because of his handy work. Fisk's strokes are masterful, long and fruitful. The motion becomes faster and steady. His strident handjob is now synchronized with the firemen's fucking.

I should leave; really, I should. Instead, I stand open-mouthed and stern, disbelieving the drug dealer's sexual potential. How amazed I am at his gyrating hand and dildo-filled bottom. How unbelievable it is for me to watch him in motion with the two male actors on the screen. Fisk is an animal with his hand and cock, a maniac on a mission of sexual accomplishment.

His fist rides up and down. Again, he pulls the dildo from its hole and immediately pushes it back inside. A testosterone-boosted grunt escapes his gliding body. His stroking becomes stronger with the progressive movement of the plastic tool in his ass. Fisk's face turns completely red as he heaves for breath. His eyes become wide, and his mouth opens with ecstasy.

It's too late to stumble away now. Let the ooze-fest begin. I want to observe Fisk in his final act of pornographic bliss as he blows his load.

White shoot twirls out of his cock's head when the firemen come on the big screen. The juice splatters against Fisk's clean-shaven chest, decorating his nipples. Moans escape his writhing torso. More sap fires out of his hose, glazing his bod. He continues to pump his beef with the same rhythm he pumps the dildo in and out of his ass.

Fisk groans.

Fisk continues to shoot.

Fisk pushes the black tool into his man-sliver, as far as it will go.

It's over quickly. The firemen are turned off, and the drug dealer lies limp on his floor.

I think about quietly slipping out of his apartment, just as I have entered, but can't.

Fisk rolls onto his left side and asks, "Did you like watching?"

"Was I supposed to?"

"You bet your faggot ass."

"I'd rate it an eight out of ten. You can do better, of course."

"Above average. I can handle that."

"I'm sure you can. A guy like you only wants to grow in life, right?" I walk to the sofa and pick up his clean, cotton towel. I toss the towel to him. "Just for the record, I like it when a guy eats his own goo."

"It's not too late," Fisk says. He finds some splatter on his right nipple with two fingertips and slips them into his mouth. Once his treat is over, he asks, "Do you want a lick?"

"I'm not into that."

"Shame on me. I should know what you're into, Derek." He starts to clean up his mess with the towel, using slow and wide strokes.

"To tell you the truth, I'm into a straight guy on the fourth floor."

"Mr. Chaz?"

I'm not surprised Fisk knows him. Fisk gets around the complex like the flu. "That's him."

"Get in line. Everyone likes the architect. No queer in this building has licked or fucked his body yet. Your odds are better if you try for someone else like me."

I don't kiss and tell (sometimes). I keep quiet about my tool-rising adventures and sex games with the architect for the past six months. No need to start gossip about myself, right?

Fisk covers up his private parts with the towel. He pats the spot beside him on the floor. "I'll let you fuck me if you want."

It's cheap but flattering. "Maybe next time."

"You don't know what you're missing, Derek. I can be a handful, if you know what I mean."

I shake my head and lie. "I don't like it rough."

"Of course you don't. Pretty boy you probably like it smooth and slow, right?"

We've never broached this topic before. Fucking 101 exhausts me, and I simply blurt out, "Felicia's pain is increasing, and I need some MJ if you have any."

"How about some S&M?"

Cute. Fisk doesn't easily give up, does he? I pull out fifty from a pocket and say, "Here's the green. I'm kind of in a hurry. Can you help me out or not?"

"I'll give it to you for free if you fuck me."

Maybe if he wasn't so easy, I would. I mean, he is nice to look at: Hollywood face, porn-perfect rod and ripped torso. But why does he have to be such a guy-whore? I shake my head, find an answer, and confess, "Maybe next time. I'll take the MJ, though."

"Suit yourself." Fisk pushes his muscular weight up and off the floor, drops the dirty towel next to the sofa, and struts away in his glorious buff, vanishing into his kitchen. I hear two ceramic surfaces rub against each other; a cookie jar maybe. Fisk comes back into the living room still buck naked; his cock almost hangs down to his knees.

He hands me a paper bag.

I hand him the fifty.

"Just so you know, I've always wanted you to fuck me," he confesses.

"Maybe someday I'll surprise you and take you up on your offer."

"I like surprises. Come back anytime."

"I'll do that."

"I'll be waiting."

13

Chapter 3 – Needing Something Naughty

I have a key to apartment 1-B, Felicia Horodowski's place. Once inside, Princess Scampers meets me at the door. She is a pink-eared, all-white feline with golden eyes. The cat absolutely loves me – just like her owner. Scampers twirls around my legs and mews affectionately. I dance fingertips between her ears. Her fur is clean and soft, and she purrs with delight, welcoming my return.

Since Hilda Marchino arrives three times a week to clean Felicia's apartment, 1-B is a spotless, dust-free museum with nothing out of place. Throughout the tenant's forty-seven years, she has collected various artists' works, mostly oils on canvas. The paintings are by W. Dunbar, Zelda Zelot and Rosemary Franklin, among other vibrant works adorning the pastel-colored walls. 1-B has cherry wood floors and the faint sounds of Bach.

"Derek, is that you?" Felicia calls from her bedroom, which is down the narrow hallway of paintings, to the right.

"Yeah, it's me!" I inform, and carry the paper bag from Fisk down the hall, entering my employer's private bedroom.

The bedroom is all pink and taffeta with oversized furniture. Two paintings by Flamingo Cove's own, Desmon Writer, hang above Felicia's king-sized bed. The paintings are both oil seascapes, large canvases that take up most of the wall.

Princess Scampers jumps from the floor to the bed, and lands on the down-feather comforter. She positions herself on Felicia's left side; a statue of protection.

Felicia is stunning for a woman who has less than three months to live. She is dressed in a pale-pink silk nightie. Her blonde-grey hair is disheveled, as usual, and she drinks her favorite evening cocktail, blue gin over crushed ice.

Although she is still stunning in all ways, the once-actress resembles something dead and creepy from a horror film. Her cheeks are pitted and shadowy. When she attempts to smile an empty hollow is seen. Her face is ashen in color, and quite sunken. The cancer has caused a crime to her physical beauty. Felicia is somewhat grotesque, a ghoul on Halloween. But inside, she is sunshine, warm-hearted and radiant, a breath of fresh air in all her pollution.

Princess Scampers curls into a ball at Felicia's hip. The retired actress strokes the feline, causing the furry ball to purr. "Did Fisk help us today?"

"Fisk is the nicest drug pusher in Flamingo Cove," I say. I walk to the bed and present the brown lunch bag to her bedded majesty.

She opens the paper bag and pulls out a plastic baggie filled with pot. A smile attempts to take over her face, but the muscles in her cheeks are just not up to the work.

"Fisk says it's top-notch stuff."

"He's such a good boy." Felicia opens the baggie and lifts it to her nostrils. She inhales deeply and closes her almost-lifeless eyes. "This is so good, Derek. I can't thank you enough for fetching it and helping me. One of these days you'll be paid greatly for your kindness and services."

We have sweet tea and joints together. Felicia tries to give me money for "just because" reasons, but I kindly decline. I tell her, "The errand is already paid for."

"That's absurd. You should never decline money from an old woman."

"You are not old."

The pot is fresh, a pure plant without additives. Felicia giggles after a few puffs. I giggle. She rambles on and on about her days in the movies, mentioning her favorite films: *Web of Sin*, *The Carpenter's Wife* and *Spinvelda*.

I imagine Felicia twenty years younger in Hollywood. She was a head-turner, a bombshell. Never an Academy Award winner, but always nominated. She worked with Robert Redford, Meryl Streep and Al Pacino. Felicia was Hollywood, a star then and a star now, one of the most beautiful and talented women in the world.

We drink the sweet tea and smoke joints. She blows the pot into Princess Scampers's face and says, "Wuvie needs to get high wif Momma."

I laugh.

She laughs.

Princess Scampers purrs and twitches her tail.

"Can I tell you a secret, Felicia?"

"Oh yes, darling. You know how I adore secrets. Please share."

"It's quite scandalous."

"Even better."

I tell her about walking in on Fisk's playtime alone, the firemen porno on his LG flat screen, and the black dildo sticking out of his ass. The tale is good medicine for Felicia. She laughs as I have never heard her laugh before, which makes me happy.

Following her spell of healthy stomach pains and more pot, she demands me to share the Fisk story again, which I kindly do.

Our time is generous together. She is like the aunt I have never had. We giggle and share dirty jokes like young girls. She instructs me to raid the refrigerator for tiny cheese cubes, the cupboards for Triscuits, and whatever else will curb our munchies.

Before leaving, Felicia coaxes me to her side for a brief kiss. She holds my cheeks and says, "I have a very special gift for you, Derek."

"What might that be?" I ask, gently pulling away from her.

"Listen to me closely. Go over to my dresser and open the top drawer."

I find my way to the top drawer. "I love treasure hunts," I say, smiling from ear to ear. I open the drawer and see wads of money inside, twenties and hundreds just waiting to be spent. There has to be over two thousand dollars in the drawer.

From her bed, fully potted, but still alert, Felicia instructs, "Count out four hundred dollars."

She's very wealthy; I've always known this. The money in the top drawer is chump change to the retired actress. Her account at Flamingo Cove Bank has over twenty million in it from her Hollywood days. Removing four hundred from the stash is nothing. After counting it out, I return to Felicia's side.

"Take the money and buy something beefy and Italian. He must have brown eyes and a sturdy frame. Have him do what Alex did. Think of it as a little gift from me to you."

Alex Ponovich was from Prague and visited the United States to study engineering. I found him at a gay bar called Pallyo on Pelican Way. Felicia wanted to gift him to me. He was God-like with chiseled arms and legs. His skin was dark and his eyes were a creamy brown, which caused me to melt a bit. Felicia had the twenty-three-year-old strip down to his bare bottom, dance to Donna Summer tunes and jerk off. Just for me! A gift! Alex's bill came to just under four hundred dollars.

The Alex episode was three months ago. Felicia, to my surprise, is feeling generous again, which will prompt another visit to Pallyo; not that I'm complaining, since the gay bar is top-notch fun.

"When would you like this to happen?" I ask, standing over her.

"Whenever you decide, darling."

My phone buzzes. It's Mr. Chaz, who probably wants to finish what he started earlier. I'm horny and decide to take his call. After excusing myself, I head into the hallway.

"I'm hard for you, Derek. Why don't you get up here, so I can make your day?"

"What if I don't want my day made?" It's total bullshit, but hey, playing is fun.

"Every young buck needs his day made. Get up here, so I can yank on your bolt."

Mr. Chaz's command is gruff, hot, and everything I want. A semi-boner comes to life in my jeans from his dirty talk. Droplets of juice leak into my white briefs.

"My apartment is open. Come in and take advantage of my skin."

A shiver of elation climbs through my body. I'm greedy for whatever the divorced architect has to offer. My lust is unstoppable. "I'll be right up."

Back at Felicia's side, a frightening grin spreads across her face. "Is someone going to get lucky this evening?"

"Duty calls. Another tenant needs my attention."

"And affection, darling. Go have fun. You can share all the juicy details later."

Chapter 4 – Duty Calls

"I'm giving you the glory to undress me," Mr. Chaz says, standing next to his Swedish sofa.

The view of the Gulf is incredible from his apartment. I'm not interested in the Florida palms, waves or romantic skyline, though. My gaze is hooked on Mr. Chaz. His dress shirt is open, and I count his hairy abs. beneath his soft looking coat of fur are perfect ripples and a kissable navel. Furthering my eye-investigation, I admire his pert and bronze nipples. My gaze falls to his center and I am awestruck to witness his zipper undone. He sports an eight-inch cock, which stands erect, at attention. His tool is damn fine looking: solid and veined with a mushroom cap. I lick my lips, hungry for it and all his other body parts.

Our rapport is elementary: Daddy is the sexiest guy in my world. Someone I want to curl up with for a long time and be held in his strong arms. The man is a release for me from reality. A sexual icon for my dirty boy needs. An idol of sorts that I like to spend time with. Our connection is not mundane or typical. We enjoy sex together, role playing often. When Daddy feels horny, he calls me. When I feel horny, I end up at his apartment door and beg to be licked, sucked or fucked by the man. Never do I spend nights. Never do I share breakfast with him. And never, do we make plans to spend the rest of our lives together, although I want to.

He pulls his boner away from his torso. The tool is immediately released and its length thwaps against his tight stomach and jeans. A welcoming grin promises a fun ride for me. He says, "Why don't you try this in your mouth?"

I'm hungry and horny for him. Positioned on my knees in front of him, I'm ready to lick the head of his tool. Mr. Chaz looks down at me and says, "Take it all. That's the way I like it."

The meat is hard like a hammer and hairy at its base. Its eye stares at me with a need of its own. Just as I'm about to take its purple mass into my mouth, he places his palms on the back of my head. With one quick motion, divinity is found, and he shoves his firm pole into my mouth and down the back of my narrow throat.

I gag by the shock, more so than the cock's mass. Air is lost, and I become dizzy. He shifts to and fro, smacking my face. My nose and eyes become temporarily buried in the V-patch of hair between his legs, repeatedly.

The architect laughs above me, enjoying his rough play. He calls down to me, "Suck it hard, Derek. This is how Daddy likes it. Suck it like the boy you are."

The sting of his sweat surfaces on his stomach, which I can feel on my forehead. Mr. Chaz smells wonderful above me, of ash soap and thick musk. He continues to hold the back of my head with his palms. His hips jut into and away from my face. He grunts like a wildebeest.

I pull the fabric down to his knees. Pleasure overwhelms me and I run my fingers up and along his hairy chest. I sport a chub in my jeans, which feels as if it will explode in a matter of seconds. My fingers find his nipples, and I pinch them with skill, one at a time.

He moans and groans. The sexy architect calls me "boy" again and again. His cock plummets down my tight throat, pulls out, and plummets again. This action continues for the next ten minutes: Daddy pumping his boy's face.

I play with his balls, rolling fingers over their smooth and hairless orbs. I choke and gag on his goods. I'm called bitch-boy and boy-whore, which (for some odd reason) turns me on. I let Mr. Chaz fuck my mouth until he can't fuck anymore.

"I'm blowing, boy! I'm filling you with my juice!"

Bittersweet ooze shoots into my mouth, layering my teeth, tongue and throat. I relentlessly continue to choke and gag, tasting his generated sap. The liquid rolls out of the corners of my mouth, down and over my chin, dripping to the V-spot of my neck.

Mr. Chaz is still at work on my face, pushing and pulling on his rod as he blows. Graphic language escapes his mouth as he gyrates. His fingers find my blond hair, and he begins to pull on it.

A geyser of his sticky syrup is swallowed. I become intoxicated by the spew, firm like steel between my legs, inside my jeans. Some of the thick ooze drips onto the floor between us. More shoot drips onto my clothes. Some of it ...

Mr. Chaz's doorbell rings. A key is heard in the lock. The door is just about to swing open when the architect pulls his still-erect plunger from my mouth and points to the bedroom.

I rise with an erection between my legs and bolt. In a matter of seconds, I'm in his bedroom, and close the door behind me.

The bedroom is very *GQ*. Everything is uppity and arrogant. Nothing is out of place. It looks like the rest of Mr. Chaz's apartment: top-of-the-line architect at work. I stand behind the door, listening.

The unannounced guest is his son, Corey. Mr. Chaz says, "This is a surprise." (I'm sure he has his jeans pulled up, and he begins to button his shirt.)

Corey says, "I was just in the neighborhood and thought I'd stop by."

"A notice would be nice. What if I was fucking someone?" My employer speaks sharply, unpleased with his son's intrusion.

"Look, Dad," Corey explains, "if you don't want to see me, just say so. I understand."

I can't see anything. I'm sure Corey faces his father, and Mr. Chaz has a perturbed look on his handsome face.

"I want to see you. You just need to call before you pop in."

"Look, I'm sorry," Corey says. A father and son begin to make up.

Trapped in Mr. Chaz's bedroom, I look around. A private bathroom is connected to the bedroom and I seek shelter here. His ooze is starting to dry on my cheeks so I decide to wash my face. Quietly I turn on the water and begin to scrub my cheeks with liquid soap, which takes about two minutes. I'm about to dry my face off when the bathroom door opens, and Corey stands in the doorway looking stunned at my presence.

"Hello," I say, dripping wet and displaying his father's sticky ooze on my neck and clothes.

Corey is amazingly hot: reddish-blond hair, azure-colored eyes, broad shoulders, frame of a high school wrestler, pale cheeks, a long nose, and next to no eyebrows. Our eyes meet for a second ... two seconds ... three seconds, and now he asks, "Dad, who the fuck is this guy?" Now he ignores me as he continues to irritate his father, yelling through the bedroom and down the hall.

Mr. Chaz arrives at the scene. "My houseboy," he says. "Derek cleans and does my errands."

I've cleaned his cock and balls with my tongue, but never his apartment.

"Is he why Mom's pissed at you?"

"Your mom's pissed about everything and always has been," Mr. Chaz says.

"He's my age, Dad. Couldn't you fuck someone older?"

Mr. Chaz pulls his son away from the bathroom door and asks, "Is it possible for you to mind your own business?"

"He's how old, Dad, twelve?"

The architect pushes the bathroom door closed. "Shut the fuck up, Corey!"

"Mom pegged you right. All you think about is your cock and what little boy you can shove it into next."

I hear a smack! Mr. Chaz has obviously slapped his son across the face. He barks at Corey, "Respect! Grow up and show me some respect!"

Corey says, "I'm outta here!" probably holding his right cheek with a palm, feeling his flesh sting.

Harsh footsteps echo down the hallway. A door opens and slams shut. I hear Mr. Chaz say, "Christ, that was awful."

I open the bathroom door and see the architect in the bedroom. He leans against a wall, crying. It's kind of sexy and nice. I don't know why I go to his side and hold him, but I do.

Chapter 5 – Homo Sweet Homo

I live in apartment 1-F with Quinn Buckham, who happens to be my best friend. Quinn is in the kitchen making a protein drink when I get back from Mr. Chaz's place. He is dressed in nothing more than a pair of Nike shorts and shows off his upper body. The guy has always been into his body and looks good. He has zero percent fat, works out six days a week, and never ingests sugars, fats, or anything unnatural. Quinn is twenty-three and resembles the boy next door, except he's bulkier. He works down at Push-ups Gym as a manager, dates only the cutest jocks, and spends most of his time trying to find Mr. Right. Some people think I'm the slut of the century, but Quinn has me beat. The last time I looked inside his little leather diary of unabridged fuck tales he was up to 245 men/boys. I'm only up to fifty.

"I made us dinner, Derek. Something healthy."

"It's not grassy again, is it?"

"Of course not. It's very nutritious with high fiber and mucho protein. Check it out. It's on the top shelf in the fridge."

I open the Kenmore and see two greenish-yellow patties on two plates. I pull one of the plates out and hold it up. "What the fuck is this?"

"Squash and beef casserole. Don't knock it until you try it."

"I think I'll pass." I slide the plate back into the fridge. "I'm really not that hungry."

"Fuck off. Whatever." Quinn gulps down his protein muck. Between swallows he says, "Rocco is looking for you."

"Rocco who?"

"Rocco with the dark purple eyes and tight ass."

I don't know a Rocco, let alone one with dark purple eyes and a tight ass. "Did he say what he wanted?"

"Of course not," Quinn says. "He did leave his business card, though." He points to the countertop next to the flattop range.

I pick up the white card and read: ROCCO MALONNI – 555.421.7782. My attention hangs on the unfamiliar phone number. "He's local."

"And about as cute as Peter Pan." It's one of Quinn's favorite expressions that never gets old.

"He didn't say what he wanted?"

"Nope. Besides, it's N-O-M-B." Quinn's been speaking text message language for the past two months, which is starting to grate my nerves.

"Knock it off with the text talk."

"Will do, Nancy Drew."

I notice Quinn's green-and-white soccer jersey hanging over one of the kitchen chairs. He reaches for it and slips it over his strapping torso. He says, "I have a date tonight. Don't wait up."

"Who's the lucky boy?"

"Tank Carson."

"The bouncer? I thought you never wanted to see him again."

Tank is a dreamy-eyed, brawny Kentucky boy. He talks more than a woman, never stops eating, and manages always to drink too much in Quinn's presence, possibly bridging on being an alcoholic. No matter what his downfalls are, Tank is one of Flamingo Cove's best bouncers, and he's not so shabby to look at, either. The guy is built like a steel building and works out almost every day. He has muscles out the wazoo, slate-grey eyes, and a military haircut. Tank wears a size fourteen shoe, wife beater shirts to every event, and never a condom (according to Quinn's diary, which I sometimes read).

The last time Quinn dated Tank was three months ago. Tank got excessively drunk at a Gay Pride party and fucked a queer wrestler in a Jacuzzi. Quinn was embarrassed and escaped the scene with just a sliver of his humility left. My roommate said he never wanted to see the man again, which he didn't, until this evening.

Maybe Quinn is horny and Tank is exceptionally easy. Maybe Quinn is giving the hot bouncer a second chance, which really isn't out of his character. Whatever the answer to this evening's arrangement is, Quinn looks good in his shorts and jersey, ready for some one-on-one fuck-stuff with a steamy musclehead.

"Love is in the air," Quinn says sarcastically.

"Love is a fuck buddy."

"Whatever it takes, Derek. I need a healthy cock, and Tank's the guy to shove it up my ass, among other places."

Did I mention that Quinn and I used to date? We were juniors at West End College in Erie, Pennsylvania. He asked me out to the movies. I thought him cute and charming, sort of geeky, and agreed to spend an evening with him. It turned out to be a nice time, some laughs, and an incredible session of heavy-duty kissing.

After the movie we went back to Quinn's dorm and fucked like wild dogs. Our intimacy was top-notch porn stuff. He could stay rock-hard for over an hour, and ride my bottom for just as long. Sex became our mutual connection. Although different in many ways, our bond grew for the remaining semester. Our peak was a run of four days of nothing but hard sex. Sex against the wall. Sex over the couch. Sex on the floor. Sex everywhere. Once the marathon was over, Quinn vanished. I didn't see him for two weeks. I questioned him regarding his distance, and he said we would make better friends than lovers. Plus, he wanted various partners in bed, which I was perfectly fine with. It felt as if we were dating one minute, fucking crazily the next, and then we separated. It was one of my fastest relationships.

How shocking that we are still friends and roommates to this day. Occasionally, Quinn sneaks into my bedroom at night and finds me in bed. He plays with my chest, kisses my neck, and we share some naughty for an hour or more. We are not committed to each other. Love is not a chapter in our lives. He has his arrangement of boyfriends, and I have mine. It seems to work out well this way, even if we sometimes fuck.

Quinn looks down at his Fossil watch and says, "I really have to run."

"Tank awaits his fuck-fest," I say.

"And cuddling. It's not always about fucking."

"Since when, my friend?"

I watch him leave. He is out the door in a matter of seconds, down the hallway, into the sun, and at his Toyota truck in no time, speeding away. I'm left with the disgusting greenish patties in the fridge and Rocco Malonni's business card on the counter.

My stomach rumbles. There's no way I'm eating Quinn's prepared dinner; I'd rather die. I open the freezer and see nothing yummy. A couple protein bars are in the cupboards. It's Quinn's turn to do the shopping; I'll be damned if I'm paying two times in a row.

My attention is drawn to Rocco's card again, and I listen to my stomach call out for help. Fuck it! I pick up the card, press the stranger's phone number into my cell phone, and listen to it buzz two times. His voicemail is just about to click on when he picks up and says, "This is Rocco."

He has a sexy voice. Definitely Italian. Definitely hot. It's curt and sort of dreamy-rough, a voice I don't mind listening to at all.

"Is this Rocco Malonni?"

"Who's this?"

"I'm Derek Reed."

Silence. Rocco's thinking. Maybe scratching his chin. Maybe squinting in thought. The file manager inside his brain currently works overtime, attempting to skim through a DEREK REED file, finding something – anything – about me.

"You stopped by my apartment today at Flamingo Cove and left your card."

"You got the wrong Rocco. I don't know what you're talking about."

"You gave your card to my roomie, Quinn Buckham."

"I don't know no Buckman."

"Buckham. Quinn Buckham."

"Fuck off, man! I don't have time for this shit." Rocco hangs up on me.

Unimpressed with his attitude, I press his number into my phone again. It rings two times. He picks up. "Rocco?" I say.

"You got some kind of problem?" He's hot under the collar. If I were standing in front of him, he'd bust me.

"You contacted me!" I burst. "I'm standing in my kitchen holding your business card. What the fuck do you want?"

"Hey, no one talks to Rocco that way."

I press the END button, satisfied. My stomach growls. The cell phone rings and I pick it up.

"You in apartment 1-F?" Rocco asks, obviously calming down.

"That's me."

"What's the business card say on the back?"

I never thought to flip it over before. Shame on me. I flip it over now and read, "Fisk Deveraux."

"You know him?"

Half of me wants to lie, but I don't. "Yeah. Everyone knows Fisk."

"I just need to know if you know Fisk."

I speak before thinking. "I do."

And just before Rocco hangs up, he quickly rattles off, "Good. Meet me at Sambone's in one hour. I'll be at the bar. Don't be late."

I think about blowing Rocco off, but hunger pains scream for one of Sambone's Caesar salads, which are the best in the city. Even if Rocco doesn't show, I can fill my belly and have a better evening. If Rocco does show, which I predict he will, we'll discuss Fisk Deveraux to the fullest possibilities and have salads together. Either way, I win.

What does Rocco want with Fisk, anyway? It's probably a sex gig or something like that. Fisk is good about getting himself involved in questionable activities. I'm sure it's a threesome between Fisk, Rocco, and an unnamed third party. Fisk has always been known to do a few homemade movies; threesomes just happen to be his specialty. Fisk sells the naughty flicks to Woody Woodcock who uploads the porn on his home-based Website called *Down with Dirty Dudes*. This is another form of income for Fisk, a means of his survival for the businessman.

Sambone's on Pilsner Street is relatively a straighties place to hang; rumor has it that only the wait staff is queer. The restaurant has a bungalow setting with a pit of angry and hungry gators in the back. The alligators reside in a fenced-in swamp. The teal lights add a soothing ambiance, as well as the Jimmy Buffet music. When Jimmy's not playing, Gulf waves can be heard; a nice touch to the comforting environment.

Two men sit at the bar. One just happens to be Carlos Gillespi, the restaurant's owner. Carlos is one hundred percent Cuban, fluent in three languages, and milks a Bud Light, taking a break from his duties. The second guy at the bar is about twenty-six years old and definitely Italian with black stubble on his chin and cheeks. His olive skin reflects nicely in the dim light. My gut instinct kicks in, and I know it's Rocco Malonni. When he catches me studying him, he shows off his dark purple eyes and exuberant smile. The sexy guy sports wide shoulders, which taper to a narrow waist. He is dressed in jeans, a royal-blue dress shirt, and black leather jacket. I observe Rocco's stomach through his shirt, which is all muscle, ab after constructed ab. Hanging from his neck is a gold crucifix on a matching chain. His black hair is thick and short, and his bangs are sprayed with product and pricked. I realize he's sexy-handsome, well built, and surprisingly pleased to see me.

"You Derek?" he asks.

"The one and only," I say, and walk up to him.

We shake hands. I determine Rocco has a strong grip, and his skin is pretty smooth.

"Have a seat. What do you drink?"

I sit down. It's seven o'clock and I'm ready for something strong. "Aboslut with Sprite. And a slice of lemon."

Rocco gives my order to the bartender, a lightweight blond with bony shoulders. He then directs his attention back to me and says, "So, Derek, tell me everything you know about Fisk Deveraux."

"The same Fisk that lives in my apartment building?"

"Yeah, him. What do you know about the guy?"

The twig-of-a-bartender serves my drink. Rocco places a ten on the bar, and the bartender scoops it away. I take a sip of the drink: strong, refreshing, and exactly what I need. "Why do you want to know about Fisk?"

"That's none of your business."

I'm annoyed, losing my patience. This is a ridiculous conversation with the handsome Italian. It's absolutely pointless and a waste of my time. Angered, I ask, "If it's none of my business, why am I sitting here with a complete stranger at his request?" Needing my drink, I take another sip of the liquid concoction, which goes down smooth.

Rocco's voice changes. It becomes more direct, almost rude. "Don't get cute with me, Derek. Work with me on this, and you won't get yourself into any trouble."

So much for getting a salad; my appetite is now lost.

He becomes pissed at me for no reason. I have every right to ask questions. Hell, I don't even know him. In fact, I don't even want to know him. Fuck! What the hell is going on? Why does he become so brazen when I'm harmless? Rocco's sweetness seems to vanish instantaneously, and he morphs into an asshole. He is not smiling anymore, and his body language says: I'm on business here, and I don't want to listen to your bullshit.

"Look," Rocco continues, attempting to calm down, "I have some serious business with Mr. Deveraux, and I would greatly appreciate your help."

"One question."

Rocco rolls his eyes. "What?"

"How do you know that I have any information about Fisk?" It's a good question. Point for me.

"Let me just say that Fisk is being watched."

"And those who visit him are being watched, too?"

31

"I would imagine so. I'm not personally doing the watching, but I'm pretty sure it's being done."

"Who's watching him?" I ask, intrigued and mystified.

"That's none of your business."

I sip my drink, which causes a tingle in my head, and stand. "It's a shame you're so brazen, Mr. Malonni, because I find you very attractive." I walk away from the bar, exit Sambone's, and end up on Pilsner Street.

"Derek, stop!"

I feel Rocco's firm grip on my right shoulder and stop walking. He spins me around. The look on his dark-skinned face is absolutely adorable. He resembles a little puppy in a window, up for sale and just waiting to be snuggled. His eyebrows are curved upwards with question, and his lips are slightly pursed. "Look," he explains, "I was being a total dick back there. There was no reason for me to act that way. You seem like a nice guy and deserve better."

He's right. Rocco was giving me shit for no reason. Point for him to admit it. And, point for me that he turns into a nice guy after his bad behavior in the bar.

Rocco reaches out and touches my right elbow, concern in his dark purple eyes. "Let me start over, if you'll let me."

I nod my head. Why not? He's amazingly sexy and cute, apologizing for being an ass. I've been on worse dates, honestly.

Rocco grazes his fingers on my inner-arm. "Lets take a walk together. What do you say?"

So we walk down Pilsner Street, side by side. It's not Madison Avenue or Rodeo Drive. It's approximately a mile from the building in downtown Flamingo Cove and near the beach. Nothing screams beautiful about it. The street is dusty and littered with fast food wrappers. Dilapidated apartment buildings line the sidewalks, and a rank smell of city sweat lingers in a fermented cloud overhead. It's something like a back street in Miami, where hookers and drug dealers are found. Not a good place to hang out unless you want some trouble.

Rocco slips my hand within his own for a second. When he realizes his oops, my hand is dropped. Our shoulders touch, too, a nonchalant graze. It's like we're on a date for the first time, but honestly … we're not.

Rocco says, "Fisk is in a lot of heat, and I want to help him out."

"What kind of heat?"

"Drug money."

"How much money?"

Rocco sighs. He knows he shouldn't tell me, but does. Maybe it's my good looks; I'm not sure. "Two hundred K."

"That's a lot of dough."

"And a lot of drugs."

"So you know I buy pot from Fisk, right?" I might be queer, but I'm not stupid. Momma didn't raise an idiot.

Rocco nods his head in agreement. "And, I know you give it to Felicia Horodowski, who suffers from stomach cancer."

I stop walking.

Rocco stops walking.

We face each other like cowboys in a dual.

I ask, "Do you also know when I fuck my boyfriend?"

"You don't have a boyfriend, but you do occasionally fuck an architect on the fourth floor of your building" he supplies, sharing an irresistible grin with me that demands: let's cut the bullshit.

Dammit. He knows everything about my petty life, and I know nothing about his. What the fuck? Rocco has done his homework on Fisk, and me. I don't know exactly know how, but he has, which leaves me confused about what he does for a living and how he is really connected to Fisk.

I'm stubborn and foolish when I have to be. I'm always polite and mostly daring. I say to Rocco, "Look, I don't know what kind of bad business Fisk does, I just try to help out a friend with cancer. It doesn't make me a hero or a villain, just human."

Rocco puts his hands up, surrendering to my concern. "I'm not here to break your balls. I just need a few questions answered about Fisk."

"You the police or something?"

"Let's go with or something."

"What kind of something? Tell me. I have every right to know, since I feel involved somehow."

"Trust me, you don't want to know."

I'm about to repeat my question to him, but a scene at the corner of Pilsner and Darling unfolds, gaining our attention.

The action transpires behind us. A midnight blue Charger rails the corner, its tires squealing. I see smoke from rubber burning, all black tinted windows, and stainless hubs. The Charger zooms down Pilsner, straight at us. The front passenger's window is cracked and a gun's muzzle pops out. Bullets scatter around my body as I scream. Rocco pushes me to the sidewalk and drops on top of me, meeting our chests. More bullets fire into the brick wall behind us and ...

It's over. I stop screaming. The Charger is gone. Rocco lies on top of me: chest to chest, legs on legs, cock kissing cock. We're both breathing heavily like we've just climaxed together after heated sex. I shake under him, scared shitless.

Rocco asks, "Are you hit?"

I'm fine. I'm just wondering what the fuck is going on. Why were we just involved in a drive-by? Who is Rocco Malonni, anyway?

"You hit?" Rocco asks again, concern locked in his tone.

"I'm not hit."

"You're shaking."

"Who the fuck was that?"

"Bad guys. I'll explain it all to you in ..."

There's too much excitement and craziness going on. I've almost been gunned down. I can't even begin to comprehend the danger. My eyes simply close, and I pass out under Rocco's medium-sized build. My mind fades to black and emptiness, immediately.

Part Two – Bad Boys

<u>Chapter 6 – The Skin Tour</u>

I wake up in an unfamiliar bedroom: everything is steel, silver, white, black and very contemporary. I smell sandalwood soap or shampoo. Light streams in through a window on the right side of the room. Silence is present, I note. This place is almost too quiet, wherever I am. It's surreal, clean, and ...

I've died, haven't I? My days on Earth are over. I've made my way to heaven, and this is the recovery or processing room. I'm an angel now. I'm going to visit God and all the saints: Truman Capote, Rock Hudson, Freddie Mercury and Marilyn Monroe.

I'm not dead. I'm not in heaven. I'm alive and breathing just fine. I lift the white sheet, which covers my body, and look at my naked skin for bullet holes, wounds or bandages. My flesh is unharmed, perfectly suntanned and muscled. I haven't been shot. There are no bandages. I've lived through the drive-by on Pilsner Street, which totally leaves me awestruck with confusion.

How long was I out for? Two hours, seven hours, a day? My Swatch is missing. So are my wallet and my clothes. I'm completely naked.

"How do you feel, Derek?"

Rocco is positioned on my left side. He sits in a black leather recliner in a pair of royal-blue shorts and drinks something red with alcohol. The stranger is bare-chested and reads a book by Peter Cameron.

"I don't know. What exactly happened?"

Rocco walks me through the dangerous scene on Pilsner Street. He says, "I threw my body against you for protection. You hit the back of your head on the sidewalk and eventually blacked out."

I rub the back of my head, checking for a bump. One's there. Egg-size and tender. "Who tried to kill me?" I ask, fingering my skull.

Rocco shakes his head and says, "No one was trying to kill you. They were after me."

"Who were they?"

"Let's not get into that right now. You need to rest. After you passed out, I brought you back here to my beach house. I called your roommate, Quinn, to let him know you were safe."

"How long have I been asleep?"

"Twelve hours. It's about eight in the morning now. I'm sure you're hungry. Are you up for eggs and bacon, or blueberry pancakes?" Rocco stands up from his chair and places the hardback copy of *The Weekend* on his seat. He walks over to my side and gently caresses my left cheek.

"Can I start with a glass of juice? My mouth is dry."

Rocco is extremely hot in nothing more than his shorts. He has a chiseled body that sports zero fat and all muscle. His olive-colored abs and biceps look like hand-size balloons. His chest is covered in a thin pelt of dark hair, which I perceive to be freshly manscaped because it is very short. He continues to caress my cheek and says, "Juice is coming right up."

Off he goes, escaping my side. I'm left alone in the room with a tiny throbbing sensation at the back of my head. Obviously, I'm in some kind of danger. Where is Rocco's beach house anyway? What's going on? What the hell is happening? ... Someone tell me!

Rocco returns with the orange juice. I sit up in the bed and take the glass of juice.

"It's freshly squeezed and will give you some energy."

As the juice soothes my mouth and throat, Rocco sits on the side of the bed. The smell of sandalwood soap or shampoo becomes more evident. I stare at his solid stomach and hairy chest. His good looks feed me more energy than the orange juice. I finish the liquid to the last drop and ask, "Where am I?"

"Flamingo Bay. My beach house. I thought of taking you home but didn't know if Quinn would look after you." Rocco takes the empty juice glass from me. "Do you want another hit?"

His nipples are tiny mountains, perfect for my tongue to explore. Rocco has a wrestler's shoulders, which are absolutely generous with molten muscle. The man is like a tasty buffet of eats just waiting for me to properly consume. I can look at him, sniff his skin, and fuck him all day long, but only if he'll let me. He stands at the side of the bed with the empty glass in his right hand. His tube of hidden cock stares at me: all seven soft inches of a man's pleasurable wonder drug tucked in Rufskin shorts.

I lick my lips, hungry for his built body to mix with my own. There's nothing better than some heavy-duty man-on-man action first thing in the morning.

"The juice has excited you," Rocco informs, gazing down at the cotton sheet, which is now a tent covering my middle.

"Trust me, it's not the juice."

The stranger adjusts his goods with his free hand, teasing me. He says, "We should get something solid in you, Derek," continuing his adjusting.

I wouldn't mind his nine inches of beefy plug inside me. I'm just about to tell him this when he says, "How about a slice of toast?"

Toasted 12 grain bread doesn't even come close to nine inches of naughty in my behind. I politely pass on the toast and attempt to push my unexpected boner away.

Rocco is still at my side, holding the empty glass. He scans my torso in the bed and says, "I admit, you're sexy as hell and totally my type, Derek. I just don't think it's a good idea to over-exert yourself with some guy-play."

"I like an honest man. You let me know when I can rock your world."

"That sounds like a good plan," he says, spinning around and leaving my side.

Rocco finds it necessary to put some clothes on while I rest. No longer is he sporting his sexy Rufskin shorts. The stranger is decked out in jeans, Crocs, a sky-blue tee, and an expensive looking pair of sunglasses, which decorate his spiked bangs.

It's almost noon, and he makes us Mint Juleps, which we enjoy in his living room, an open space with very little furniture and two large paintings by a Maine artist named Pam Dover.

I wear a pair of his cotton briefs, which have tiny red fire trucks all over them. Before the Juleps, Rocco offers me a matching tee to wear, but I cordially decline, wanting to show off my upper bod for his needy pleasure.

Like the spectacular view from his bedroom, the living room's vista is equal, if not better. The summertime waves are beautifully melancholic. Sun blisters across the August heavens. Rocco's private beach is decorated with heaping white sandy dunes and yellow-green grasses.

"Would you like to go out on the patio?"

I do. We make our way with the drinks, finding half-shade on the patio. We sit beside each other at a Tropicana table with four matching chairs.

A warm breeze caresses my face and bare torso. I take a sip of my Julep and study the expansive view. We are totally secluded on the Gulf, miles away from Flamingo Cove. There are no sunbathing beefies or steamy lifeguards present. As far as I can see to my right and left, we are completely alone.

"My father bought me this place a few years ago." Rocco sips his Julep.

"He must really love you."

"We're a close family. Our blood is very thick." He looks out at the ocean; I can see he loves it by his steady stare. "How close are you to Barbara and Melvin?"

Shit. How does he know my mother's name, and her current boyfriend's? This is far too strange. There's no way I've heard him right, so I ask, "Who's Melvin?"

Rocco takes another swallow of his Julep, turns his head to me, and shows off his adorable smile. He informs, "Melvin, the rug dealer. He owns Carpet Ride on Tarpon Street. He's been dating your mother for the past two years."

Fuck! Rocco's right. I want to know how he is privy to this information exactly, and ask, "Are you Melvin's friend or something?"

"Not quite. Let me just say that I know certain things about certain people. Like Fisk Deveraux for example. He's made a few bad decisions in the past month, and I have the responsibility to clean up his mess."

"What kind of mess?" More questions surface within my mind: Is this how I'm involved? Does the shooter on Pilsner have something to do with Fisk? Who are you, Rocco? Who do you work for? Tell me what's going on and how I'm involved? I'm eager to learn all these answers. Calmly, I take a sip of my Julep and observe him in an uncanny and mysterious manner.

He laughs at me. It's belittling and a little arrogant, but kind of sexy, too, in an odd sort of way. He finishes off his Julep between hearty bursts of manly laughter and now inquires with surprise, "You really have no clue who I am, do you?"

I obviously don't. And personally, a sliver of me fears to find out, since I was almost murdered in his presence the night before. I try to humor him though, and say, "You're the sexy bad boy who secretly likes to seduce good boys like me."

Rocco shares more laughter. This time it's light, airy and playful. "Do you like sexy bad boys?"

"I admit, I find them hot as hell," I respond. Will he mind if I reach out and touch one of his erect nipples through his tee? Every sexy bad boy needs some playtime, right?

"You flirt a lot. I find that appealing."

"I only flirt with guys I know nothing about." I give Rocco a wink, which all the men in my life seem to go for.

"Point taken. Let me tell you a little about myself, the drive-by on Pilsner, and Fisk."

41

I learn more than I should. Shame on me for listening. Rocco's father is Antonio "Boss" Malonni III, a Mafia godfather based in Miami. According to Rocco, he's a badass motherfucker with over two-hundred million dollars. Rocco calls him a loving and caring father, a good guy, and says, "When I was nineteen I came out to him. He called me ballsy and classy. He said he didn't care who I fucked, as long as I was safe and happy doing it. My father is very supportive of my being gay."

"You seem very happy and healthy."

"I'm a very lucky young man."

"This is good to know."

Rocco fills me in on Fisk. "Fisk works for my dad. He was doing an undercover job at the Baskin Fish Company, which is illegally importing cocaine from Columbia into Florida. Long story short, my father gave Fisk two-hundred K to buy the goods, setting up the Baskin bad guys, his nemesis. My father and a guy by the name of Mr. Drago are the epitome of enemies. Actually, I'm surprised they haven't murdered each other yet. Both work in the same territory. And, both want the territory to themselves. Anyway, Fisk either lost the money or embezzled it. The money is still missing. My father should have known he was an amateur at doing gigs and would fuck up a big job. Fisk was given the benefit of the doubt, though. My father believes the goons from Baskin thieved the money from Fisk. This is what I'm working on."

"And, I'm involved because I know Fisk, right?"

"I need to question everyone who talks to Fisk. It's not like you're the only connection to Fisk that we have."

"Did your rivaling goons do the drive-by on Pilsner?"

Rocco nods his head. "That's a possibility. Everyone has a few enemies."

"Because you work for your father?"

"Let's just say I help him out."

Rocco places his Julep down and plays sexy bad boy with me again. He rises from his chair and ends up in front of me. He reaches out with his right hand and grazes two fingertips against my left nipple. He says, "You have a killer chest, Derek. If I didn't have meetings this afternoon with some bad guys, I'd stay here and take a skin tour of you."

Rocco's big-time into me. As he continues to play with my nipple, I say, "That's too bad. I think I would enjoy it."

We are face to face now. I realize he's even more drop dead handsome up close and personal. My cock twitches in the fire truck briefs, ready for some blazing action between dudes. I practically catch on fire in the patio chair, this is how hot the moment between us becomes.

Rocco gives my nipple a little pinch. He asks, "Can I have a rain check for the skin tour?"

"Any time, any place."

He leans into me for a kiss. Rocco uses his tongue, which drives me wild. His fingertips find the center of my chest and fall to my navel. He plays with my blond treasure trail and now goes for the stiffening pleasure between my throbbing legs. The sexy bad boy weaves his fingers over my growing, cotton-covered tool, and he now begins to stroke my rod with his entire hand. Cotton and his palm agree with each other. I'm ready to shoot a few bubbles of pre-spew on the fire trucks, but his cellular buzzes, and he pulls away from me.

Fuck the pink-assed gods! I'm having the time of my life with the queer mobster, which ends abruptly. The only thing I'm left with as he takes his important call in the sun is a cement statue between my pulsing legs and dribbles of Rocco's tongue-saliva in my mouth.

Feeling disgusted, I reach for my Mint Julep on the table, which I casually enjoy during his call with a man named Mickey. Again, I hear things I shouldn't hear: "Don't leave a trail ... Stay underground for a few more days ... Don't attempt to reach Hurricane Brass ... Stay low ... Someone will contact you from Miami."

Rocco ends his call and swaggers up to me. He says, "Sorry about that."

"You really do work for the mob, don't you?"

"What you see is what you get. My apologies for the imperfections."

What I see is a hot mobster with fall-into eyes and a Prince Charming grin. Personally, I really like what I see, and I tell Rocco this.

I feel his fingers on my chin and listen to him say in the most debonair manner, "I like you, too. Unfortunately there's business to attend, and I have to leave. Promise me you'll make yourself at home while I'm gone."

"I will."

Rocco rolls his thumb over my bottom lip. "I could look at you all day."

"What if I'm not here all day?"

"Remember who I work for. I'll find you."

"I hope you do find me."

Our meeting ends with an intoxicating kiss that only happens in gay films. It's passion-driven and sultry, and everything a young man like me desires.

When our connection breaks, I feel as lively and wild as the Gulf. What an amazing feeling! What zeal!

Rocco waves goodbye, walking toward the sliding glass doors that lead into the house.

I say, "See you around."

And, he completes our romantic mid-day chat with: "Remember, I'll find you."

Chapter 7 – Lust at First Sight

After Rocco leaves, I shower and head to the kitchen in the buff. A glass of chilled water calls out to me. Passing through the foyer, the front doorknob twists and the door opens. Of course, I expect it to be Rocco, returning to the beach house after forgetting something. To my shocked embarrassment it is not Rocco. The surprise intruder is a red-headed delicious looking male at the ripe age of eighteen or nineteen. He has sparkling emerald-colored eyes, perfectly sculpted side burns, and freckled cheeks. The bouncing boy is as surprised to see me as I am of him. His beautiful face blooms a rose-red hue, and he stutters, "Who ... who are you?"

I cover up my Johnny and his two male-pals with both hands. I cross my ankles and reply with wide-eyed terror, "I'm Rocco's guest, Derek Reed. Now, if I may ask, who the fuck are you?"

"Farrell MacCormick. I'm Mr. Malonni's houseboy."

So, Rocco's found himself an attractive leprechaun to run his errands, clean the beach house, and carry out whatever else a mobster's son needs to accomplish. How interesting. It's the scoop I was looking to obtain while prying through his drawers and cupboards before my shower, but sadly came up empty-handed.

Farrell is not looking at my eyes like a proper young lad. The Irish cutie scans my body from head to toe. Without taking his emerald peepers off my skin, he pushes the entrance door closed behind him.

"Do you like what you're looking at?" I ask sarcastically, toying with the boy.

"Pull your hands away from your privates, and then I'll make my decision."

I call Farrell's bluff and release my palms and fingers from my middle. I uncross my ankles and ...

"Christ, that's the best wanker I've seen in days."

Am I blushing? I think so. Embarrassment doesn't come easy for me, but Farrell's comment certainly pinks my cheeks. I'm so caught off guard by his statement, I cannot respond.

Obviously Farrell has a covert agenda of his own and quickly pulls off his white T-shit. The cotton is dropped to the foyer's steel-colored marble floor. He runs a hand between the firm pecs on his Irish-pale chest. It is visibly evident that the young man works out at least five times a week. He maintains a better build than I do. He sports shoulders of a wrestler, and deeply cut abs line his stunning torso. His pecs are muscularly plump with erect nipples, both are pierced with thin, silver bars. Veins on his lower tummy are from excessive squats and fall into his hip-snug Diesel jeans.

Using my left hand, I continue to toy with him, beginning to stroke my soft tool in a southern direction.

"You'd better stop that if you don't want a foyer-fuck," Farrell warns while deciding to kick off his Nikes. He unbuttons his jeans, sports curly-red pubic hair instead of Candyman underwear, and pushes the Diesels down to his feet.

I admit, it's lust at first sight between us. I want Farrell as much as he wants me. In truth, I'm fascinated by his red hair and athletic body. I've never become busy with a leprechaun before, let alone an extroverted houseboy. His treat of being fucked can certainly be worth my time.

"Dude, I'm going to suck you dry." Farrell drops to his knees in front of me and positions his left hand around the base of my swollen rod. Hungry for what I have to offer, he opens his mouth and begins to lap at the tool's mushroom-shaped head with the tip of his slippery tongue.

Above him, I state, "Damn, Farrell, you don't waste any time."

His straying tongue tastes every inch of my stick. Farrell finds pleasure in sucking on one ball and then the other, slurping like I'm a popsicle. His free hand rolls up and down my tight stomach while he continues to suck on my fuzzy man-sack. He discovers my left pec and gives its pointed nipple a gentle squeeze. He does the same with my right nipple, pleasuring the both of us to his fullest capacity.

I'm in heaven, dizzy from his suck-job. I roll fingers through his red hair, push his face forward, and jam my shaft into the back of his narrow throat. Quickly I pull away from his face, push into it again, and pull away. Bliss is found with my swift and erratic motion. I become lost in the movement, swishing my hips to and fro, continuing this gyration for the next few minutes.

He gags and laughs on the hearty meal. It's slippery work with too much salvia, but it rocks for both of us.

I have to push him away or I'll explode inside his mouth. I huff, puff, and say, "You're totally naughty."

Farrell wipes a hand across his mouth. His erection stands at full-mast between his legs. Still on his knees, he provides a boyish grin, and says, "Put your face against the wall. I'm not finished with you yet."

The leprechaun has me pushed against a foyer wall and spreads my legs. One of his palms spanks my tight bottom, and he warns, "I'm going to rock your fucking world."

Tingles of man-getting-it-on-with-man rush through my body. The underneath side of my stiff cock rests against the smooth wall. My right cheek is pressed to the wall and my palms are flat against the paint. Farrell kisses the nape of my smooth back. He plays with my ass cheeks and pink manhole with an index finger and whispers, "I can't wait to nail you," while pressing two fingers inside me.

My eyes close and I grit my teeth because of the generous pain. I spread my legs more and welcome his dry and invading fingertips inside. I crave his steel prick to take residence inside my bottom. I'm eager for his thumping while he hangs onto my narrow hips. I want him to bang my bottom until there is no banging left.

Fags in heaven! The tip of his tongue drags down and along my spine and eventually touches my sensitive opening. Farrell takes one, two, three laps at my hungry hole. He uses all ten fingers to casually pry my glory hole open and – I swear to God! – I feel his slippery extension inside. He darts his tongue in and out, fucking me.

I become weak against the wall. Thank the queer gods it holds me up. I melt above/in front of him, lost by his tongue-dance. Continuous shivers erupt through my pulsing body. My sensitivity to his tongue-touch is dynamic and sinful. I want Farrell to continue this all day, long into the night.

He shares a dozen or more licks. Another spanking is carried out with his right palm, slapping my tight bottom. He says, "Dude, I think you're all lubed up and ready for me."

Sex. It's a timeless affair between or among the most deviant. Sex between a clergymen and a boy is not the same as a husband and husband. Sex among male students in the back of a college library is undoubtedly not like the sex between a hustler and his trick. Sex between beach buddies is nothing like sex between two strangers in a foyer, like us.

I think of this before we fuck. I think there is no depth to our connection. We know nothing about each other. Our temporary fuck-scene has no substance, except for Farrell's nine-inch cock in my ass. Who is Farrell MacCormick, anyway? We will always be strangers, no matter how close our naked bodies become.

Here and now. Farrell finds a condom in his jeans on the floor. He applies the plastic over his tool and stands behind me. One of his hands clamps to my hip. The other hand holds his cock at its base and rails its mass inside me.

"Jesus-pleases!" I groan as one inch, two inches, three inches of his plastic-wrapped tool begins to plow my hole.

Farrell likes it rough and fast. He now holds both of my hips, pushing all of his stern meat into me. Grunts and murmurs escape him as another two inches plunder within me. Farrell says, "Take all of it, dude. Hang on for the ride."

The last of his nine healthy and swollen inches spread me apart. Erotic pain scurries throughout my middle and the train of my spine. I feel split in half, broken in a good way. Forceful hurt opens me, and I become intoxicated with it. Perspiration decorates my back and chest, still flush against the wall. I become windblown, breathless and disoriented. There is no ground beneath me. My body is weightless. Farrell has me exactly where I want to be.

The sex is unconditional as our bodies combine, waving in motion. His lengthy prick teases my asshole to the fullest. This affection between us is sex and sex only. There is no tie between us other than the raw beauty of sex itself. It's men fucking to the limit. Men who only desire to blow their pent loads.

Farrell is a porn star in motion. He rides my ass wildly, digging fingertips into my flesh. Bolts of chaotic bliss seal his pick to my pink opening. Thrust after harsh thrust become his sexual act. The houseboy pounds my hole with all his might. He moans and groans the naughtiest names while bucking my backside: dick-rider, ass-slut, queer-whore.

The stranger removes his left hand from my hip and finds the plump poker between my quivering legs. Still thumping my center, Rocco's houseboy informs, "I'm going to make you shoot your fucking load all over the wall."

Indeed, he will. Farrell carries out a few light strokes to my Johnny. He builds up a synchronized rhythm with his handjob and ass-pounding. Again, he calls me unthinkable names: cock-eater, ball-sucker, cum-swallower.

I writhe in front of him. Jolts of ecstasy rock my world. Farrell's continuous stroking and pounding is mind-blowing. There is no way I can keep my cream contained, certainly not for the next ten minutes of ass-splitting and rod-jerking. I confess, "Farrell, I'm going to shoot."

He pulls out of me and stops playing with my ready-to-burst dong. He rips the condom off his own tool and says, "Spin around and feed me lunch."

It's sex. Nothing but sex. It's hot and sweaty, cheap and easy sex, without inhabitations. It's dirty and playful. It's ...

Farrell is on his knees again, choking his beef up and down with his right palm. He says, "You'll like this. Watch me come," and tugs his meat, moaning. His palm glides north and south on his rod. Sweat covers his entire torso. He spits on his cock's head and uses the fresh saliva as lube, stroking the tool up and down, vibrantly. A final groan escapes his teeth-clenched mouth. Farrell stops jerking himself off and holds the base of his rod. A playful grin shines on his cute face. He holds back his explosion for just a few seconds and eventually blows. White sap shoots in four arcs out of his flesh-pistol. The juice splatters against his torso. Ooze sticks to one nipple and just beneath his chin. Sap glazes his abs. He stares up at me, satisfied with his work, and says, "It's your turn to shoot. Make sure you aim for my mouth."

This is insane, but in a good way. I stand over the leprechaun's spent body. His face and shoulders are a fiery red from his orgasm. His green eyes glimmer with deep satisfaction from our afternoon flesh-fest.

He requests, "Let me finish you off, dude," and grabs my erection. The houseboy begins to tug on my protein with some hearty pulls. Farrell is a pro at the handjob; one of the best experiences for me.

I let his fingers manipulate my skin. Uncontrollably, I move against his pleasurable stroking, which causes friction and enlightenment between us. I stand with my hands on my swaying hips and allow him to carry out the rest of the work, all by himself. Sweat drips from my chest. I become breathless and numb. Pre-bubbles of jizm leak out of my pole. Farrell leans forward, extends his tongue to my capped rock, and licks the goo away. Following this dick-cleaning ceremony, he whispers, "That was yummy, feed me more."

And so this compromised act between queers continues. I jut my hips toward his mouth. I pull away, hump his throat, and pull away again. I fuck his hand and face, elated, on fire, frantically ready to blow.

Farrell pulls off the rod for a second and instructs, "Feed me, fucker. Shoot it on my face," eager for his bittersweet meal.

A stream of all-natural cock-juice fires out of my Johnny and splashes against his nose and mouth. Some of the spent sticks to his chin and cheeks. The explosion is unstoppable and nothing of the norm for me; it's as if I've been saving up my juice for the past week, just for this moment with the houseboy. I shoot until my sex-spigot is fully drained, leaving me spent and exhausted, ready to fall to the foyer's floor.

Farrell is hungry. No, he's ravenous for the cum. I watch him lap up every drop from his face, using two fingers. He sucks and licks the fingers like a little boy eating an ice cream cone, delighted with his untidy chore. Our loads are cleaned up in a matter of seconds. The houseboy becomes smear- and droplet-free of ooze. His face and chest are now spotless. No wonder he's a houseboy; Farrell seems very much into cleaning up sticky messes.

We don't cuddle following our fuck-time. We don't kiss. We don't even shower together. Farrell stands in the foyer, panting like a dog, and says, "Thanks for the good time, dude. Maybe we can fuck again sometime."

"Maybe," I respond, feeling awkward and naked, again.

"Just for the record, I really like the taste of your shoot."

"Cool." It's all I can really find to say, unsure of how to finalize our foyer-fuck connection.

Emotionless, Farrell says, "You can let yourself out. I'm going to shower."

"I'll do that," I respond, watching him escape upstairs. I'm not surprised that our bond ends like this. Hell, it was sex with a stranger; I shouldn't expect anything more.

After clean-up in the downstairs powder room, I head upstairs and find myself in Rocco's bedroom. Here, I steal one of Rocco's Polo shirts and a pair of Blackpool jeans, just to get home in. Once dressed, I call a cab, which takes me back to Flamingo Cove, leaving Rocco out of my mind and life ... for the time being.

Chapter 8 – Bottom Tales

I almost forget about my appointment with Walter Landing, Flamingo Cove's out-of-the-closet author. Walter is sixty-nine years old and has such paperback mystery titles on the local book store shelves as *The Candy Boy Murder*, *The Prince Charming Massacre* and *The Queer Cowboy's Hanging*. He's been writing mysteries since he was a junior at Flamingo Cove University. Before retiring as a full-time writer he worked the beat in Fort Lauderdale for over twenty-five years. He's pudgy, bald, and quite serious regarding his fictional work.

Walter is not uninteresting or bland. Like Rocco Malonni, he keeps an arrangement of male doll babies at his service, all of which are paid very well, including me. I do occasional work for Walter; he usually calls me, and we arrange an appointment to meet and discuss my next phase of employment with him, like our meeting this afternoon.

My position does not entail sexual favors like his other young pups. Nor do we sit and drop acid, which he is known to partake in at least two times a week. Vicious rumors proclaim that one of his boy-employee pups – Philip Berg, I believe – is a major whore, banging Walter every other day. Vinnie Rock will definitely give the old man a blowjob for cash. And Ted Martin, a sassy vixen in our small community, will get on his knees and lick the writer's rectum with pleasure, for a full week's pay.

My business with the author includes running simple errands, purchasing Mont Blanc pens, and mailing off his bills. I occasionally pick up his lunch at Pyro's Deli, or purchase mysterious tools at Killer Whale Hardware, devices that inspire Walter to create his fiction. All in all, it's a harmless job with good pay.

Walter sometimes lets me read his manuscripts, a chapter here or there, but rarely. This act is a total honor for me, since I'm like a nobody. He gives me a red or green medium point Integra pen, and instructs, "Two things. One, find my mistakes. Two, find my mistakes."

In truth, I like to read his work before it's published. My opinions are weak and tawdry, but Walter doesn't seem to mind. I hardly ever share a substantial idea of criticism, but he always finds a way of complimenting me. "You've been very helpful, Derek. I will gladly take your comments into the deepest consideration."

Today, we meet at one of his favorite watering holes, Timely Books on Palm Way. Walter likes to cuddle up in a booth and spend his afternoons writing here. Most of the time, though, he's more into the Vivaldi playing on the speakers, or all the cutie queers coming and going. Walter disguises his people-watching by arranging three Mead notebooks in front of him, two of which are filled with notes regarding his newest work, and a third that he uses to write in, if ever. He is afraid of laptops and the Internet, which doesn't surprise me, since he's sixty-nine. The Mead notebooks are his safety and comfort, leaving him feeling repugnant of the computer world.

Occasionally, he shops in the store for Marilyn Monroe biographies and drinks cappuccinos. He always leaves Carlos Menendez, Timely Books's owner, a fifty dollar tip at the register, paying for his hours in the store.

To my surprise, I am not late for our appointment: three o'clock sharp. Bonita Espana is behind the register area, a sixty-two-year-old *conchita* from Palisades Springs, a neighboring community to Flamingo Cove. The lovely Cuban prices a new stack of Nora Roberts paperbacks. When walking through the store to meet Walter, she yells, "*Hola, bambino!*"

"Hi, Bonnie!" I call out, zooming to Walter's booth.

Walter wears a marigold beret today, which is no surprise for me. I notice the new mustache above his lips, and reading glasses. I inquire, "Are we incognito today, Walter?"

"Hush, darling ... You were almost late. I've simply become the character in my new novel. You can explain your almost-tardiness over a cappuccino." He raises his right hand and a red-headed cutie – jumping Jesus does he look like Farrell! – takes his order. Once Farrell's twin escapes the booth, Walter says, "You look refreshed. Tell Uncle Walter who's been sleeping in your bed, Goldilocks?"

Is it this obvious that I've just gotten my bottom thumped? How exactly refreshed do I look? Like pushed-against-a-foyer-wall fresh? Or, rough and tumbled fresh? Maybe even both.

"Who has had an interest in your bottom?" Walter asks with wide eyes and a full grin, deeply interested in my Farrell-connected-to-my-ass adventures.

This is why I enjoy Walter's company. He's the gay uncle I've never had, and he always places me in the spotlight, no matter when we meet. He is a confidant who enjoys my private business, whether my tales are erotic or not, he listens with appeal.

Frankly, I know the older gentleman gets off on my risqué doings. His new mystery is titled *Bottom Tales*, and I have certainly added to its detailed contents. Walter craves my whorish behavior, able to wet his dry and aged pen, among other pointed objects he is equipped with.

I fulfill his needs and leave no detail spared regarding my almost-connection with Rocco, and my naughty doings with Farrell in the foyer at the goon's beach house.

Walter blushes, taking mental notes. He says, "I must get a leprechaun for myself."

"If I encounter Farrell again, I'll mention your name."

Joon, Farrell's twin, delivers two cups of cappuccino and a tiny plate of chocolate chip biscotti.

Walter slips the waiter a twenty and says, "You are a sunflower." He pats the boy's bottom, giggles and picks up his cup of hot drink.

To my surprise, Fisk enters Timely Books. He saunters up to Bonnie's counter and asks, "Did my copy of *War and Peace* come in?"

Something tells me Fisk is not the Tolstoy-type, possibly buying the tome for a relative as a gift. In my opinion, Fisk would enjoy chick-lit or something like James Patterson. His brain is dull around the edges and inoperative. Perhaps a Danielle Steel would suffice for his reading needs.

Bonnie tells Fisk that she'll look for the Tolstoy.

Fisk says, "What? I ordered *War and Peace*."

Bonnie rolls her eyes, shakes her head and walks away from the drug dealer.

Fisk shrugs his shoulders and escapes to the window display, beginning to finger new hardbacks.

Walter is in seventh heaven, a master at people-watching. He asks, "Who is that morsel of delicious meat that just walked in?"

Fisk is cute, nicely built, young and one hundred percent pure beef. Perfect for Walter's list of soon-to-fuck men. Fisk is dressed in a clingy pair of Lycra running shorts and a sunflower-yellow tank; the material leaves nothing to one's imagination. Walter cannot take in the pleasure of pontificating the young man's prick size or sculpted chest on his own. Basically, what you see with Fisk is what you get. His physical details are not at all hidden or disappointing.

Walter asks again, "Who is he? I must know. Tell me now."

Down boy. Hold your boxers on. I respond, "I honestly don't know anymore."

"But you do know him, right?"

"Yes. His name is Fisk. He lives in my building. He sells drugs."

"Survival of the fittest. We all have careers."

I find it best to keep my trap shut about Fisk's involvement with Rocco and the Baskin Fish Company; some things are better left unsaid. Plus, I don't want Mr. Mobster or the Boy Bangers to come after my ass; minus Rocco, of course. Business is business, I assume, and my questionable connection with Fisk is better being off limits to discuss.

"Will you introduce me to him?" Walter looks like a child again, or teenager ready to get laid. Wide-eyed and happy, he becomes hungry for some new ass.

I should tell Walter not to get wrapped up in Fisk's bad business. Instead, I agree to the introduction and say, "I'll be back in a minute."

Walter nods his head with delight, eventually taking a sip of his hot brew.

I see that Fisk holds a copy of Christopher Rice's *The Moonlit Earth* when I saunter up to his side. He seems surprised to see me, dots a kiss to my cheek, and says, "Derek, what are you doing here?"

I point to the novel he holds and say, "Buy it. I loved it."

"I like Ben Tyler." Fisk places the Rice back down in the display where he discovered it and looks over my shoulder for Bonnie at the register area. He informs me, "The cunt is never going to find my fucking book. She's looking for Tolstoy and I want *War and Peace*."

I correct him with class, "Saint Bonnie is the goddess of books and will unquestionably find Tolstoy's *War and Peace* for you."

As Fisk absorbs my information, I look over my shoulder and observe Walter in his booth. The writer waits patiently for my return with news on the drug dealer. I turn my attention back to Fisk and ask, "Have you ever met Walter Landing?"

"The queer author from Coconut Key?" Fisk's eyebrows raise with excitement, fully interested.

"The one and only."

"I absolutely love his mysteries."

This is a shock. I've never taken Fisk as the mystery reader. I go with it though, and ask, "Would you like to meet Mr. Landing? He's visiting here today."

"Are you kidding me?" Fisk's voice raises an octave. He gawks around me and sees Walter. "Holy fuck," he whispers, "I see him. Take me over to him. I'm not leaving until I shake his hand."

"Let me lead you astray," I say.

Fisk obeys, following me to Walter.

Walter and Fisk sit beside each other in a booth. I decide rather sensibly that they should get a room and fuck their brains out. It's absolutely disgusting how the old man is all over Fisk. It's more disgusting to watch the drug dealer accept Walter's groping hands. Walter gets a good grip on his bicep, ass and cock – whatever is graspable. He unconditionally flirts with Fisk, fawning over the drug dealer. Fisk is a whore for the attention and takes it all in, every nipple-pinch and penis-tug. He likes to be the center of attention, particularly in the company of a famous author. He's not at all perturbed with the old man's dancing fingertips across his abs and between his legs. Nor does the tenant of apartment 8-F seem to mind when Walter slips a few fingers down into his skin-tight shorts and begins to travel where many men have traveled before. Fisk doesn't jump away. He takes it like a man, enjoying himself, loving every minute of Walter's hunger.

A fluffy discussion of *The Prince Charming Massacre* takes place between the two. Fisk sounds ridiculous when he says, "I have all your books."

"And a nice cock," Walter whispers. He rubs Fisk's tool under the table – I just know he is. "Bring the books by my beach house tonight, and I will personally sign them." He is smooth, just like how the Gulf's tide rolls in and out, a master at seduction, obviously.

In truth, the only thing Walter wants to autograph is Fisk's poundable bottom with his extended tongue.

Fisk takes the bait, though, smiling from ear to ear, and says, "I'll be there."

Walter, with his free hand, finds a business card with his name, address and personal numbers on it. The card is sunflower-yellow with black lettering. He hands it over to Fisk and instructs, "Show up at seven. I hate tardiness. I'll have dinner prepared for us."

Saint Bonnie calls out from her register area, *"War and Peace!"*

Fisk looks up and shifts his view to Bonnie.

Bonnie waves the mega-novel overhead.

Fisk turns his attention back to Walter and says, "Wow, I can't believe this is happening."

What's happening is simple: after laying some pretty sturdy groundwork, Walter has just landed his next fuck. He is not at all interested in the Danielle Steel reader's mind, though. What he wants is to selfishly peal the drug dealer's clothes away from his nicely built body and process an indecent tour of his skin. He desires nothing less than to touch and taste Fisk's summertime tan. In doing so, Walter will fully investigate Fisk's private areas with fingers and mouth, later this evening.

An impatient, and perhaps humorous, Bonnie yells out, "I've got your fucking book over here, mister!" She drops the seventy-pound novel to her counter, waking those who are reading James Joyce or Henry James.

With an outlined boner in his shorts, Fisk escapes the booth. He excuses himself from the mystery writer's side. "I can't wait to see you tonight."

Walter is glued to Fisk's plump cock. It looks like a balloon/sausage/telephone pole. Walter says, "I can't wait for you to come."

I roll my eyes.

Fisk vanishes, covering his popper with two palms.

Walter heavily sighs, in love.

Fisk, while paying for his hardback copy of *War and Peace*, and attempting to discreetly push his boner away, does not comprehend that he is being watched. I am watching Fisk. The writer watches Fisk. And a third party also watches Fisk; a male somebody sits on a wooden bench outside the bookstore, peers through Consega sunglasses, and is half-hidden behind a daily *Flamingo Cove Tribune*.

Who is the handsome stranger in his black denim pants and clinging white tee? He resembles Ashton Kutcher, whom I have always had a major Hollywood crush on. Does the stranger work for Rocco, or is he a goon belonging to the Baskin Fish Company? No matter who he is, Ashton is not the employee of the month. He wears a black watch/radio transmitting device on his right wrist, which looks quite ultra-modern and sexy. As he watches Fisk, Ashton speaks into his banded wrist. And once Fisk is through at the cash register, leaving the bookstore, it is quite obvious that Ashton follows the drug dealer down Palm Way.

I don't intervene. What happens between Ashton and Fisk is none of my business. There is no reason why I should become involved in Fisk's missing money mess. Ashton will just have to accomplish what he wants with Fisk and ...

"I can't wait to get inside that young man's pants, Derek," Walter shares, breaking my attention away from the Ashton and Fisk scene. Is Walter this oblivious to what has just transpired outside Timely Books? Or, is he far too concerned about slipping his cock into Fisk's mouth, among other orifices?

"You're a horny old man," I preach.

"Is it that apparent?" Walter takes a nibble of biscotti and washes it down with a sip of his cappuccino.

"You reek of desperation. If I didn't know any better I'd say you were ready to fuck Fisk right over this table."

"Stop, Derek. Pointing out the obvious is rude." Walter blushes and waves a hand in my direction. "Besides, I would never do PDA at my age."

"It's too late for that, my friend. I think you already have."

I will honestly never know what transpires at Walter's private, one-attendee dinner party and book signing. The only picture I can muster of the event is what he allows me to review in Chapter Four of *Bottom Tales* early next year:

F arrives on time. He smells of light sweat and the need to be bitten ... F has three shots of Jack Daniels. Each shot goes to his head and he finds it comfortable to remove his shirt ... He's drunk, on overload, and he says, "I want you to sign my books while I'm fucking you." ... Sticky semen shoots on the pages; the mystery novels are ruined ... Post-sexed, while cuddling, F decides to spend the night and ...

The chapter is unforgettable, fully naughty beyond one's expectations. Although I am not certain that the narrator is Walter himself, and the character simply known as F is Fisk, I surely would place a hefty bet that suggests the chapter is more biographical than bogus, and certainly not a figment of the author's imagination.

Questions remain unanswered: Did Walter drug Fisk and take advantage of him? Was Fisk willing to share a bottom tale with the author? Are the two secret lovers, no matter the steep number of years separating them? Perhaps a remaining chapter in Walter's developing work will compile the answers and enlighten me.

We get down to business. Walter pulls out a manila-colored envelope from one of his Mead notebooks. He passes the envelope to me, which is semi-thick and durable. Walter says, "Once again, young man, I desire your services."

"Another wedding?"

"Oh yes. Not a year goes by without attending three weddings and just as many funerals. When you're my age, it's all you'll have to look forward to."

It is not uncommon to be Walter's paid guest at uppity functions. Throughout the past three years I have accompanied him to various events: book readings and signings, banquets, award ceremonies, brunches, auctions and birthday parties. The events are always trendy and exciting to attend. Plus, the pay is very steep. Taking on the role of supporter, assistant, lover, griever, boyfriend, pool boy, listener, and pet is one of my uncanny skills. Walter calls me a natural, and always compliments me on my dashing manners, wardrobe and social skills.

The invitation is no surprise at first. I finger and admire it with deep pleasure. I see that the envelope is addressed to Mr. Walter Landing & Guest. I pull out the already opened invite, reservation card and directions. The heavy-weight Vellum paper smells of lavender. Each document is cream-colored and gold-embossed. There are no tacky ribbons or confetti, thank Jesus. I find the invite portion, flip it over to read, and feel my heart immediately drop to my knees.

The invitation is to attend a commitment ceremony between Mr. Andrew James Chaz & Mr. Worthington Philip Lewis. The ceremony is being held at the Gulf Bay Stables; a very posh property approximately two hours south of Flamingo Cove. The date is set for a Sunday in late August.

I drop the invite to the table as my entire body tenses. I attempt to construe the misconstrued in my mind, but can't. Color washes from my face. I freeze with shock, terror, something raw and poisonous flushing through my body.

61

"What is it?" Walter questions.

I cut to the chase, bitter and bold, "Mr. Chaz is the guy from apartment 4-E. The architect I'm fucking."

"Oh dear," Walter whispers, bathed in embarrassment. "I'm sorry, Derek. I didn't know." He finds the abandoned invite on the table and hides it away.

"Of course you didn't know."

Walter reaches across the table and pats the back of my left hand. "Do you want something strong to drink? You know I carry a flask of whiskey with me at all times."

I shake my head.

"Really," Walter soothes, "I'm sorry."

He can obviously see and feel my heartbreak. Although Mr. Chaz and I have not pursued our relationship in full, I was willing to give him a shot. I am broken now, torn and crumpled. There is no way I can see him again, no matter how handsome and professional he is. We are no longer anything, I declare emotionally.

"Honey," Walter says, "don't cry." He passes me his napkin for my eyes and nose.

I sniffle and ask, "Who is this Worthington guy?"

Walter seems apprehensive at first to further discuss the matter. He comes around, though, and shares, "I'm surprised you've never heard of Worth Lewis."

I shake my head, sniffling. "I haven't."

"Christ," Walter whispers, uncomfortable with our conversation. "He's a tycoon in the gay film industry. Think Chi Chi LaRue without all the drag. Worth is a billionaire who walks and talks gay money. He owns the film company Gladiator Media Limited and Pandom Press, my publishing house. This is how I know Worth. He is basically my boss, and personal friend, which explains the invitation."

"Stop," I instruct. "I've heard enough. This is ruining my day."

"Yes, of course. I completely understand. I'll find someone else to attend the ceremony with me. I can ..."

I cry like a baby and can't sit here any longer. Mr. Chaz has attempted to murder my heart and embarrass me. He has not only lied to me, but he has also humiliated me. I stand and quickly say, "I have to go, Walter. All of this is too much to consume right now."

Walter understands and apologizes again. While I bolt away, exiting the bookstore, he calls out, "Derek! Derek, honey! I'll be thinking of you, sweetie!"

I'm long gone, though. Out the door I go, into the wild, wild world of mobsters, and a heap of new trouble and confusion.

Chapter 9 – Demands
of Boyfriendhood

That dick-licking freak! That creepy fucking bastard! Loser-whore! Two-timing ass-eater! This is what I think of while walking down Palm Way, pissed off at Mr. Chaz and his future commitment ceremony to Worth Lewis.

The Florida sun belts me across the face. It's the time of day when it will rain for approximately ten minutes, and then abruptly stop. I don't care if I get burned or wet. Whatever Mother Nature has in store for me, I'll take it from the bitch. Fuck the action of taking a cab back to the apartment building. I need to walk and calm down after my visit with Walter.

If Mr. Chaz is in his apartment, he'd better watch out. I'm ready to chew off his balls. If he's a lucky cocksucker, he won't be home. He'll be thanking Jesus to live yet another day!

I still can't believe the news: Mr. Chaz is permanently hooking up with Worth, whomever the fuck he is. The information leaves me distraught and catty. The architect cannot possibly be involved with another man when he's semi-involved with me. Worth is just someone Walter devised in his fictional-fuck-world. The invitation he showed me was bogus. This is a joke – it just has to be!

It's not a joke – I can feel this deep inside. Mr. Chaz is no longer my Mr. Right. He has turned into a lying bastard, like the other sleepovers in my life. The commitment ceremony is real, just like the invitation. There is nothing bogus about ...

A white van pulls up beside me on Palm Way. This is not a shocker, though, since Florida has about seventy million white vans driving around. What shocks me is how quickly the side door slides open and one, two, three guys in ski masks jump out and surround me on the sidewalk. The trio is all decked out in black from head to toe. Two hold automatic pistols.

Mr. 3 yells at me, "Get in the fucking van!" and does a bear hug on my body.

Mr. 1 and Mr. 2 have their automatic pistols aimed at my head.

Mr. 3 pushes me toward the van. Eventually he lifts me up and tosses me inside. Seconds later, he jumps in behind me.

Mr. 1 and Mr. 2 leap into the van behind him.

Mr. 2 slides the van door closed and hops in the passenger's seat. The van zooms away, burning rubber.

"Don't even think about moving a fucking inch," Mr. 3 sits across from me. He holds what looks to be a .9mm silencer at my chest. The guy is on the chunky side and smells like pizza. I notice his very blue eyes, which are sort of attractive. He asks, "What the fuck are you looking at?"

Mr. 2 yells from the front seat, "Don't ask him any fucking questions!"

"Who are you guys?" I inquire, foolishly.

Mr. 1 has green eyes, a muscular build, and smells like musk. He points his own silencer at me and rattles off, "Don't worry about who we are."

Mr. 3 removes my cell phone and wallet. He quickly passes my belongings to Mr. 2 in the front seat.

Mr. 1 asks Mr. 2, "Yorkie, do you want him blind-folded?"

"He's a feisty fairy. Give it a try."

Mr. 1 places a blindfold over my eyes. Before doing so, I try to get a glimpse of the driver. She has coal-black hair and flamingo earrings dangling from her earlobes.

Yorkie instructs, "Bind his wrists and ankles together. Put some tape over his mouth. Just don't remove his clothes."

Shit. This is serious stuff. I'm in trouble. These guys (and Miss Earrings) are rough bitches and mean business.

I hear either Mr. 1 or Mr. 3 rip a band of duct tape off a roll. One of them slaps the band across my mouth. In a matter of seconds my ankles and wrists are zipped together with plastic ties. Now, one of them puts the muzzle of his gun to my right temple and says, "Don't do anything stupid, or we'll blow your fucking head off."

These guys are not into circle jerks or watching gay cinema together, are they? They seem a bit too serious for me, and way too straight. I'd better be on my best behavior if I know what is good for me.

Yorkie instructs from his front seat, "Knock him out, Joey."

I expect a blow to the head or fist-punches to my face. This doesn't happen, though. Joey holds my right arm up and sticks my bicep with a sharp object. He says, "You're going to feel sick to your stomach for a second, and then you'll fall asleep."

Someone says, "Just relax, Derek. Ride it out. You have a meeting to attend in Miami."

I do ride it out. My stomach turns and I become dizzy. Blackness settles behind my eyes and my thoughts are lost. Before I black out, losing consciousness, I hear Yorkie say, "Mr. Malonni is going to be roaring pissed if we're late. Speed it up, Bev."

I hear running water. Just a sprinkle. Somewhere close. Is it raining outside? Is someone taking a piss next to my head? Did Quinn leave the tap on in the kitchen again?

Tink. Trickle. Tink.

My head feels like a bowling ball. I can barely open my eyes. Everything is a misunderstood fog. I can't move my legs or arms. I know I'm lying on my back, but where?

"Mr. Reed? ... Derek Reed?" It's a female's voice, possibly Bev's, the van's driver during my unexpected abduction.

"Let him wake on his own, Bev," someone says. It's not Joey or Yorkie. The voice is more sophisticated and sounds arrogant. "He's going to be very thirsty when he comes around. Fetch Mr. Reed a glass of water."

In my grey state of disturbia, I smell roses and Usher cologne. I blink a few times, but my vision is blurry. I continue to hear water running: Tink. Trickle. Tink.

"Is he going to be okay, Boss?" Yorkie's familiar voice asks.

"Absolutely. It's just a minor sedative."

67

I hear footsteps nearing my body.

Boss says, "Thanks, Bev. Put the water on the table in front of Mr. Reed."

Someone brushes fingers through my hair; I can feel long fingernails against my scalp. Are they Bev's or Yorkie's? Honestly, I'm not sure.

"I want to be left alone with him," Boss says.

A parade of footsteps exit the room. I imagine a line of my abductees leaving my side. I hear a door close behind them, silence and … Tink. Trickle. Tink.

The man named Boss says, "Mr. Reed, I know you're groggy. It's just a minor side effect from the cocktail my men gave you. You'll be able to see and sit up in a just another moment or two."

My mouth is dry. I open and close it. I begin to feel my legs and arms again. My upper lip is no longer numb, as well as my neck and back. Little by little, I regain life. My wrists and ankles are no longer bound by plastic ties. My mouth is duct tape-free. I'm alive. Thank God.

A statue of David stares at me. He pees inside the room; the fountain I've been hearing. The floor is black-and-white tile. The ceiling looks like the Sistine Chapel. Louise the XIV furniture is scattered about the massive room. I lie on a stiff settee across from a man who looks like an older Rocco.

Boss says, "Drink some water, Derek."

I reach for the crystal tumbler next to an arrangement of aromatic tea roses on the exquisite coffee table and take a sip. I place the tumbler back on the table and sit up.

"I just want you to know that I'm not going to hurt you. We have some minor business to take care of, and then I'll send you on your way." Boss clears his throat, lightly coughing into one of his fists.

The guy totally resembles Rocco, or vice versa. I know the stranger has to be Antonio "Boss" Malonni. Rocco has the same eyes and lips, which are both handsome. Rocco even said he was given his daddy's good genes, which is now apparent to me.

"I'm sorry about my men and the van incident. Sometimes I realize my staff can be a little rough." Again, Boss clears his throat.

"Mr. Malonni, with all due respect ..."

"I know you don't want to be here, Derek. I apologize for any inconvenience, of course. I just have a few questions for you regarding Rocco, if you don't mind." Boss's voice is tender and smooth. One would never guess by the sound of it that he's a Miami mobster.

I ask without attitude, on my best behavior, "Is Rocco safe?"

He nods his head. "I'm glad you have a positive interest in my son. There is no emergency. Rocco is in Tampa on business at the moment." He picks up a cell phone-size black box to his right and presses one of its red buttons. He says, "This meeting between us is a personal and private matter. I thought it best to let Rocco handle a job elsewhere."

A red light flashes on the black box. Boss says into the unit, "Joey, send Bev in." He places the black box down on the coffee table separating us and says to me, "Your interest in my son is very keen. Do you want to tell me about that?"

My eyebrows automatically lift and my mouth turns instantly dry again. I want to reach for the tumbler of water in front of me, but keep still, half-frightened I might just do something wrong in his presence. I swallow dry air, feel befuddled and fully on alert.

"You don't have to comment, Mr. Reed. In truth, I have pictures of you with my son."

I wonder what kind of pictures and hope they are not of the two of us on Rocco's beach house patio. This would be far too embarrassing.

"It's quite obvious my son has a crush on you, which concerns me, and ..."

"Look, we were just having some fun together," I interrupt.

Boss smiles. It's not cold or calculating. The smile is actually warm and effectively smooth.

Bev, the van's getaway driver, walks into the room. She carries a white box and places it on the coffee table, next to my tumbler of water.

"Thank you, Bev," Boss shares.

The driver exits the room, silently.

Boss leans forward and opens the white box. Inside is a pearl-handled pistol of some unknown caliber. I suppose he's going to shoot me and hide my body in a cement floor somewhere. Maybe he'll chop my appendages off and send them to Quinn. Whatever he's about to accomplish with the pistol will not be joyous, I'm sure.

He places the white-handled pistol on the table between us. Underneath the pistol is a stack of 4x6 glossy photographs. Boss removes the stack from the box and says, "Rocco would shoot me if he knew I shared these with you." He passes me the photographs. "Just so you know ... that boy is my pride and joy. Since your little accident on Pilsner Street with him, you're the only guy in his life that he talks about."

The photographs are enlightening and amazing: a boy-Rocco in fifth grade with buck teeth smiles graciously at the camera; Rocco builds a snowman in January 1987; a seventeen year old Rocco sports a navy-blue suit, standing beside one of his brothers on Easter Sunday in April rain; Rocco sunbathes in a yellow trunk on some unnamed beach; Rocco naps on a couch at twenty-two; Rocco reads *Paradise Lost* under an oak tree in the shade at a summertime picnic.

I pile the photographs up the way Boss handed them to me. "These are fascinating. Rocco was just as normal as any other kid growing up."

Boss reaches for the stack of photographs and replaces them inside the white box. He says, "Remember, this is our little secret. Rocco doesn't need to know about it."

"Of course," I share, keeping my word – forever.

Rocco's father places the pistol on top of the photographs and closes the white box. He sits back and rests his hands on his lap. He says, "I have a lot of respect for you, Derek. You lead a very clean and safe life. You make wise decisions. I think you're a very acceptable boyfriend for my son."

I'm not taken aback by this discovery. I don't want to sound arrogant, but I know I'm a nice guy and have a clean record.

In truth, I'm not at all surprised that Boss knows everything about me. He is the godfather of a powerful group, right? Control is his motto, and protection of his "family" is at the top of his priority list. Boss is the mob. Carrying out kidnappings is a typical occurrence in his daily life. Knowing everything about his mob-son's friends and boyfriends is nothing out of the ordinary. It's just another day in the life of a goon, I'm sure.

"How do you know Rocco wants me to be his boyfriend?" It's a realistic question without prying too much. Honestly, I'm just curious to know. Does he always choose his son's boyfriends? I wonder. Something tells me he does.

"I know everything my son wants. We're a very close family, which comes first in our lives together. Why wouldn't he want you as his boyfriend? You're charismatic, intelligent, honest and charming. You're a good catch for Rocco." He finds his remote again and presses a green button this time. A second later he says to me, "I'm ordering us a drink to celebrate your boyfriendhood with my son."

Shouldn't we fill Rocco in first? Shouldn't he be present for this unexpected announcement and celebration? Boyfriend keeps shifting from one side of my brain to the other. I quickly become confused. I really just don't understand what has transpired in the last few minutes. Has Boss bequeathed me as his son's boyfriend? I think so. Is this how the Mafia works? Again, I think so. Do I have a vote in this matter? I don't think so.

I have to be honest with myself: Rocco Malonni will not make a bad boyfriend. The world is filled with losers, and I perceive that he's not one of them. There's just one problem, though: I have Mr. Chaz in my sights to become my boyfriend. Is Boss aware of this information? Is Rocco?

Joey returns to the sitting room and places a silver tray on the coffee table between us. The tray holds two martini glasses, a silver shaker, a tiny crystal container filled with olives on one side and toothpicks on the other.

Boss whips up a dry martini and passes it to me. He now makes himself one and toasts my new romance with his son: "To a beautiful relationship with Rocco."

This is insane, I realize. But if I don't agree to it, Boss will pop my head with a twin set of bullets, knocking me off. Of course I'm going to agree to his terms. If he wants me to be his son's boyfriend, I will. I'm dealing with the mob now. People who are very dangerous. Villains who can wipe someone like me off the face of the Earth in a split second. I'll do anything to live another day – honestly.

"To us," I say cheerily, sharing the toast.

We drink. Boss relishes his beverage; a smooth look on his mouth surfaces. Relaxed, out of the blue, he asks, "You have no plans of becoming involved with Fisk, correct?" He takes a casual sip of his martini. "Listen to me, Derek. Fisk Deveraux is trouble. He's not a very smart young man. He's dangerous and harmful. I highly suggest you stay away from him."

I shake my head, agreeing not to have any connection to Fisk. If I don't agree, Boss still has access to the white-handled pistol on the coffee table and will pop a bullet into my right shoulder or skull. It's better to follow his rules instead of making up my own. "I understand," I whisper, complying to his wish.

Boss says, "I know you buy illegal items from Fisk for Felicia Horodowski. I respect this, Derek. I comprehend the woman has stomach cancer, and you're just trying to help her. Felicia is a good woman who just happens to be in severe pain. Purchasing medicine for her does not make you a bad person. In fact, it probably makes you more civilized."

I feel awkward. This conversation with Rocco's father is far too bizarre. What have I stumbled into, anyway? Now, I'm Rocco's arranged boyfriend and have permission to buy Felicia more pot. Today is just fucked up to the highest degree, an unexpected dream of sorts that is totally out of control.

"Derek?"

I'm all eyes, feeling drained. I don't want the martini any longer. I just want to be back at "the building" and on my couch, napping. "Yes, sir?"

He finishes off his drink and pours himself a second one. "As for Rocco's houseboy, Farrell, I highly suggest you keep your skin away from his. Farrell's very frisky, and I would prefer you didn't cheat with him behind my son's back."

Fucking flamingoes! Does Boss really know about my foyer-affair with Farrell? Obviously, he does. How about the other dudes I've casually played around with in the sack, among other places of interest? I'm sure Boss has a mental list, ready to fire off names and my favorite fuck positions.

He says, "Don't be embarrassed. We all need the occasional houseboy to fuck. I certainly have nothing against sex with strangers. Let me just say that from here out, you will be faithful to my son. Do you understand?"

I nod my head, nervous as hell.

"I'm glad we had this little chat this afternoon. I feel that our relationship is quite strong, and growing." Boss's cell phone chirps with a new text message. He reviews the message and heavily sighs. His attention is now drawn to me and he says, "I'm a very busy man, Derek. I must respond to this." He stands with his fresh drink and walks to the door where Joey comes and goes. Before leaving, he spins around and rattles off, "I'll have Bev fly you home. She'll return your wallet and cell phone. A Mercedes is parked out front for your convenience. From here you will be taken to my private plane. Bev will explain the rest."

As I sit inside a Cessna plane with Bev playing pilot, confusion is found. What has just transpired in the past twenty-four hours?

A list of notes/facts begin to form inside my mind:

1.) Rocco's father really is a mobster, and some rough fuckers work for him.

2.) I have officially become Rocco's boyfriend, and he doesn't even know it yet.

3.)   I've agreed to stay away from Fisk. No problem. I can accept this. Boss is right, Fisk is trouble.

4.)   Farrell MacCormick is totally off limits to fuck, among other guys in the queer field. I'll have to resort to some heavy-duty masturbating, unless Rocco decides to put out.

I take all of these details serious. There has to be some type of rationale for the list. How significant is the list to me? What objective do I really have pertaining to these ...

No, there isn't a single drop of rationale. I'm still confused. Baffled to the fullest. Whatever. My life is still going to go on, in misery or happiness, I guess.

But hey, at least I have a really hot boyfriend, right?

Chapter 10 – Guys Get Wet Night!

I have things to do and people to see:

Mr. Chaz is not in his apartment; so much for ripping him a new asshole regarding his upcoming commitment ceremony with Worth Lewis and lying to me.

Fisk is nowhere to be found. Of course he's not found. The man is accused of stealing two hundred thousand dollars from Antonio "Boss" Malonni, the biggest mobster in Florida. I still need to ask Fisk if he'll perform a masturbation scene for me. If he cordially rejects my offer, then maybe he'll know of someone at Pallyo who can fill the position for him.

I want to tell Felicia everything about my morning and afternoon, leaving no detail spared. To no avail, I discover her dozing in the sun on her patio and decide to leave her be.

Back in my apartment, Quinn wants to take a nap together. We snuggle in the shade on his queen-sized bed for over an hour. Afterward, we eat cold chicken salad sandwiches for dinner and watch a movie.

When evening falls, Quinn wants me to go to Pallyo with him, a local gay bar, in hopes of getting laid by a jock, cowboy or construction worker. He stands in front of the bathroom mirror and plays with the tips of his hair. Quinn sports a plum-colored cotton towel around his nicely built waist. He looks extra beefy and just right, still a little damp from his shower.

My roommate is physically beautiful in all aspects of the word. A jock who wants to be fucked by a jock. He is horny and confesses to me, "I'm ready for some guy-behind-guy action. It's the only thing on my mind. Can you relate to me?"

Not really. I've had half of Rocco and all of Farrell today. I'm doing pretty good in the "getting laid" department. I say to Quinn, "If you find a hot Italian tonight at the bar, I need to know."

Quinn fingertips product into his hair. He asks, "You hungry for some Italian?"

I'm ready to hop in the shower. I've just finished brushing my teeth beside him, drop my olive-colored shorts to the bathroom floor, and step into the shower. I turn on the warm spray, position myself underneath it, and inform Quinn that Felicia wants to hook me up with an Italian fix.

"I can totally dig a woman like her," Quinn says. "Fisk is Italian. Would you enjoy a jackoff scene with him?"

I shampoo my hair: start at the temples, work to the top, and move fingertips to the back. "Fisk is definitely a candidate. Unfortunately, he's missing."

Quinn scares the Jesus out of me. He pulls the shower curtain back with a quick yank.

Surprised, I drop Lever 2000 to the stall.

He informs with a broad smile, "Buddy, Fisk is hot to the core and would do a porn star-perfect scene for you again." Quinn is completely naked. His cock is limp, hanging down to his knees. He drops his head and studies his thatch of bristly, triangular-shaped hair. He asks, "Do you think I should shave my boys?" referring to his drooping balls.

I bend down and pick up the bar of Lever, which I roll against my firm chest, creating suds. "How fuzzy are they?"

Quinn lifts his cock with two fingers and inspects his boys. "They're not soft like the guys at Pallyo like them."

"Then you should shave, my friend."

He tugs the curtain closed and heads back over to the mirror and his cordless Norelco. Quinn calls through the curtain, "By the way, are you working out more? Your body is rocking tight these days."

"Let's chalk it up as good sex."

"Thatta' boy," Quinn laughs. He has the cordless shaver on, manscaping.

I've always found it a turn-on to watch a guy shave his steamy goods. I discreetly pull back the curtain. Quinn has a full erection against his flat torso. He holds its mushroom-sculpted cap with three fingertips. His other hand holds the Norelco, and he goes to town with the buzzing device on his sack. Fuzzies of his dark pubic hair shower the floor; he'll clean them up later. For now, he works like an artist, sculpting his fuzz like Leonardo Da Vinci painted the Sistine Chapel.

I flag a boner in just a few seconds. My joint firms up, needing a piece of Quinn-ass. Enough with the sex thing, though. My cock maybe needs a break. Sex isn't mandatory all the time, is it? I push my roommate out of my mind and think how Mr. Chaz is breaking my heart. What a piece of ...

"By the way," Quinn turns off the Norelco and says from outside the curtain. "Rocco's looking for you."

"What for?"

"He didn't say."

What does the sexy hotshot want with me? This is nice to know. I digest it with appeal and reply, "Rocco's my Mr. Right. I could easily see me long-term with him."

Quinn finishes his manscaping. Without notice, he climbs into the shower and stands directly behind me. He grabs the bar of Lever 2000 out of my right hand and begins to soap up my strong back. I feel his rock against my firm bottom, which makes me forget about Rocco. His soapy hand reaches around my right side and greets my solid chest. I inquire, "What are you doing back there, *compadre?*"

Quinn says, "I shouldn't give you a handjob," as his fingers lather up my pecs, tight stomach, and settle on my private part.

"You really shouldn't," I nervously say. "I think I'm Rocco's boyfriend."

"You think? What does that mean?"

"Nevermind. I'll explain later."

Quinn says, "It doesn't matter, anyway. What happens in the shower stays in the shower."

"But I ..." I have no control of the situation. I shouldn't be with Quinn like this. I've promised Rocco's father to be his son's boyfriend. I've committed myself to Rocco. This is wrong what I'm doing. It's sinful and ...

The soap and Quinn's right hand feel too good to pull away from. Instead, I just go with the flow and proceed with his hand-adventure. My cock smoothly glides within his grip. I huff, losing breath, buck his soapy fist, and feel a buzz of sex-elation shift through my tense torso.

His cock is a swollen pole behind me, which generously slips between my thighs. Quinn clasps me to his upright body with one hand. His other hand plays teeter-totter with my dick. He nibbles on my neck, one earlobe, and whispers, "This is all about you, Derek. Come whenever you want to come."

Holy queen kingdom! I can only tolerate this for so long. I can't take his soapy hand on my tool. I can't ...

Quinn thumps the area between my shaking legs with his inflated beef. He is not inside me, but the action is just as fiery-hot. He whispers, "Do it, Derek. Fuck my hand. Think of it as my tight ass. Fuck it hard and long. Shoot your load into it. Fill me with your cum."

He continues to toy with my nipple, laps his tongue against my neck, humps my thighs, and does an incredible handjob on my Johnny. It's all too much to take on at one time. It's impossible not to come.

I warn him, "I'm spraying."

"I'm ready for it. Let it fly."

A beautiful vibration of orgasm sweeps through my interior. I shiver at Quinn's touch, exploding a stream of man-syrup from my dick. I writhe with passion, unable to breathe, trapped within his hands. White fluid fires into the shower from my spigot, spraying out like a cleaning agent.

Stroking my joint, Quinn coaches, "Pump all the juice out, dude."

"Quinn," I say, "you shouldn't have done this." The last of my sap exits my thumper, dripping to the Spanish tile.

He loosens his grip on my cock and chest, knowing I am post-sexed. My roomie turns me around with his sticky fingers and kisses me on the lips.

The kiss is rather shocking with some intense fire for men who just happen to be roommates and friends; shame on me. I really don't like to kiss Quinn, but this one is pretty magical. It's something I never thought we could share and enjoy at the same time. It's a real kiss, long and sensual, and better than some kisses I've shared with long-term boyfriends. If Boss Malonni knew about it … he'd kill me. And Rocco himself wouldn't be too pleased either, since he is now my boyfriend.

In a matter of seconds he escapes the kiss just as quickly as he plants it on my lips. Wide-eyed and dick-hard, he says, "I've wanted to shock you like that for some time now."

"A shock it was." I reach out and grab his upright tube of beef. "Do you want me to do the same thing to you?"

Quinn steps around me and finds himself under the spray. He does a quick rinse, tells me he's taken up too much of my time, and steps out of the shower. In doing so, his left hand pushes my palm and fingers away from his erection. "I'm saving myself for tonight. This was all about you."

"That was pretty intense and selfless. I never knew you had it in you."

Beyond the shower curtain and my grasp, he informs, "That was just one of my specialties. Maybe we'll do it again sometime."

"It's an open invitation. You're welcome back any time." I find the bar of Lever 2000 and wash up. I rinse, step out of the shower, dry with a fresh towel, and bolt to my bedroom and closet to choose something tight, colorful and smashing to wear to Pallyo.

In doing so, I tell Quinn about my abduction by Rocco's father, and how I was bestowed Rocco's new boyfriend.

Quinn is about as shocked as me, and exclaims, "You have got to be kidding me?"

"It's the truth."

"So the mob is already working you, isn't it?"

I laugh, slipping into a pair of swimming trunks for the night, and confess, "In truth, I'm a little bit flattered that Boss Malonni thinks I'm good enough for his son."

"That's the craziest thing I ever heard."

"I know, isn't it? But hey, you have to work with what you've got."

Oh my god! It's a GGWN (Guys Get Wet Night) at Pallyo, and Quinn smiles from ear to ear, confirming that he's getting laid. GGW nights are Quinn's whore nights. Random sex with a group of drop dead gorgeous strangers is a top-notch event for him. He claims it's better than X with Absolut, one of his favorite combos.

Pallyo has massive rafts and inner tubes decorating the boy-infested floor. Beyond the dance floor are plastic palms and Jurassic Park-size ferns. A tiki bar with a bamboo canopy welcomes all the queers to buy their favorite drinks. All the drinks showcase umbrellas and fruit. The far left wall is a photo-image of a Cancun or Aruba beach. Upright surfboards and sprawling lawn chairs decorate the area around the bar.

The bar is a beach party for the raunchy. A let-your-cock-out-and-play night for guys only. Pallyo is a dude-playground. It looks rough around the edges on the outside, but inside, it is tease-me perfect. Boys are high-strung on everything from Magic to K. Any pill I want is available at arm's reach. Boys are bare-chested in their skin-tight trunks. Some pop boners, ready to be blown. Others drink alone, sucking up the feisty scene. And the naughty boys – the blowers, ass-munchers, and butt-pounders – get their sexual grooves on (or off). Their bodies are here and there; a scattering of orgies in all directions. Colorful beach balls bounce off spray tan bodies. Bottles of Rolling Rock are poured over bottoms and biceps, and quickly lapped away by straying tongues. The sting of a sexual smell lingers and wavers about the place. The floor has condom wrappers everywhere; the used condoms are tossed in selected stainless steel pals marked: DUMP YOUR BOYS HERE! This is the party of the month, one the guys around Flamingo Cove will be talking about for weeks.

To the right side of the bar is a pile-up of eight young dudes who are freshly doused in cheap beer. Three of the guys still have their trunks on, eating twenty-two year old bums and performing blowjobs on blue rafts. The other five guys are lined up on the inflatables with their legs wide open, sticking straight up, welcoming tongues and lips to mingle with their private parts.

Beyonce sings about a wedding ring. The place rocks with booze, boys and boners. Some hottie who looks like the porn star, Josh Harting, passes me a beer and whispers into my ear, "You want to fuck me?"

I politely decline his proposal and keep the beer. "Josh" vanishes into the crowd, searching out a pitcher to play with. I lean into a pole that holds up the rafters and observe the sex-ruckus around me.

Quinn yells in my direction, "They need a man to get the job done!" and points to the orgy of eight on the plastic rafts. He yanks off his shirt, passes it to me, and vanishes toward an evening of fun. I find an empty stool, drop the shirt on it, and watch Quinn at work on the group of eight dudes.

Digital cameras snap and film the action. The nine-man pile up (including Quinn) is doused with a fresh spray of beer. Quinn looks absolutely delicious with the dots of golden, urine-like liquid dripping down and over his carved torso.

It is not Quinn's first performance in adult films. He starred as a queer banker in a low budget skin flick called *Buck Fucking*. He also did a jackoff scene for a Website called *Meaty Solos*. Other resume-enhancing bottom-performances include *Daddy Shoots His Gun*, *Naughty Night Nurses* and *Beefcake Buffet*.

Quinn is proud of his video work. Although he is not a queer icon or banked a million bucks from his sexual escapades, he showcases his low budget DVDs in our apartment with exuberant pride. It is not uncommon for a queer guest to remove one of the flicks from a shelf and find a bare-bottomed Quinn on its front or rear sleeve. How shocked the guest becomes when they see Quinn naked in the sun and climbing a rock, on a tractor in the buff, or tied up to a bed with leather straps.

I must admit, I'm also proud of Quinn's dick-licking and ass-munching on the five young men in the bar. With chaotic and hungry energy, he goes from one performer to the next. The last of the five bottoms is ready for his needy attention. A blue-eyed blond dandy makes chemical eye contact with Quinn and the crowd goes wild. It's Walt Disney magic between the queens. Quinn kisses the fag on his lips, sucks his nipples, and lands his mouth over a steeping, seven-inch pole.

BC (Blond Cutie) thumps his entire body into Quinn's face. Cock throttles my roomie's slim mouth and causes Quinn to choke. BC is wicked with his hips. He is a rough little fucker that holds Quinn by his head, fucking his face.

There is nothing to panic about. Quinn is a master with the men and boys. Some heavy-duty face-pounding is nothing for him. He is no amateur on GGW nights, and will probably take on maybe four or five guys before deciding to spend the night in one of their beds … and arms.

BC is a maniac and keeps Quinn to himself. The other seven dudes carry out a blowjob circle, having the time of their youthful and dangerous lives on the inflated rafts. BC is one raunchy man-mouth fucker. After a continuous action of rod-plummeting-throat, BC is ready to shoot his load. ABBA is too loud to hear him announce that he's coming; the look on his face – a half open mouth and squinting eyes – is enough for me to comprehend that his cum is going to fly.

BC shoots his boys all over Quinn's chest. Goo slaps against my roomie's nipples and abs. And following his burst, he becomes a die hard player and goes to town on Quinn's chest with his tongue. He licks and laps up his sap with a great big smile on his face, happy to be here at GGWN again.

Once Quinn is fairly clean by tongue and beach towel, BC lies face down on a bright orange inner tube and waits for Quinn's services. He looks over his shoulder and his boyish eyes say: My ass needs the hardest pounding.

Quinn has never rejected a man's bulbous ass to fuck. He certainly can recognize a tight little man-bottom that needs some sufficient grinding. Like the amateur porn star that he is, Quinn promptly drops his trunk to his ankles. No matter how many buddies he boinks, he's safe, and grabs a condom from a beer mug on a nearby table. He opens the condom with his teeth, applies it to his boner, ready for some action.

A spanking is in progress. Shame on BC for being a naughty boy. Quinn knows the little shit has it coming and smacks his behind.

Cherry-colored welts bloom on BC's bottom. He squints in pain, yelling out repulsive vulgarities that are unheard in the crowd because "Take a Chance on Me" blasts from the surrounding speakers.

Of course Quinn knows a cameraman is present; some local by the name of Woody Woodcock who operates his own Website called *Down with Dirty Dudes*. Woody's all over the shit between Quinn and BC, almost in their faces. He moves around the duo for fifteen minutes, since Quinn jumped into the line of boy-bangers. There is no doubt in my mind that Woody will use Quinn's adventure on his site. My roomie obviously has the talent and all the right moves that viewers like, and Woody knows it.

Quinn pushes an inch of his swollen meat into BC. Two inches. Three inches. All of his cock generously slides into BC's used hole. It doesn't take him very long to pull out his tool with a hearty movement. He pushes it in again, pulls it out, pushes it in again, and builds up a fine rhythm between dudes.

Woody's gotta have a woody, because I do. The friction between Quinn and BC is mouth-watering. It's one hundred percent porn fun. Hell, I would even pay the $2.95 per minute for *Down with Dirty Dudes* just to watch the two guys go at it.

Quinn is not a surfer, but he rides BC like a surfboard. All he really needs to fulfill the surfer role is sun block on his nose and a nearby shark. He rides BC's ass with some Cancun passion. Quinn rams his find, pulls out, rams the ass again, pulls out, and just about makes me cream in my trunk.

The guru behind his Sony digital camera has to be loving the dick-hardening scene. Woody goes in for a few close-ups of cock-connected-to-ass, pulls back, and goes in for another close-up.

Quinn sweats up a storm during his BC workout. Perspiration glistens on his chest and thighs. Even the back of his palms sweat, which dig into BC's hips.

How long does Quinn thump BC? I'm really not sure. In truth, he'll be at it all night. For now his time is with BC. From BC he will go to Boxer, Jock, Twink and Olive-Skinned Mechanic. Quinn will have sex all night long, if they don't kick him out of Pallyo first.

I decide to leave my pole and Quinn's sex antics. The dance floor calls out to me. Rainbow Gods, a local band with a new hit, blasts from the speakers. I'm just about on the dance floor when strong arms and hands wrap around my torso, and Rocco says in my right ear, "Derek, I found you."

It's nice to be his catch. I spin around and give him a kiss to remember tonight by, and lead him to the center of the dance floor, ready to see what he's made of.

We dance like high school boys on a drug called Heat. Body parts are discreetly fingered. Hips come together and separate. Mouths embrace and tongues do a dance of their own.

Rocco looks good in an all-black trunk; all the dudes under the glittery disco ball eye him up and down as if he is sweet candy. I scowl and become catty to those who come too close, keeping him in my proximity, all to myself.

He wears a T-shirt that clings to his built torso. I peel it off his skin during a song by The Bathroom Boys, finger his delicious looking chest, and dance with him like a queen of the night.

After three more grooves I drag Rocco to the bar. We order vodka tonics and stand chest to chest among the drinking dudes. I ask, "Did you follow me here?"

"Did you want to be followed?"

Clever. Answer a question with a question. I give him a vodka tonic-kiss and reply, "I'm okay with you following me. You're my personal bodyguard."

A wet body contest begins. Twelve extremely chiseled guys line up on the stage. One of them just happens to be Quinn in the buff, ready for a spray-down of cheap booze. His deflated cock swings between his legs like a chain. Quinn makes eye contact with me and shares a thumbs-up regarding the hottie mobster beside me. He gets hosed down with beer by a bald boxer, smiling like a jock in a bathhouse.

Following one more vodka tonic with Rocco, watching three contestants on stage shake their tight asses and gyrate their goods, Rocco suggests, "How about we get out of here and have some alone time?"

I'm good with the idea and let him lead me through the crowd of screaming and drunken fags. Before I know it, I'm outside with him, under the moon and stars, swept away by his charm and debonair style.

Chapter 11 – Buoy Fun

Pallyo sits next to the Gulf on Pelican Way. We head to the beach and lapping waves. Rocco holds my hand and gently swings it to and fro. He says, "You were hot on the dance floor. I really like your moves."

"You weren't so bad yourself."

"I was the International Champion of Disco for two years," he jokes.

"Don't forget, the best looking mobster in Florida, too."

"Of course. Daddy passed his good genes onto me."

We reach the beach, hidden by the grassy dunes. Rocco releases his hand from mine. He says, "Let's strip out of our trunks and sandals and enjoy the breeze." He kicks off his expensive sandals and goes for my tee. Rocco pulls the fabric over my head and admires my chest in the blue-spirited moonlight. "Your body is rockin' fine. I like how you take care of yourself." My shirt dangles in his left hand while his other hand drags up and down my torso in a rather seductive manner.

"Trust me, my metabolism does most of the work for me. I'm a sucker for strawberry milkshakes and not working out."

"Could have fooled me," he says, touching my navel with a few fingertips. The wind mixes with his fingers; both feel great against my body. He finds a nipple, a few average-size abs, and my navel again. Rocco fingers the rim of my swimsuit and he pulls me toward him. His lips find my mouth, and he indulges in a hearty, windblown kiss that about knocks me off my feet.

We end up like the cover of a gay romance novel: a gentle breeze laps at our hair; our heads are slightly tilted forward, connected in a sultry kiss; Rocco's masculine palms are flush against my bare chest; my shirt lies on the glittery and magical sand; a crescent of silver-blue moon and fairy tale-like clouds make up the backdrop. The cover is quite ominous, but delicious-looking. A best-seller in Greenwich Village and West Hollywood.

Rocco breaks away from me. His shirt is lost somewhere in the bar, and he sports a centerfold-perfect torso. I can't help myself and carelessly dive my mouth to his chest. My lips meet a pointed nipple, a second nipple, and the center of his furry abs. I'm ambitious and lift his right arm. I take in a strong whiff of his man-scent, which makes my cock bounce inside my trunks. I lower his arm and lick a bicep and eventually pull away, preventing myself from a spicy meal.

"Take your suit off," Rocco says, fingering its cotton strings.

I slip out of the suit, now bare-ass on the beach, ready for whatever happens between two guys who just happen to be attracted to each other.

Rocco pulls his suit down and steps out of it. The blue moonlight exemplifies his cut and long rod. Every inch of his body looks like steel. My eyes take in his thighs and hips, scanning his muscled skin. I determine he is more attractive than I. Rocco is David or Adam by Michelangelo. He is sculpted to perfection, the epitome of what a Greek god should look like.

"I'm ugly," he jokes.

I touch one of his nipples and say, "I don't have any problems with ugly."

He shares a hearty laugh.

I return a laugh.

Rocco finds my fingers on his chest and he strolls me to the ocean. Together we walk into the water and feel the waves at our hips. The tide is pretty strong and he faces me, holding me up.

I say, "We're going to drown out here, aren't we?"

He sounds confident, and says, "You'll be safe with me. No matter what the situation is, I'll be there to rescue you."

"You promise?"

"I promise."

I always thought of myself as a tie-me-up-and-fuck-me-hard kind of guy, but this isn't so bad. I'm not into the over-the-top romance shit, but this moment with Rocco is sort of Walt Disney-perfect. His promise reeks of Hallmarkian beauty, which I like, too. Now, what's next? I wonder.

He wraps our naked bodies into a hug and kisses me; the icing on the cake. I'm waiting to hear Celine Dion sing that Titanic song, of course, but the Las Vegas princess has better things to do with her time. In truth, the kiss is perfect and doesn't need Celine. Rocco kisses like a pro: softly, smoothly, and with just a little bit of man-spittle, which I like.

There are no Mafia goons present. There is no Boss Malonni watching our homo-connection. We are alone on the coast, indulging in a kiss that I will remember for a very long time.

I believe our degree of affection is limited, though. Sex between us will not ensue after our shared, coastal embrace. We will not bump-and-grind in the rising tide. Something tells me Rocco wants to wait for as long as he can before fully seducing me. Hugging for now is acceptable, as well as kissing. Fingering my private parts, or possibly licking such areas that queers tend to enjoy, is always an option for Rocco to carry out. He is not like me, though, and chooses his flesh-buddies with careful picking. A night of random fucking is lost from the equation.

Rocco admits, "I'm crazy about your ass," grabbing it with both palms and giving it a gentle squeeze.

"It's crazy about your cock," I say, reaching down into the water and grasping his upright buoy. I add, "You want me to introduce the two?"

"I wouldn't have it any other way."

So, I'm wrong about Rocco. He obviously wants to get it on with me. Becoming naughty with me is definitely something he has in mind. How shocking is this? How ...

We are just about to share some guy with guy action that will totally blow our minds when a tsunami-like wave crashes into our connected bodies and we separate. The undertow grabs at my legs, arms and cock, pulling me into the Gulf. I swallow two mouthfuls of saltwater, trapped and helpless inside its wicked current. A teasing and taunting black world under the water's surface captures me. I try to swim, but the undertow's strength is too mighty, wrapping its smooth body around my own and keeping me its prisoner.

I do have a gold medal for a killer backstroke from my senior year at Mermanda High School. I have never been afraid of water, certainly not the Gulf. I'm trim and fit, and occasionally still swim in the Florida waves when the mood strikes. Unfortunately, none of these attributes assist during my quasi-drowning. The undertow is far too powerful and holds me in its ferocious grip.

My life flashes before my eyes: grade school and being called faggot by Danny Martin; being picked last in gym class; trying on Elizabeth Tyranny's double-pleated chiffon skirt at a Friday night party in eleventh grade; kissing Rudy Baltimore against a lab table in Mr. Kirmy's chemistry class; coming out to my mother and father over the Labor Day weekend when I was eighteen; slipping Vinnie Testaverde's nine-inches of uncut cock down the back of my throat and almost chocking to death; attending my first Gay Pride parade at twenty-one; getting slammed by Jordy McWilliams; slamming Jordy McWilliams; picking up a Nordic hitchhiker on Route 1 and having unsafe sex with him on a nameless beach along the coast; sex with Ivan Comstock, Jody Nike, Christopher Badlinski, Corey Mezzanine, Doyle Walton, Chi Zan and Bradley Hellsingberry; running errands for Walter Landing and Felicia Horodowski; waking up to Rocco and ...

An arm firmly wraps around my middle and pulls me to the Gulf's surface. Stars, night and oxygen greet me. I cough for air, spit up saltwater, and hear Rocco's soothing voice say, "I have you. You're safe with me. I'm going to swim you back to shore."

I bob in the water, being rescued. Rocco braves the undertow's vicious temper and swims to the beach.

Once on land, he wants to perform CPR, but I'm conscious and breathing, lying still on my back. I spit up more Gulf water and cough like a smoker during a New York December.

Rocco wipes water away from my face. He says, "That was some tow. I thought I lost you."

Lost me? Is he really into me this much? We hardly even know each other. We haven't even ...

I feel his lips against my lips. His right palm rests on my chest, between my pecs. He is so happy I'm alive; this is what his kiss suggests. I'm safe against him, unharmed and protected. Rocco pulls away from my mouth and says, "Don't scare me like that. I thought you drowned out there."

I'm drowning right now. Is Rocco Malonni real or just a figment of my imagination? How much more romance can he muster? Is he an angel disguised as a mobster's son?

"Thanks for rescuing me," I say. "That was a killer swim."

Again, Rocco runs a palm over my face, removing Gulf water from my lips and forehead. "Let's not try that again. What do you think?"

I think ... I think Mr. Chaz will forever be forgotten ... I think Rocco will be my permanent boyfriend ... I think ...

"You're totally hot lying here like this," Rocco says. "If you didn't almost just drown, I'd severely be putting the moves on you."

"Severely?" I question. "That's pretty serious."

"How about just a kiss for now?"

"Ain't nothing wrong with just a kiss," I agree.

This has got to stop. Rocco's dignified and Prince Charming all the way. I'm rough and wild, and have very few morals. We come from two different worlds, yet here we meet on the most perfect night that can easily be considered romantic.

Is he purposely attempting to get me to fall for him? Is this sandy beach/moonlit tide scene his way of getting to my heart?

No! Absolutely not! It's too soon for heartstrings to strum. In truth, I'm not really sure what's going on. This chick flick moment is absolutely feasible, though. His endless attention is top-notch stuff. Whatever Rocco's processing, it's working.

Rocco's kiss is a little bit Redwoods mixed with Brokeback Mountain. I'm under its spell in a matter of seconds and become weightless by his touch.

Although we are naked, he does not discover the semi-boner between my legs. Most of me wants him to man-handle the tool and have his naughty way with it. He is a complete gentleman, though. Shame on him for being a good boy.

The kiss ends. Rocco pulls up and away. It's too bad our lips cannot stay together all night long. Instead, he realizes I'm fine from the undertow incident and mentions his father. "I know what my dad's employees did to you, and I'm sorry."

I play dumb, and ask, "What are you talking about?" looking into his dark but softly-rounded eyes.

"My father had you abducted outside Timely Books. Four of his men tossed you into a van and drove you to see my father in Miami."

"Honestly, it was three men and a driver named Bev."

Rocco shakes his head, embarrassed by my details. He sighs and explains, "My father is always looking out for my best interest."

"It just proves that he loves you and never wants anyone to hurt you."

"You're way too understanding, Derek."

"I have to be. Remember, you just saved me from drowning."

He lies on his side, one elbow is planted in the sand, and a palm holds up his head. Rocco pushes blond curls back from my forehead in a sensual manner. "Can I ask you a question?"

Keep it honest and real, Derek, I think. Too many relationships start off on the wrong foot because of bogus shit. Honesty is a road without bumps. "Ask away, Mr. Malonni."

He brushes fingertips over a cheek and my lips. The fingertips work their way over one of my shoulders, between my ribs, and lands at my navel. "Were you really drugged? Did one of my father's men jack you up with a ..."

I don't want this evening to be ruined by too many details and decide to complete his question with: "It was just a minor sedative that made me groggy."

"You've got to be kidding me? My dad drugs you, and you're here with me?" Rocco heavily sighs. "I'm surprised you didn't try to drown me in the Gulf. I told my father a long time ago to stop abducting the guys I like. It's not good for my dating life."

I laugh. For many reasons. For the obvious reasons. And after laughing, I ask, "So, you like me?" My voice lifts like a seventh grade boy heading straight into puberty.

"A little."

"I think it's more than a little."

"Probably."

I sit up on my elbows and kiss him. It's steady and quick, but more than a peck. I melt the way actors melt at the end of a romantic movie, and gently pull away. "I probably like you, too," I whisper, overwhelmed.

Rocco removes his hand from my navel; it's been there the whole time. "Look, I don't know where this is going, but ..."

I interject, "Didn't your father tell you I'm your boyfriend?"

"What are you talking about?" he asks, befuddled by my news, completely caught off guard.

"Your father ... he says we make a pretty great couple. He accepts me, and he bequeathed me your boyfriend."

"Hold on a minute," Rocco says. He leans into me with such skill, inches away from my lips, and says, "Start at the beginning. I'm not getting any of this."

So I start at the very beginning and tell him about my abduction, how I woke up under his father's care, and detail the fountain of David, Bev's earrings, and ...

"Shit," he whispers. "Leave it to my father to do this."

I feel broken inside, used and abused. "What, you don't want to be my boyfriend?"

Rocco shakes his head, and replies, "It's not that at all. My father needs to mind his ..."

I reach for his hand on my chest and slide it down and against my groin. I interject with something totally out of character, but mean it, "Life's an undertow, Rocco ... Ride it however you like."

He kisses me again, open-mouthed, perfect.

The undertow traps me again, and the conversation is dropped.

Following some heavy-duty kissing, we find our trunks, shoes and cell phones on the beach. Rocco asks, "Do you want to head back into the bar for a drink, or would you like me to take you home?"

"How about we have a drink at your place?"

"Only if you want to."

"I want to," I confess.

"Then drinks at my beach house it is."

Rocco's hunter-green Hummer pulls into his private drive. He parks the gas guzzler at the garage door and says, "I never park inside. I secretly never throw anything away. It all ends up in the garage."

"I don't see you as a junk hoarder," I say, climbing out of the Hummer.

"Did you see me as a mobster?"

I chortle, "Not quite."

"Exactly. We all have our dirty little secrets."

"Yes, we do," I respond, following him up a flight of wooden steps. At the top, standing behind him as he fidgets with keys to open the door, I hug his back and ask over his shoulder, "What's going on?"

Rocco says, "The door is unlocked. I always lock it."

"Another unsolved mystery of the world. I'm sure you just forgot."

"Maybe," Rocco says, pushing the door open and stepping inside the beach house.

As he searches for the foyer's light switch, I hear a sharp click and feel cold metal at my right temple. I hear a second click and instantly know that Rocco also has a gun to his temple.

Someone in the pitch-black room gruffly instructs, "Don't fucking move, or we'll plug you both with lead."

Chapter 12 – The Wrong Guy

I hear a thump and Rocco lets out a growl. "Leave him alone," Rocco says in the dark, "he's the wrong guy. He's got nothing to do with this."

"Where the fuck is the money?" one of the thugs asks, jabbing me in the back with something metal and heavy.

"I'm telling you," Rocco explains, "he has nothing do with this. He's the wrong guy. You want Fisk."

The next sound is Rocco's body falling to the floor.

"Turn on the fucking light!" the thug behind me instructs.

Gold-white light fills the foyer. The first thing I see is Rocco splayed out at my feet on the marble floor. A stream of blood at his right temple drips down and over his face. Rocco is out cold, motionless on the floor, but alive.

A skinny bald guy stands in front of me. He has ebony-black eyes and a pock-marked face from a bad dose of teenage acne. Ugly Face holds a Colt .45 at my head, aiming its small barrel between my eyes. He says, "Tell me where the green is, and I won't fucking kill you, faggot."

I now have two guns pointed at my head, and a blunt object digging into my spine. How the hell am I going to get out of this situation? Ugly Face and his partner are not going to believe me if I explain that I'm not Fisk. Nor will they comprehend that I have no idea where their money is. If Fisk doesn't have it, and I don't have it, and Boss Malonni doesn't have it, where is it? Ugly Face and his fuck buddy have IQs that equal a squid's ass. Neither will believe that I'm Rocco's arranged boyfriend. What the hell, though, I try anyway. "Look, I'm Derek Reed. Rocco is my ..."

The guy behind me steps around me with his lead pipe. I'm stunned to see that it just happens to be Quinn's off and on boyfriend, Tank Carson.

"Tank, what the fuck are you doing here?" I ask, flabbergasted beyond realism.

Fuck! What's going on? Since when does Tank have connections with the bad boys at the Baskin Fish Company? Like Fisk Deveraux and Rocco Malonni, Tank obviously has a hidden identity. He is a secret badass motherfucker with an undercover agenda that nobody knows about, including his sometimes boyfriend, Quinn.

"Tank, what's going on?"

Ugly Face looks confused. He turns his attention to Tank and asks, "You know him?"

"Doesn't matter. Let's get the job done," Tank responds.

"Tank, what's going on? Can you put the gun away? Can we just talk about this?" I'm confused, panic settling into my voice.

Tank has always been a nice guy to me. Tonight he's a monster in rare form, all business and no play. He quickly passes the lead pipe to Ugly Face, balls up his free hand, and swings his fist back. The hand rushes forward, open-palmed, and slaps me across the face.

My head flies to the right and blood splashes out of my mouth, splattering across Rocco's torso. Pain dives through my skull. I taste sweet blood in my mouth. My vision is lost for a second, two seconds, three seconds, and surfaces.

Tank blares at me, "Shut the fuck up!" and pulls back his hand again, ready to nail me with a second blow. When the hand flies toward my face, I block it with one arm, catching the cocksucker off guard.

Ugly Face yells at Tank, "Knock this shit off! We need information from him before you decide to kill him!"

The professional bouncer (among other surprise careers) is all muscle from head to toe. I can see in his stern looking eyes that he's ready to break me. The dude is three times my size and can easily paralyze me with a single flick. Tank says to Ugly Face, "He's a piece of shit."

"You can hurt him later. Right now, we need to get him out of here." Ugly Face slips his weapon into the belt on his right hip. He pulls out plastic zip-ties and a roll of duct tape from his back pocket.

"No funny stuff, fucker," Tank informs.

Ugly Face ties up my wrists behind my back and duct tapes my mouth.

If I live through this, Quinn will die when he finds out that his calm, cool and supposedly collected off and on boyfriend works for the Baskin Fish Company. Shit will surely hit the fan. Quinn despises liars and cheats. I guarantee that ...

Tank nails me across the face with a third, open-palm blow. Blood oozes from my mouth and begins to sting my face. I yell at him, "Come on! You don't want to do this to me! I'm Quinn's roommate! I never did anything wrong to you! I've known you for almost a year!"

Tank bashes me a fourth time, which really hurts, knocking the wind out of me. So much for the pretty boy look this fall. Dammit! It feels like a bowling ball has just rolled into my face. It feels like faggot-bashing outside Pallyo on a rough Saturday night. It feels like ...

Tank is a total prick; not all the cute ones are nice. He calls me something profane, clamps his right fist into a ball, and undercuts it into my chin.

I drop to the marble floor next to Rocco and hear Tank yell down at me, "I told you to shut the fuck up!"

A screen of blackness takes over my vision, and I fall into unconsciousness.

Bad guys suck; it's why I try not to date them. When I come to on a wooden floor in a windowless room, Tank sits approximately four feet away from me on a steel chair. He has a dumb look on his face that says: You're not so pretty now, are you?

Groggily, I ask, "Did you fuck me?"

Tank doesn't crack a smile.

I sit up. My body shifts a little to the right, then to the left. Boards creak all around me. The fish smell is rank, like a go-go boy's ass after a seven-man train. I ask Tank, "Are we on a boat?" but he is stern, a total dickhead, choosing not to answer me.

My face hurts from his blows. I wonder what I look like: blood caked to my mouth, black-and-blue eyes, a swollen left cheek. I'm sure I look like hell. After all, Tank did try to murder my face.

Physically, I'm not at my worst right now; I just feel like it. My arms are weak and my stomach twists and turns. My energy level is low, and I'm hungry and thirsty. Truth is … I could be worse and know it.

Tank finally speaks. "Bolt will be here in a few minutes to ask you some questions. I suggest you work with him. If you think the dose of shit I gave you was bad, his will be twice as bad."

"Who's Bolt?"

"Don't ask me no questions."

Nice grammar. Quinn really knows how to pick them.

I'm in no position to antagonize him and decide to keep my next question under wraps: What does Quinn see in you, anyway? Tank has already damaged me, and I don't want a second dose of his potent shit. I don't need a broken arm or jaw. Instead of being a smartass, I keep quiet, subdued for the moment, hungry as hell with stomach pains.

To my right is a wooden tray with a plastic tumbler filled with water. The tumbler accompanies a salami sandwich; hold the cheese, lettuce and tomato. I look at the combination and Tank says, "Go ahead. It's not for me."

The white bread is dry and the salami is warm; who cares, some food is better than none. It's dreadful to think that this is going to be my last meal. I take a bite of the sandwich, drink some water, and take another bite. I slowly eat and Tank watches me, which doesn't thrill either of us.

There is a door behind Tank; wooden with rusty hinges, a bar for the handle.

Tank studies my interest in the door and states, "The door is locked from the outside. Don't get tricky."

Of course not. Between bites and mouthfuls of water, I study the familiar Modey leather band on Tank's right wrist, and ask, "Is that the watch Quinn gave you for Christmas last year?"

"Eat the fucking food," Tank says in a grumpy manner. "Leave Quinn out of this."

The sonofabitch. It is the watch that Quinn gave him. An expensive gift that he bought on line from Spain, just for Tank. "Can you at least tell me the time?"

Tank shakes his head. "I can only tell you that Bolt is coming."

"How long was I unconscious? Where am I? And tell me what happened to Rocco."

He is not pleased with all my questions. Tank jumps out of his steel chair and rushes toward me. His arms are wide and his fists are balled up like a mechanical monkey's on a jewelry box. Just before he is ready to bash my skull in, I raise my empty tray and say, "I'm done with the goodies. I'll be quiet for now."

Tank rips the tray out of my hand and tosses it aside. He backs off and sits in the chair again. With crossed arms over his chest and daggers shared, he says, "I'm not the bad guy you think I am. I'm the nice guy you know outside of here. This is my job. A gig like this pays my bills."

I've learned to keep my mouth shut. It's better not to piss him off more than he already is. There is no reason to get my ears boxed in. I keep quiet, as promised, and hold my tongue. Today, I want to stay alive.

Tank continues: "You know I'm a pussycat. I really do care about people. I'm the opposite of this. I'm not a monster, Derek. You of all people know this about me."

I feel like Dr. Phil and Tank is my patient. His confession does not change my mind regarding the simple fact that he will kill me. Tank works for a high power group of badass motherfuckers. His little pony show is falling on deaf ears. Too bad.

"When you get out of here, you tell Quinn I want to hook up with him again. He's husband material, if he just learns to keep his cock in his pants. Tell him I'll stop by the gym, and we can work out together. He likes to do that with me."

Is Tank serious? I want to roll my eyes, but decide my life is too important, and on the line. To humor him, and to prevent my death, I say, "Quinn really likes you. I'm sure he can't wait to hear that you want to hook up with him again."

"Don't you think we make a cute couple?" Tank semi-smiles, talking again ... always talking, and saying too much of nothing important.

I play the game hard and well. I have every intention of getting off this boat alive. To appease him, I say, "You do make a cute couple."

Tank is all butch and bad. He sits up in the steel chair and points at me. "You tell him that! Tell Quinn that we make a fucking cute couple and ..." Tank stops speaking and looks over his right shoulder at the wooden door, which now swings open.

Tank is big, but Bolt is even bigger. Bolt is Sumo wrestler big. 350-plus pounds, easy. He has a handlebar mustache, hoop earrings, and onyx-colored eyes. Bolt has tats along both arms and around his neck. He sports a black wife beater shirt, ripped jeans, and black leather boots that a Skinhead would die for.

Once Bolt enters my wooden cell on the fish boat, Tank leaves. Bolt takes over the chair, which looks as if it will snap under his Shamoo weight. He plants his palms on his knees and says in an almost laughable, petite and high octave manner, "Where's the two hundred grand?"

Is his voice for real? Bolt sounds like a little girl. In truth, it's very difficult not to lose my composure and laugh. He truly does sound like a circus freak. A cartoon character. Robin Williams on crack. I hold it together, though, and reply, "Fisk knows where your money is. He was working for you. I have nothing do with this."

"Fisk says you have the money."

Fuck. This is news to me. If I had two hundred thousand I would be long gone. Cancun would be too hot. Alaska would be too close. Paris just might fit my bill. I don't have the bling, though. I'm the wrong guy. I attempt to bring this point to Bolt's attention, but he's a mobster who runs cocaine on a line of fish boats, and doesn't want to hear my defensive crap story.

"Tell me where my fucking money is, and I won't kill you!" Again, the girlish, circus freak voice escapes him.

I shrug my shoulders and proclaim, "If I had your cash, I would gladly return it to you. Fisk is mistaken, though. I'm flat broke. I barely have enough funds to buy toilet paper to wipe my ass. I'm the wrong guy."

Bolt is not pleased with my honesty. He abruptly stands from Tank's former chair and closes the gap between us. He hovers in front of me with his legs spread, hands planted on his hips, and his belly in my face. He scowls down at me, sharing eye contact that says: "I mean business. I'm talking a broken face stuff. I'll pull your body apart if you don't start working with me."

Don't fuck with a fucker; I've learned this throughout time. Up to this point in my life, my theory has not benefited me in any way. I think about lying to Bolt and telling him that I know exactly where his cash is. A lie like this will only endanger me more, though. It's best to keep my trap shut, and continue my plea of innocence.

Bolt's fish-smelling tummy is nauseating. I think he's about to drop his jeans and smack my cheeks with his limp, tattooed dong. He keeps his belt buckled, though, and his denim up – thank Jo-Jo in Heaven, again. Instead, he pulls out a silver switchblade from a hidden hip pocket, and flips the blade open like a Jet in *West Side Story*. Bolt positions its sharp point at the center of my throat. Tattoo guy grins down at me like Charlie Manson, and whispers in his girly manner, "Listen to me, Buster, and listen to me closely. This is not penny candy shit we're running on this boat. You seem to think all of this is a joking matter when it's not. My question for you is simple: How serious are you going to be after I knife your body full of holes and you start to bleed to death?"

I'm petrified, ready to piss myself. The knife's blade digs into my throat, pushing against my skin. My heart thumps erratically within my shivering chest. I can easily die from a heart attack at this very moment, right here and now; this is how frightened I am. Sweat bubbles up on my forehead, under my arms, and on the back of my hands. I plead for the very last time for my life, "I don't know where your money is, honestly."

"You do, and you're going to tell me!" Bolt is on fire, boiling with anger. He is just seconds away from shoving the stainless steel blade into my esophagus.

"Please, I don't know."

"Fuck!" Bolt screams, a little girl monster coming to life, exploding.

He doesn't slice my neck open, though. Nor does Bolt slide the gleaming blade into my chest or other body parts. Out of nowhere, completely unexpected, his left fist swings upwards and bashes me in the jaw.

Blood and pain mix in my mouth. Teeth bite an inside cheek. I see three Bolts instead of one.

Bolt girl-yells at me, "I know you're the right guy! Stop fucking with me!" and powers a second blow to my jaw.

I fall to the left and thump against the cabin's wooden floor. Bolt screams something unintelligible down at me. As unwelcomed pain skies through my head, I close my eyes, drift into blackness, and fall under a hypnotic spell identified as unconsciousness.

Chapter 13 – Bad Boy Action

I stand against a wall in an all-white padded room with Rocco, Quinn, Farrell, Mr. Chaz, Tank and Fisk. The half dozen men are completely naked and lined up shoulder to shoulder approximately fifteen feet away from me. All six men sport erections, smiling from ear to ear.

Tank says, "Take your clothes off, and let's get busy."

I stand in front of the men feeling horny. My wardrobe consists of winter Moon boots, a polar bear fur coat, cherry-red scarf and matching gloves. I look stunning, catwalk material.

Fisk moves his right hand down to his boner, pushing on it like a lever. The dick bounces upwards and snaps against his firm stomach. He says, "We don't want to hurt you, Derek. You're the right guy for us. It's just a little gangbang. There's nothing to be afraid of, honestly."

Quinn rolls both of his hands up and down his chest. Fingers eventually meet nipples; he hardens them to fine points. He says, "Did you ever have four cocks inside you at the same time?"

I shake my head, nervous as hell, and realize the full content of this dream: Derek Reed becomes the center of attention at an all-male gangbang.

Mr. Chaz teases his upright yanker. He says, "Do you want this in your mouth or ass? It's your choice. Just tell me where you want it."

What I want is to wake from this prelude to a naughty scene and be cuddled in Rocco's arms, holding me throughout the night. The dream continues, though. All six men begin to close the gap between us, and I have nowhere to run or hide, unable to move.

Rocco's adorable eyes twinkle like stars at night. Gosh, how can someone be so handsome? He makes me dizzy; this is how smitten I am with him. He informs me, "We're going to find the two hundred grand in your asshole's cavity. We know you're hiding it there, and we're going to fuck it out of you." His cock is twice its size, an anaconda between his legs, thick as a tree and solid with thick veins, pointing north and touching his navel.

Like a scene in *Night of the Living Dead* the line-up rushes toward me.

Fisk yells, "Fuck him!"

Tank hollers, "I've got dibs on his ass!"

Mr. Chaz says, "I'll hold him down."

Farrell exclaims, "I'll plug his mouth and keep him from screaming!"

Quinn bellows, "It's time for some pounding, Derek!"

And Rocco commands, "Get him!" in a ferocious voice that comically raises my eyebrows with surprise.

They're all over me within seconds. My winter gloves and jacket are torn from my body. Moon boots are pulled off my feet and tossed aside. My jeans and tee are ripped from my flesh. Tank uses his bare teeth on my Aussiebum briefs and yanks them from my middle, elastic and all. I'm pawed and scratched at. I'm bitten and growled at. I'm on the icy-white floor being spanked and pinched by their feisty hands and fingers. I'm licked and kissed all over. I'm ...

Like a prophecy that comes true, the six men work as a team on my flesh and begin to take a skin tour of me:

Fisk and Mr. Chaz use their mighty hands and pin me to the floor.

Farrell steps up to my head, hunches down, and slides his rock-hard dick into my mouth.

Tank rushes to my legs, spreads them apart, and pushes ten inches of his swollen spear into my bottom.

Quinn moves up to Farrell's side, hunches down, and slides his stick into my throat, right next to the leprechaun's thick pipe.

Rocco is last to make his move on me. He steps up to Tank's side, man-handles his cock into my ass, and carries out a synchronized rhythm of motion with Tank, fucking me.

I'm dizzy beneath the men, feeling estranged and bemused. I can't breathe because of the two plugs in my throat. Their sweat drips all over my body. My butt burns with Tank's and Rocco's picks thrusting in and out of it.

Fisk leans over my torso in a perpendicular action and takes my rod into his mouth, blowing me with porn flick ambition.

Mr. Chaz finds my chest irresistible and toys with my nipples. First, he licks at them with a cleansing manner, and now he begins to bite at their points with his sharp, dog-like teeth.

The six-on-one action continues for the next fifteen minutes. I become catatonic under their power, numb from their humping, fucking, holding, gagging, licking and biting. The festivities soon turn into a sex-train and the men line up between my open legs, ready for some ass-play. Since Rocco and Tank have already had a shot at my rump, they wait at the back of the fuck-line with their still-hard erections.

Fisk goes first, banging all he's got into me.

Quinn is next, holding my ankles with tight grips, plowing his meat-god into me.

Mr. Chaz is third, pounding the hardest, fastest and longest.

Farrell plays with my poker as he glides smoothly in and out of my rectum, building up a sweat.

Tank is virile, an animal visiting my hole, popping in and out/in and out/in and out.

And, Rocco is last, riding me like a rodeo cowboy. He swings his hips into me with the most power, pulls away with speed, and rams my core again, smiling his pearly whites the entire time, proud of his ripping ride.

They do it again:

Fisk.

Quinn.

Mr. Chaz.

Farrell.

Tank.

And Rocco.

They go for a third round:

Fisk.

Quinn.

Mr. Chaz.

Farrell.

Tank.

And Rocco.

On the fourth and final round, they spray me with their ooze:

Fisk shoots it on my asshole.

Quinn fires his load on my nipples.

Mr. Chaz decorates my balls.

Farrell fills my navel.

Tank paints my cock.

And Rocco aims for my mouth, nose and eyes, tagging all three areas.

Spent men; this is what they become. They breathe heavily, half-exhausted from their work. They are not weak men. And, all six know they are not finished with me just yet.

Fisk uses two fingers and spoons his cream out of my asshole. He draws the fingers to my open mouth and feeds me a dream-meal.

Quinn brushes a fingertip across one of my nipples, collecting his sticky sap. He shoves the digit into my mouth.

Mr. Chaz cups my balls with his right palm, glazing his skin with his own shoot. He now positions the palm at my lips and instructs, "Lick it off, Fido!"

Farrell sucks his warm spew out of my navel, meets my mouth with his mouth, and feeds me like a little boy bird.

Tank wipes his mouth against my still-solid pole, demanding an open-mouth kiss from me afterward.

And Rocco, my bad boy of bad boys, kneels by my face, bends over me, and lathers his cock with his own man-goo. Once his erection is smeared with the glue-like substance, he holds the tip of his tool at my mouth, and instructs, "Take this inch by inch and clean it off, Derek."

"Derek? ... Derek? Wake up. You're in good hands now. I found you again."

I smell Rocco's breath against my face. He brushes a damp hand through my hair, comforting me. I sit up and see that he looks like Ian Fleming's 007. Rocco wears an all-black SCUBA suit. His face is painted black; I can only see the whites of his eyes.

"Can you walk?" Rocco asks.

I can, nodding my head.

I'm still on the fish boat, a prisoner in the small cabin.

"How badly did they hurt you?"

I feel my swollen lips and my head rings. My body aches as if a bulldozer has just plowed over me. "A guy ... Bolt ... He tried to beat my face in."

Rocco whispers, "No offense, but it looks like it."

"There's a nasty one named Tank, too. He wasn't very nice to me."

Rocco knows the names; I can see it in the whites of his eyes. He caresses my right cheek and says, "Tank can be the meanest fucker out of the lot."

"Do I have black eyes?"

"Chalk it up as a Goth night at Pallyo."

"My whole face is swollen, too, isn't it?"

"You look good. Let's keep our heads in the game and get you out of here."

I find the strength to grab his arm and ask, "How'd you find me? ... How long have I been knocked out? ... Where are we?"

Rocco answers my question with a brush of his lips to mine, which stings a little bit, but I welcome them. He says after pulling away, "I'll explain everything later. We don't have much time."

Behind us, the cabin's door flies open and a new face appears. The six-two brute looks German with his white-spiked hair and piercing blue eyes. He holds an Uzi in his hands, ready to scatter us into pieces.

I have to hand it to Rocco; he's the gay James Bond all the way. He pulls out a black-handled Chinese dagger from his SCUBA garb and flings it through the cabin with just the slightest arch. He aims at the German's heart, obtains a bull's eye, and drops the white-haired bitch to the cabin's boarded floor, all in a matter of seconds.

Rocco turns to me, helps me up, and pulls me against his chest. A quick squeeze is shared that completely delights me. We walk over to Mr. Dead German. Rocco finds the Uzi with his free hand, lifting it for use. He passes me the Uzi and informs, "Use this for protection. There's more bad boys on this boat."

I watch Rocco pull the dagger out of Mr. Dead German's chest and slide it back into its SCUBA sheath, blood and all. He instructs, "Keep low and follow me."

I've had some pretty intense boyfriends since high school. Wayne Nelski was into motor crossing and broke his leg on a super fly. Blake Black was in the Navy and gave the best "don't ask, don't tell" blowjobs in the history of queer men serving our nation. Austin Martinburger was a bridge builder/acrobat, fearless of heights. And Shawn Mozart worked for the F.B.I. and knew how to catch top-notch bad boys, even serial killers.

Rocco isn't very far behind Mozart in the "man" category. He is mean for all the right reasons, apt to destroy, and makes me melt. His butch side is a major turn-on for me. The guy is like a superhero at work, saving my life. No wonder I'm a puddle next to him.

We exit the cabin and enter a narrow shaft without doors. At the end of the boarded shaft are steps leading up and into another cabin. He pulls out a palm-size .40-caliber Glock from his SCUBA gear and holds it up with two hands. Rocco awaits some vial action with the

Glock, stands perfectly macho-still, ready and willing to blow a bad guy away.

"Is this a Baskin Fish Company boat?" I ask.

Rocco nods his head and immediately hushes me.

What transpires next is something like Vin Diesel going ape-shit crazy in one of his high body count, action-packed movies, destined to blow a criminal away.

Bubba steps out of a hidden doorway and thunders down the narrow shaft toward us. He holds a double-barrel shotgun with anger in his midnight-black eyes. Bubba is Rocco, plus me, in size. He is all fat and grime, bottom of the ocean stuff. He fires off his shotgun and blows a hole in the boat's port side, just ten feet in front of us.

Rocco fires his Glock, aiming at Bubba's head. The gun snaps but doesn't go off; it's probably soaked from his The Little Mermaid swim to save me.

Bubba fires his shotgun a second time. Scattershot blows a hole in the wall to our left. Wooden splinters fly in all directions.

My He-Man is not a happy superhero. He flies around, snatching the Uzi out of my hands, ready for some low-profile action.

I think Rocco is going to Swiss cheese Bubba, but he doesn't. While Bubba reloads his shotgun, Rocco bolts down the shaft with the Uzi in tow. Once in Bubba's reach, Rocco swings the Uzi around to the slime's center, and blasts him in the side of his head.

Shotgun shells roll out of Bubba's right hand and down the shaft toward me. Bubba's double-barrel flies over Rocco, onto the shaft's floor. The slime is knocked backwards, to the stairs.

Rocco doesn't fuck around and smashes the Uzi into Bubba's head a second time. A third blow – something mixed with Rocco's anger and grade-A testosterone – knocks the pig into a fatty slump.

I rush down the shaft toward Rocco and stand behind him. He deserves a rugged, kick-ass kiss for his bravery, but there is no time.

Two new thugs appear at the top of the stairs: Baldy and Walrus. Both hold high-caliber pistols, firing down at us. Bullets spray around our bodies and into Bubba, killing him.

Positioned behind Rocco, I cower like a little girl. He is not to be fucked with, and retaliates with the Uzi. Baldy and Walrus turn into a bloody mess. They roll down the steep steps, joining Bubba in a slump at the bottom.

On the way up the stairs, Rocco snatches up Baldy's .9mm and passes it to me. "Don't be afraid to use this."

"Does it work like a hair dryer?"

"Even better."

A kitchen opens up at the top of the stairs. There is a stainless steel table littered with fish guts. A battered, two-burner range sits between a rusted refrigerator and restaurant-size sink. The sink is filled with blood-stained knives of various sizes. The room is empty of Baskin bad guys. This doesn't mean some lunatic like Tank or Bolt won't rush into the kitchen armed, ready and willing to cream us.

To the right is a single wooden door with three Yale locks. The locks are all Pentagon-tight. At the bottom of the door is a white powder dusting the floor. Obviously this is one of Baskin's coke boats, and the locked room is where the drug stash is located. I wonder if Boss Malonni's two hundred thousand is inside the room with the missing coke. Maybe a couple of corpses are in the room from some bad dealings, too.

None of this matters, though. Whatever is behind the locked-tight door is none of my business. Drugs, cash and corpses are not my forte.

Rocco makes a left, leading me out of the kitchen. Some ugly motherfucker with warts all over his face steps out of a cabin. He holds a semi-automatic pistol, on task and ready to blow the two of us away.

Baldy's .9mm is the handiest weapon. I find the balls and aim it at Ugly's head. I pull the trigger twice, and thump! Ugly's on the floor with a new pair of eyes in his forehead.

Two more uglies appear in the hallway. Bullets fly around our bodies. Rocco pops one of the uglies in the heart, dropping the rogue to the wooden floor. The second ugly gets another two shots off. One of the shots nails Rocco in his right shoulder, and he falls to the floor. His blood splatters my feet and one arm. He lets out an umpff sound that he's hurt, and leans into my legs for balance.

Chapter 14 – Skin-Diver Here

I've shot a load, a seductive look, Jack Daniel's, and now a .9mm gun for the second time. Once Rocco is down, my defense goes up, and my finger finds the gun's trigger. Bullets nail the second ugly in his chest, and he falls to the floor, bleeding all over the place.

Rocco stands, groaning with pain. Blood is splashed against his shoulder. The SCUBA suit is mangled, completely ruined. No matter how much pain he is in, though, he still leans into me and provides me with a full-mouthed kiss that I will remember forever. Pale and losing blood, he says, "Thanks for that, macho man. What do you say we get off this float?"

"Here, take this." I hand the .9mm to him. "That thing brings out the bad boy in me."

"I like your bad boy side," Rocco confesses, warming up with a smile. He pockets the pistol in his SCUBA gear and kisses me again, which blows me away. Once the kiss is over, he pulls away and says, "I like it when you go butch. It gives me an instant woody."

"Maybe later we can play queer A-Team. For now, get me out of here."

We walk over the uglies' bodies and to the end of the hall. A wooden door greets us, which Rocco attempts to open. He turns the rusty knob, but the door doesn't budge, obviously locked.

Blood coats his SCUBA-covered chest. There is a hole in the rubber where the bullet went in, but didn't come out. The bullet is still inside his shoulder. I'll have to make some effort to share a remedy of good old-fashioned TLC once we're through this.

"Stand back, buddy," Rocco says. He points the Uzi's barrel at the door's lock and knob, and squeezes the trigger.

The wooden door splinters into a thousand pieces. The doorknob falls out of the remaining plain of wood and drops to the floor. Rocco kicks debris to the side and asks, "Are we having fun yet?" cringing from the pain in his damaged shoulder.

"I'll play Nurse Derek after you save us."

"Deal," Rocco supplies, pushing the door open and discovering another flight of stairs.

The night is filled with twinkling stars and moonlight at the top of the stairs, which is a sign of relief for me, since I'm ready to end this escapade. The meany of all meanies blocks most of the enchanting view, though. Bolt's bulky shadow looms in the narrow opening. He clutches what looks to be a long pipe in his right hand. He swings the end of the pipe into his left palm, growling like a tempestuous feminine bear.

I say, "Oh shit. He looks cranky."

"Get up here so I can fuck the two of you over!" Bolt yells down the stairs in his little girl-voice. He swings the pipe into his palm again, sneering with dark madness in his stare.

Rocco raises the Uzi and attempts to blow him away. The gun jams, making a locking sound. Rocco yells, "Fuck!" as angry as Bolt.

Bolt tilts his head back and provides a girlie laugh.

I don't know exactly what surfaces in Rocco, but it's major hot. Even with his damaged shoulder does he manage to find enough strength to let out an obnoxious growl and supercharge up the stairs. He swings the Uzi like a baton, and his disgruntled growl turns into a full masculine scream, meeting Bolt face to face.

I follow Rocco up the stairs; quite possibly the most foolish and masculine thing I've ever accomplished.

Rocco swings the Uzi above his head and almost nails Bolt's skull. Bolt acts fast and blocks the attack with his pipe. This does not stop Rocco, though. He swings the Uzi again, nailing the brute in his ribs.

Bolt is on fire, acting like a demon who has just escaped hell, ready to gobble Rocco up. He lets out a girl-yelp, falling backwards. Bolt almost tumbles on his back, but finds his balance at the very last second. He attempts to bash the pipe against Rocco's right temple, but Rocco impedes the hit with the help of his Uzi, using it as a shield.

Rocco obviously has superhuman powers, or he just has a pretty solid background in street fighting. No longer does the bullet wound in his right shoulder seem to have any effect on him. Rocco uses the Uzi like a knife and stabs Bolt in the stomach, pulling the weapon's trigger in hopes that it will now operate correctly.

One shot is fired.

A second shot is fired.

Bolt drops the lead pipe and falls to the ship's deck.

Rocco holds the Uzi in his good arm, spins around, and says to me, "I didn't want to do that, but the stupid fucker had it coming."

I feel like a damsel in distress and Rocco is my knight in shining armor. He says, "It's safe now."

I kick Bolt's bloody, bullet-ridden torso, and burst, "That's for being a bitch to us!"

Rocco wraps his arms around my back with the Uzi hanging from his right hand. He shares a robust and starry kiss with me that totally rocks my world.

I try to close my eyes and take the kiss in, but Tank creeps out of the shadows and steps up behind Rocco. He places a .44 Magnum against the back of my boyfriend's head, and says, "Mr. Malonni, we meet again. I thought I blew you away on Pilsner Street."

So Tank was the shooter at the Pilsner Street drive-by; no big surprise. I imagine Bolt was the driver.

Rocco stares into my eyes. We are nose-to-nose and lips-to-lips. I feel his heartbeat against my chest. By the look in his eyes, I can tell he's planning an escape. Rocco confirms this by winking at me.

How far is the mainland from the fish boat? Are casino and boardwalk lights visible from our position? I'm not sure. We could be miles from the coast, unseen and unheard, the perfect place for two murders.

"Did you two faggots honestly believe you could get off this boat?" Tank asks.

Rocco keeps quiet.

I keep quiet.

"I'm sure you both know all parties come to an end," Tank shares.

Rocco is exhausted by Tank's bullshit and drops the Uzi to the deck. He swings his left elbow backwards with the force of Vin Diesel and cuts it into Tank's chest. Rocco spins around with a gymnast's skill and knocks the .44 Magnum out of Tank's hand; the gun lands somewhere behind the villain. Rocco jumps and kicks out his right leg, chopping Tank in the gut.

Tank looks as if he's going to vomit; getting the shit kicked out of him is not something that transpires every day in his life. Once he finds his balance and takes Rocco in, he jabs his left fist at Rocco's wound, punching it with three quick thrusts.

Rocco screams at the top of his lungs in pain, filling the night; a sound I will never forget. He drops to the deck, inches from my feet.

I actually freeze, unable to move. Some inconceivable spell looms over me, causing me to become dazed and useless.

Tank stands over Rocco and kicks him in the side. He yells down at the mobster, "Who the fuck do you think you are?" and shares a second kick into Rocco's ribs.

Mafia man lets out a horrendous roar that is doused with masculine pain. The two kicks to his torso do not keep him down, though. He bounces off the wooden boards like a cat and his foot tags the bouncer in his chin, twice.

The musclehead falls to the deck and blood oozes out of his mouth. Tank's beautiful smile is lost. Now he is missing a few teeth and possibly has a broken jaw.

Rocco kicks Tank in the balls. He uses all his force, driving his sack and cock into his intestines.

Tank whales, spitting up blood. He swears at Rocco, "You mudder fudder!" and gropes for his private parts with both hands.

My mobster hero lowers himself to Tank's level. The two men are now face to face. Rocco says, "You're a piece of shit," and balls up his right fist. Quickly, he smashes the fist into Tank's face, three times.

Tank is knocked out and goes limp. So much for kicking our asses.

Rocco turns to me and says, "We gotta bust this boat before another maggot comes out of the woodwork and tries to kill us." He leashes his left hand into my right and leads me to the boat's railing.

For the first time I consume my surroundings: the wind is vigorous and electric; a storm blows in from Texas; Flamingo Cove's city lights resemble a Lite-Brite; Orion decorates the night's canopy among distended clouds; the moon is a crisp-white crescent, half-hidden; sprinkles of rain fall from the heavens in a delicate manner; the fishing boat is approximately one hundred feet long and rusted to the gills; four by four steel buckets are filled with ice, fish and bagged cocaine; a steel crane looms overhead like a fifty-foot tall stick figure. It's actually an ominous night, overwhelmed with goons and gunshots.

At the steal railing, overlooking the Gulf, Rocco unzips a SCUBA-hidden pocket and pulls out a cellular phone. He flips the phone open, presses a few numbers on its screen, and says into the phone, "Skin-diver here ... Starboard side ... One hundred meters. Over." Rocco snaps the phone closed, directs his full attention to me, and asks, "You ready to play Neptune with me?"

"Neptune? What the hell is that?"

Rocco points out at the Gulf. "I've got a guy meeting us in a speedboat out there. We have to swim one hundred meters for a pick-up."

"Can you do that with your fucked shoulder, Skin-diver?"

"You'll be surprised what I can do," he flirts with me.

"Promise?"

"I promise. Now, it's time to jump and ... you're first."

I study the Gulf and see some very angry waves. The fish boat rocks from side-to-side because of a frisky wind and soon-to-be thunderstorm. The wind seems to kick up a notch, offering a nasty forewarning to something dangerous. Shit. I'm first to jump. Why? All I can think about is the night before and almost drowning in the undertow. Fear envelops me and ...

"Hey, I have your ass out here. I won't let the current take you under," Rocco says, touching my right cheek.

I have to trust him. What other options are there? How do I survive this ugly situation without his help? How do I ...

Bullets fly around our heads. Two bad guys use pistols, heading toward us from the bow.

"Jump!" Rocco yells.

Like a gymnast I pull myself onto the steel railing with him, and balance my weight for just a second. I take in the blue-grey-black waves, feel Smith & Wesson bullets zoom past my ears, and leap overboard in Rocco's arms.

Rocco and I break apart. The Gulf is swift and cold during the rainstorm. I expect it to be like a sauna, rather warm and relaxing, but it isn't. My eyes close and everything goes black. How far do I sink into the ocean? Twenty feet? Thirty feet? I'm really not sure. I come to under the surface, observing two sunken treasure ships that are glittery gold. A dozen or more mermen with rainbow-colored fins swim around me. The chiseled mermen with their graceful fins perform a synchronized show for me under the water. One by one they kiss me, welcoming me to their friendly underworld. A merman who appears to be Triton fingers my chest and nipples. Another merman, Poseidon, brushes a hand against my cheek and then my chest. He seems to smile at me with delight, taken by my human and mortal looks. They continue to circle me, touching parts of my body, kissing me again and again. I'm given a seashell crown and golden trident. Each merman kindly shares a hug with me. Some are very cordial and grope my biceps, ribs and inner thighs, exploring my body. And eventually, the exotic mermen create a bed with their raised arms and hands. I lie down on the devised bed and they gently push my body upwards, toward the water's surface.

Once I break through the water and enter night, gasping for breath, the mermen vanish from beneath me. I have to tread water to stay afloat. I keep my mouth closed, fearing I'll gulp down saltwater and drown. I see the cocaine boat's shadow approximately one hundred feet away. I recall Rocco's quick cellular call and its helpful details. I have a little more than two hundred feet to swim until I meet Rocco's rescue team.

Lightning cracks across the heavens, chasing the playful thunder. Rain begins to heavily fall as I wonder where Rocco is. Did he drown out here? Did the undertow pull him beneath the water's surface and have its ferocious way with him? Has he already been rescued out of the Gulf, searching for me? Did a bullet nail him in the skull when he jumped overboard? Did one of the bad guys ...

Rocco swims up through the saltwater and bobs at my side. He uses his good arm, treading the Gulf. He spits up some Gulf water and says, "I'm fish bait if we don't start swimming."

"Can you make it?" I ask, worried about his safety.

"It's either swim or become shark food. Let's go with the first choice before I lose all my energy."

We swim, bob, float – whatever it takes. Rocco is a trooper with his bad arm, but he goes under a few times, and I help him out. I carefully wrap an arm around him and swim him away from the Baskin fish boat. He loses a lot of blood and goes limp in my arm. His head falls forward, into the Gulf, and I pull it up and back, so he doesn't drown. I say, "Hold on, man. Someone is going to save us," but he doesn't respond.

Thunder wrecks havoc overhead and rain pounds the Gulf. The fish boat becomes smaller behind us, a blurry metal and wooden figure in the storm. We swim over two hundred feet, but there isn't a small rescue boat in sight. I bob up and down with an unconscious Rocco and begin to panic. I peer across the water's surface in a left to right motion, searching out rescuers. My heart thumps wickedly within my chest. If the rescue boat doesn't show, Rocco and I will die one of three ways: by sharks, drowning, or being shot at by a remaining villain on the fish boat.

"Fuck," I whisper, "this can't be happening. This is a horrible way to die."

My legs and arm start to go numb. I don't know how long I can keep Rocco afloat. I won't let him drown, though – certainly not after he rescued me from the fish boat, saving my life.

"We're going to do this, Rocco," I mumble, gulping down some saltwater. "I don't know how, but we are."

My treading is weak, and we begin to sink under the water's surface together. There are no mermen this time. No Triton. No Poseidon. No treasure ships. No crown. No golden trident. A strong sense of panic rushes through me. I fiercely paddle with my empty arm and kick my legs with all the energy I can muster. In a matter of seconds, we break through the water's surface and I gasp for air. Rocco is completely limp against me; maybe it's too late to save him; I'm not sure. More panic settles within my chest and ...

Thank Jo-Jo in heaven! A fourteen foot speedboat glides out of the darkness and floats next to our bodies. Someone from its deck faintly calls down to us, "Skin-diver?"

"He's been shot!" I call upwards. "I think he's still alive, though!"

The rescuer on the speedboat tosses me a white life saver with Princess Dune painted in red letters around its curved edge. I grasp the life saver with my empty arm and yell out, "Got it!"

It's Fisk Deveraux who pulls Rocco out of the water and to safety. As I wait for my turn at the port side ladder, Fisk calls down at me, "You two were bitches to find out here."

While climbing the slippery ladder, I respond in a rather pissed tone, "Fisk, I swear to God, I'm going to kill you for getting us into this mess!"

Part Three – Castlegate

Chapter 15 – Wrestling
Before Heated Sex

Four weeks later I'm at Antonio Malonni's estate near Clearwater, Florida. Castlegate is huge money. Italian marble and bronze statues are everywhere. The place overlooks a picturesque Gulf and screams private vacationland all over it. The mansion is twenty-four thousand square feet with an indoor pool, bowling alley, and a room displaying rare pieces by Jackson Pollack and Picasso, mostly from his Cubism period. Palms decorate the beach and the estate's golf course. A cricket field sits parallel to the beach.

I mustn't forget to mention the staff of nine at Castlegate, who just happen to be on hand at all times: Juan is the driver, a thirty-something Cuban hottie; Marla cooks all my meals; Tiempo and Carlos are constantly busy with the grounds; Sampson is from South Africa, and he does all of the maintenance; Gina and Sala do the housekeeping; Pedro takes care of the pools; and Miguel, a sexy-as-they-come Peruvian god, is the butler, whom I see most of the time, since he follows me around the estate like a puppy dog.

Miguel Sanchez is twenty-seven years old, likes to drink rum, and rarely leaves me out of his sight. He is all beef with Latino-colored skin, soft-brown eyes, and tiny dimples around a smooth-looking smile. Rocco hires the hunk as my bodyguard, which is currently a secret that I just happen to know about. Miguel, to my liking, is always bare-chested and wears the skimpiest shorts. To my disappointment, he is a hardcore straightie, flocking to women for sexual pleasure. One benefit that I find quite dick-hardening is that Miguel's really into his body, almost a heavy-duty narcissus and likes it when guys watch him work out. He admits that it's a turn-on for me to stand above him as a watcher while he bench presses almost three-hundred pounds. Miguel finds it sexy that I admire his muscles, sweat and bulging veins. He says he's not into guys, but gets a high when dudes ogle his body in motion.

Here I am, practically a prisoner at Castlegate, hidden from the Baskin bad guys, watching a half-dressed and fully-straight jock pressing mucho pounds like they are Q-tips. Miguel is all sweaty-perfect with a map of veins lining his chest, arms and neck. His pert nipples rise and fall with every lift. His breathing is a sexy pattern of inhaling and exhaling. Miguel's chest is freshly waxed, solidly hairless, and just right for a *Men's Fitness* audience/cover.

One lift. Two lifts. Three lifts. Miguel works ten lifts in. Now, I help him put the Q-tip back to rest where it belongs on the bench. He sits up and asks for a hand towel, which I toss to him. The jock wipes his sweaty face and shoulders off with slow strokes, smiling while doing so from my faithful ogling.

I confess, "It's too bad you don't play for my team. All the fags would be lining up to get a taste of your ass, among other succulent body parts. You'd have a full schedule of dates, and the best sex life any dude could want."

Miguel laughs. He wipes the cotton towel across his forehead and says, "I gave guys a try in college and decided I didn't like cock."

"If you change your mind, I'm sure I can hook you up with a team of jocks to rock your world."

"Thanks for looking out for my best interest," Miguel says, grabbing two bottles of piss-yellow Gatorade from a nearby Coleman cooler. He tosses me one bottle from his bench, which I surprisingly catch, and keeps the second for himself.

I take a swallow of the liquid and ask, "You doing anymore reps, or are you calling it a day?"

"I'm good for today. How about a shower?"

No way. Although I haven't seen Rocco in over thirty days, I'm hard for the mob man and want to stay monogamous. I share with Miguel, "Truth is, I'm flattered with your invitation, but I'm sticking with Rocco."

"Derek, you know I'm into women. I'm not asking for some hanky panky stuff." He drinks from his plastic bottle, his face glinting with droplets of workout perspiration.

"I would be all over you if we showered together. I have to stay honest and devoted to Rocco now that he is officially considered my boyfriend, and a man I want to keep in my life."

"I understand. Maybe next time."

"Perhaps, my friend," lying, but being cordial.

Miguel raises his bottle and says, "To friendship."

We clink plastic bottles together and drink.

Changing the subject, I ask, "Has Fisk been found?"

"Still missing," he says, shaking his head. "No one's seen him since he saved you and Rocco from the Gulf."

"He'll be found. Give Rocco more time."

Since I landed at Castlegate, I have found Miguel extremely conspicuous regarding his position as a butler. I want to clear the air about his real position and ask, "You're really not a butler, are you?"

Miguel shakes his head and shares a handsome smile.

"You're a bodyguard on Rocco's payroll. You watch me night and day. You're my protector."

He ignores my comments and says, "You can't leave Castlegate until Rocco finds Fisk."

"Is Fisk dead?"

"Not that Rocco's aware of. I'm sure the Baskin Fish Company has him."

"Where is Rocco now? And when is he returning to Castlegate?" I ask.

"I don't know where Mr. Malonni is. Nor do I know when he will return."

"How long do I have to stay a prisoner here?"

"Until Rocco thinks it's safe for you to return to the real world."

"Who's to say I won't leave on my own?"

"And get past me?" Miguel raises his left eyebrow. "You'd better think again."

"Can you outrun me?"

"You don't want to chance that. Look at me, Derek. I'm fit, strong, and I have eyes in the back of my head. If you think of running away from Castlegate, I'll be on your ass like a welt."

"Something tells me that if I stay here, you'll be on my ass, anyway."

"I told you, I don't do dick."

"Too bad. Fisk would fuck you all day and night long."

"I know. He tried it a few months ago when Boss first hired him on, but I defeated his forwardness."

I'm not surprised to learn this information; Fisk would do anything with three legs. I decide to change the topic yet again, exhausted by the thought of having sex with Rocco. I take a deep breath, let out a contented sigh, and ask, "Now, tell me how long you've worked for Rocco?"

Miguel shakes his head. "Not a chance."

"Am I asking too many questions?"

"Not yet," Miguel says again. "I'm getting a shower."

"Enjoy."

Walking away, he looks over his right shoulder and shares, "If you change your mind about joining me in the shower, I'm okay with that. You can look at me all you want. You just can't touch me. Any advancements made on my stinging-hot body and your boyfriend will have my ass in a sling."

I roll my eyes. "Thanks, but no thanks. I'm holding out for Rocco."

Miguel stops approximately twenty feet away from the weight bench and kicks off his Adidas running shoes. He drops his towel to the floor, steps out of his A&F shorts, and shows off his tight rump, which looks very fuckable. His inner thighs are muscled and his balls are a little hairy.

"You're teasing me!" I yell.

"Every prisoner needs teased, Mr. Reed!" he hollers in return. And off he goes to the shower room, all alone.

I sunbathe on the east patio, next to the in-ground pool and East Garden. I decide to go bare-bottomed, lying on my stomach, mooning the gay gods. The sun feels lusciously warm on my tush and back. I listen to birds chirp and the soft wind blowing against my right side. I drift off to sleep, napping in the rays for just a few minutes, and then turn over on my back, sunning my front.

My mind drifts to Fisk missing. Not only does the Baskin Fish Company have Fisk, and the two hundred thousand dollars, but they also have the cocaine that Fisk was buying from them. It's top-notch bad business among bad boys. I wonder if Fisk is safe under their care. Is he missing a limb? Has some loony decided to chop off one of his feet? Does he still have his tongue? And, will Rocco and his staff find Fisk, rescuing him from his torture? All of these unanswered questions circle within my mind.

When Rocco returns to Castlegate I will ask him these same questions. In the meantime, I have Miguel to play with. Not sexually, of course. Mentally. Every bodyguard needs a new game to play, just to keep active.

Enough sunbathing. I'm bored. I find my shorts, socks and Nikes. I slip into the set and head toward the East Garden. A pathway sneaks between fragrant tea rose bushes and summer navel trees, which are both in bloom. I make my way slowly between them, following the path down a narrow slope, up a dozen or more rocky steps, and end up at a fountain. The fountain is comprised of two life-size male wrestlers. Both are bronze and naked. Water sprays in a circle, away from their man-over-man position. The Greek on top has his buddy in a powerful headlock. His limp cock rests against his partner's arched back. The dude on the bottom – to my surprise – sports a semi-boner, on his knees and palms, helplessly unmovable. I mentally title the masculine duo "Wrestling before Heated Sex," and giggle under my breath at the erotic sculpture.

Moving on. I walk past the fountain, find a stone stairwell that leads into the ground between two boulders, and ...

Here, a secret room is exposed with cranberry-colored rugs, beige stone walls, candles on two Victorian tables, a matching Victorian-style settee, and a king-sized bed, which just so happens to be occupied by Tiempo and Carlos, the handsome groundskeepers.

The couple in lust do not see me on the stone stairwell. Half of me is bathed in the brutish light from above, and the other half is a mere shadow in the semi-darkness creeping up from below. I stare at their naked and connected bodies with a sense of enlightenment.

Carlos is hairy, around twenty-six, and has intense blue eyes. He lies on his back with his legs lifted and spread in mid-air.

Tiempo is broader in size, completely bald from head to toe, and positioned on his knees at the end of the bed. He strums his tongue against his buddy's pink and tight bottom.

Carlos moans and groans in full pleasure, sporting one of the biggest pieces of wood I have ever seen – a massive length of ten inches.

Tiempo strokes his partner's joint with two hands while working Carlos's rump with his mouth. He is obviously into pleasuring Carlos, since his upright flag is untouched and bobs between his stern legs.

An erection ultimately rises between my legs. Life fills my joint, and it swells to a full length inside my shorts.

No longer is Tiempo on his knees. He climbs up on the bed and begins to wrestle with Carlos. A headlock is shared with playful knuckle-punches and slaps. Carlos escapes the master hold and attempts to pin Tiempo to the bed. Boyish grunts and groans are shared by the playful two. I expect to see an Anaconda Vice or Camel Clutch, but the duo keep their sexual match basic. Kisses are shared, laughter, and Tiempo tries for a shoulder claw, but fails because of Carlos's quick defense.

I'm exhausted, watching them from the stairwell. My erection wants to be played with, but I still hold out for Rocco's touch. I can escape the scene, but I will miss out on their sexual romp. Helplessly, I decide to stick around and watch their match continue, being a voyeur.

The wrestling ends. Carlos is on his knees and Tiempo licks and laps at his ten inches of solid cock. Carlos thumps his muscled weight forward, and Tiempo takes it like a man. Tiempo's hungry for the action, needy for his friend's hearty beef. He consumes all ten inches down his throat, gagging.

Carlos moans words in Spanish, which I don't understand. He swings his hips forward, backward, forward again. His hands clamp to the back of Tiempo's head, and his rhythm grows stronger.

After ten minutes of blowing Carlos, Tiempo pushes his lover to the bed and spreads the man's muscular legs. Tiempo brushes his cock's head against Carlos's taut hole. Carlos lets out a moan that Chi Chi LaRue would go nutso over. Tiempo spits on his rod and shoves the tip of it inside his moaning lover, condomless.

Is Carlos enjoying the ride, cock-hungry? I imagine so by the look of glee on his face, which consists of an upturned smile and reddish cheeks.

I adjust my own goods, wanting to man-handle them in front of the groundskeepers. Decent behavior is found, though, and I manage only to watch their sexual frenzy unfold.

Tiempo shoves eight of his nine inches of rod into Carlos.

Carlos screams, gritting his teeth. His back arches as inch by inch of his lover's cock enters his middle.

Tiempo begins to ride his buddy's hole. His palms clamp around Carlos's ankles.

The two share some teamwork with each other; their motion of to and fro becomes passionate. Tiempo glides all of his nine inches into Carlos, and whispers naughty names down at his lover.

Carlos is in delighted pain. He spreads his legs as far as they will spread, arches his back, and begins to perspire. The man heavily pants to the movement, over-zealous regarding his enjoyment by having Tiempo's body connected to his own.

The duo move gracefully back and forth. Tiempo's cock smoothly rides inside Carlos's tight behind. Both moan and groan. Both drip with perspiration. Both continue this act of sexual-wrestling for the next twelve minutes.

I'm ready to explode in my Nike shorts. The action between the groundskeepers is far too exciting. My cock needs to be touched, licked and man-handled by Rocco. I can't possibly stand here for another second, watching the Latino team at work and play.

As of yet, I don't ascend the stairs and return to full daylight. Truth is, I can't move. The wrestling match on the bed is far too invigorating for my escape to occur. My feet are glued to the stone stairs. My gaze is locked onto the two bodies in their harmonized motion. The cock between my thighs is stiff in my Nike shorts, ready to fire off a load, without even being manipulated by fingers.

Tiempo confesses that he is ready to blow his cargo. He asks Carlos, "Do I shoot inside you or on your chest?"

"Whatever it takes," Carlos answers in his thick Spanish accent.

Tiempo goes for Carlos's chest. He pulls his stiff and wet cock out of Carlos's ass, gives it a few strokes with his left palm, and fires off a creamy-white load onto his buddy's hairy chest. Tiempo wavers to and fro above Carlos, flapping his cock around, splashing ooze everywhere. He gyrates wildly, allowing the fresh orgasm to take over his body.

"Beat me off," Carlos instructs after Tiempo comes.

Tiempo's a good listener. He strokes Carlos's ten-inch rod with both hands. Diligently, he works the rod up and down like a skilled laborer. Tiempo whispers things in Spanish, but they sound smooth and vibrant, just like his strokes.

Carlos lets out a moan and juts his hips upwards. Sticky ooze fires out of his man-spigot and spirals against Tiempo's clean-shaven chest. The sap sticks to pecs, abs and nipples. Carlos thrusts upwards again, a third time, until his cock is empty.

Spent, the two men lie on the bed, cuddling. Tiempo spoons Carlos, nibbling on his ear. They whisper things in Spanish that lovers only whisper to each other.

Quietly, I escape the post-sex scene, ascending the stairs. I leave the team to sleep and their happy afternoon dreams. I step out into daylight, become somewhat blinded by the Florida sunbeams, and hear Rocco's familiar voice say, "There you are ... I've been looking everywhere for you."

Chapter 16 – Man-Contact

I practically faint at the sight of Rocco. Thank Jesus he leashes his comforting arms around me and lifts me off the rocky ground in a compact bear hug. He spins me around, kissing my neck, cheeks and lips. Once he places me back down, he pulls away and gives me a once-over, studying me from head to toe. Rocco says, "You've been working out."

"With Miguel a little."

He grips one of my firm pecs and gives it a squeeze. "Nice job. I like it. Maybe if I find the time we can beef-up together."

"I have other things in mind to accomplish with you."

"I hope a private workout," Rocco suggests, raising his eyebrows. "I know the perfect place."

He turns and begins to pull me along the narrow pathway to the secluded bedroom between the massive boulders. Approximately twenty-five feet away from the stone stairs, I abruptly stop him and confess, "We can't go down there. Your groundskeepers are resting together after heated sex."

Rocco smiles in a devilish manner. "Did you watch?"

"Of course not. I wouldn't dare."

"You would."

"You're right," I giggle. "I would."

"And you did, didn't you?"

I sinfully smile and pull him to me. We kiss with fire in the summer sun. I can't believe how much I have missed him. My whole body tingles by his touch. My passion rises, and I'm all over him like a sex-crazed teenager at a wild rave.

"Hold on, tiger," Rocco says, pulling away from me. "We've got a few days together to get crazy."

I blush, embarrassed by my sexual hunger. Shame on me for wanting and needing him so badly. "Look," I whisper, "I haven't had any man-contact since you dumped me here. Of course I'm ready to jump you. Thirty days without queer human contact is insane. I don't think I can wait a single moment longer to get in your briefs."

"Who says I'm wearing briefs?"

"Boxers?"

Rocco shakes his head.

"Commando?"

He laughs. "I was in a hurry this morning. Besides, it's kind of sexy to go bare." He shares another hug and adds, "You're right about not having any man-contact for a month. I understand. Just promise to gently rip off my clothes."

"You like it rough, though."

"Sometimes. I'm still babying the shoulder damage."

I gently touch his shoulder and ask, "How's it feel?"

"Better, now that I'm with you. Dr. Milanos in Miami is the best, and he takes very good care of me. I'm almost back to one hundred percent."

"I'll kiss it and make it better," I say, placing my soft lips to his white tee, providing a light kiss.

"You're going to make me hard," Rocco confesses.

"I was hoping you'd say that."

He pulls away from me, and we start our walk back to the mansion. He swings my hand within his own and says, "Do you know how much I've missed you?"

"Not very. Since the fish boat thing, I haven't heard from you. They have these things called e-mail and text messaging that you'll have to learn."

Rocco rolls his eyes. "I know I should have called."

"And visited."

"Yes, and visited."

"And e-mailed."

"Yes, that, too."

"And texted me."

"Okay, I get it. I'm a very bad boy."

"A very bad boy who needs spanked for not communicating with me. I woke up the last thirty days thinking you were dead."

Rocco confesses, "Miguel knew I wasn't dead."

"Miguel was useless in the comforting department regarding your whereabouts and safety. He's the quiet bodyguard who is forever faithful to you."

"Good help is hard to find. I pay him very well for his services."

"It would have been nice to hear from you, Rocco. A simple call would have helped my wonderment."

He apologizes. It's lengthy and boy-like, and it melts me.

"Stop it!" I hiss. "It's too late for your charm."

Rocco man-handles me into a hug. We kiss for a very long time, baking in the sun.

Once the embrace and kiss end, I inquire, "Where's Fisk?"

"I don't know."

"Did the Baskin bad guys plug him and ditch his body in the Gulf?"

Rocco shakes his head. "You're imagination is running away from you. Fisk is still missing. My father's men are on it. They're on a mission to find him."

"How many men?"

"Something like ten."

"And what about Tank?"

"Missing. Ten other men are looking for him."

"What about the two hundred grand?"

135

"Still missing, too."

"And ten men are looking for it, right?"

"Don't be a smart ass, Derek."

"It's part of my charm. I can't help it." I smile with happiness to see him. It's so nice to have him next to me. It's even better that I get to touch him. I ask, "What about the coke? Was it found?"

Rocco shakes his head again. "We're working on it."

"Of course. I shouldn't have asked."

Rocco's smile fades. He holds my sides with both palms. His muscular chest is gently cuddled next to my chest. "Listen," he says in a serious voice, "I have something to tell you."

"What kind of something?"

"Some bad news."

"Shit," I whisper. "I hate bad news."

"It's Felicia, Derek. She passed away in her sleep last night."

"Oh my god," I whisper, feeling my heart sink to my wobbling knees.

"She didn't wake up this morning. Her lawyer, Renaldo Lusick, contacted Quinn this morning. Quinn got a hold of me because he doesn't know where you are."

"Shit," I whisper again. I fall against Rocco and place my head on his right shoulder. Tears begin to swell and fall out of my eyes. I tremble against his comforting body, murmuring, "I'll miss her. She was like an aunt to me." My heart stings, and my head feels numb. I begin to lose my balance, but Rocco holds me up.

Deep down inside I know Felicia wasn't going to make it through autumn. Death was at her doorstep for many days, and she was finally welcomed inside. In truth, she lived a happy life that was short but potent, blessed beyond all comprehension.

"The funeral is tomorrow." Rocco rubs my muscled back, grazing fingers up and down my bony spine. "According to Lusick, it's a private gathering, and you're invited. The service is being held at

Flamingo Cove. If you want me to go, I'd be glad to attend as your support."

"I'm not sure," I reply, flummoxed and in a state of disrepair at the moment. "I don't know what I want."

"It's alright. You don't have to." Rocco is an angel, helping me through this disheartening situation of loss. It feels nice to have him hold me, protecting me from the world's damage and chaos.

After a solid ten minutes of sobbing, he walks me back to the mansion. He escorts me to my private room on the second floor, helps me lie down on my bed, and serves me a glass tumbler filled with blue gin over crushed ice. Rocco says, "You need a nap to help you with the stress. I'll wake you in a few hours."

Minutes later, the blue gin is gone. I cuddle with two pillows. Rocco pulls the pillows away from me and tosses them to the floor. He climbs into the bed with me and spoons my shaking body. He whispers, "You're safe in my arms. I'm here to help you through this. I'm not going to leave your side until you're feeling better."

"Thank you," I groggily respond, comfortable in his gentle and soothing hold, close my eyes, and drift off to sleep.

Something is between my legs. I'm not exactly sure what it is, but it stirs me out of sleep. I hear slurping and feel hard at my middle. I feel elated, vibrating with waves of erotic bliss. I feel ...

I reach down with my right hand and discover Rocco's head moving up and down between my thighs, having a post-midnight snack on my firm rod. I whisper, "Rocco, what are you doing?"

He comes off of me for air and responds, "I just want to please you. I'll do all the work."

"You're blowing me," I confirm, knowing it's not a dream.

"I know it's shocking, but fags sort of do this thing." He drops his head and goes to town on my wood. Rocco uses his tongue and the back of his throat. His movement is strong and vibrant. He gags a few times at my width and length, but eventually masters the pole.

"You're too good at this," I whisper in the night, half-smiling in the dark room. I relax by his tongue movements, listening to the Gulf's steady waves.

Rocco fingers my bottom and balls. He grazes fingertips against my silky inner thighs and the base of my pulsating cock, driving me crazy. His licking, lapping and sucking are vibrant and noisy, which totally turns me on. Again, he comes off for air. This time he chants, "I missed you, Derek. I've been waiting to do this to you since we last saw each other."

I plug his mouth with my cock. I thrust my hips upward/downward/upward/downward. I pull at his hair, windblown and ready to shoot my load into his mouth. Something tells me to hold out, though. My breathing increases, causing my sweat-slicked chest to rise and fall. "Rocco," I whisper, lost in the moment, totally shuddering because of his mouthy exploration.

He rolls fingers up and down on my stiff rod as he sucks its mushroom-shaped cap. Using his other hand, he toys with my hungry bottom. Rocco presses two fingers to my pink and tight opening. He plays with the cove, teasing me, driving me mad.

"Hold still, Derek. I have something special for you tonight."

I'm gently kissed by my navel, one nipple, the second nipple, and turned over. Before I know it, I'm on my belly and Rocco's tongue is inside my bottom. Gently he slides his wet lips against my rump's surface. His pointed tongue darts inside me, pulls out, and returns to the hole again. I clench the cotton sheets, burying my head into the feather pillow. I murmur his name in the cotton as he continues to work on my hole. I feel his palms on my sides, caressing my flesh. I feel ...

His straying tongue is no longer inside me. I feel his pubic triangle at the nape of my back. Warm lube is soothingly smeared against my tight hole with two of his fingers. His nine inches of erect cock press against one of my ass cheeks. The tip of one finger pops inside me, and I gasp uncontrollably. A second finger pops inside me and my world spins into erratic motion. Rocco carefully works the fingers in and out, and whispers into my right ear while leaning over me, "You ready for a ride?"

I lift my head from the pillow and groan, "I'm ready."

He removes the fingers from my prepared bottom and the tip of his cock replaces them. An inch of his beef enters me, two inches ... and three inches.

I crane my neck upwards and gasp with sweet pain. I grip the sheets, under his naughty spell. "Rocco," escapes my teeth-clenched mouth.

Four inches of his throbbing, veined and stiff meat enter me.

"Jesus, Rocco!" I can't contain the enjoyment, gasping for breath.

Five inches ... six inches ... seven inches of his protein buck my burning bottom. Seven inches quickly pull out of my core and push back in. This synchronized motion occurs for the next ten minutes or more, driving me to a point of no return regarding my sanity.

Eight inches plummet into my lubed bottom. Nine inches smack into my flesh. All of his sweaty weight is against my sweaty weight. Rocco's stomach touches my back. He lies on me, wedged inside my solid ass, and whispers, "I can't get close enough to you, Derek." He nibbles at my ear and kisses the back of my neck. He rises from me, pushing off of me. His nine inches is tenderly removed from my man-cove and pushed back inside.

"Ohmygod!" I yell, lost in the moment.

Again, Rocco pulls out of me, stalls for a second, and pushes all of his nine inches inside my sensitive canal. This continues for the next twelve minutes, boinking my bottom in a slow and rhythmic manner.

I moan with ecstasy, hard as a rock between my legs. My cock rides against the cotton sheets in a pleasurable manner. I'm fucking the bed as Rocco intimately fucks me.

Nine inches in. Nine inches out. Stall time. Nine inches in. Nine inches out. Stall time.

"Rocco," I groan, "Rocco, you're so naughty."

Gently, I'm flipped onto my back with his erection still inside me. And kindly he holds my ankles, charging inside me, pulling out, and charging in again. He becomes rough with his motion and begins to grunt. Rocco thrushes his weight forward/backward/forward/backward.

He eventually removes his right hand from my ankle, letting me place my heel on his shoulder. His free hand finds my extension of plump rock. He starts to roll fingers up and down my shaft, from base to head.

I jut my hips upwards. Graphic moans and groans escape me because of our building passion. Prosaically, I move against the friction of his hand applied to my root. Oxygen is unattainable, found and unattainable again.

Rocco is still at his naughty work, riding me like a bull. Sweat clings to his fingers. His breathing intensifies. It's obvious he is ready to shoot inside me, filling my middle with his sticky spew.

I gather my composure for just a second and suggest, "Let's shoot together. What do you say?"

And so it is done. Rocco pulls out of me and leans over me. Our cocks kiss, drawn together by his right hand. His fingers and palms begin to work the combo-meat platter in a simultaneous manner: north and south motion that is unyielding.

We gasp for air together, writhing in bliss. Our bodies become one, entwined by his functioning palm. Our upright cocks swell against each other, ready to burst. Hips gyrate and chests heave with the same motion.

Rocco groans, "Shoot."

I moan, "Shoot."

Ooze fires out of our hoses. Although the room is dark, I know the sticky spray spirals upwards and falls against our cocks, his hand and my torso. Droplets of the hot sap cling to our connected embrace. The smell that fills the air is bittersweet and vigorous; an aroma of shared lust between lovers on a hot, September night.

Spent, we lie side by side. Both of us are sticky and semi-asleep. I listen to Rocco breathe, the waves, and my breathing. I smell his post-sex aroma of sweat and ooze. My heartbeat is calm, next to his side. My head is near his chest, next to his right armpit.

He whispers, "Derek, are you awake?"

"A little."

"Can I tell you something without getting freaked out?"

"As long as it's not bad news." I've had a horrible day for bad news. Finding out that Felicia passed has broken me. I'm really not into anymore negative surprises.

"Derek?" he faintly says my name, still against me.

"I'm here."

Rocco turns his head to me and his lips touch my forehead. He exhales and whispers, "I just want you to know that I ... I love you."

My heartbeat grows. I'm wide awake now. The world seems to stop for a moment. The tide no longer rises. The room explodes with colorful fireworks: lavender flowers, royal blue balloons and red stars. Truth is, though ... the room is still completely dark, my paradise.

"Derek?"

I kiss his chest, next to his nipple, but choose not to respond with the same statement, protecting myself for the time being, perhaps adrift and somewhat afraid to fall in love with him, lost but happy.

Chapter 17 – Funeral & Foe

Rocco feeds me a pink little pill called Relay on the drive north to Felicia's funeral. He promises me that the pill has very few side effects, and I gulp it down in his Hummer with a chilled bottle of water. It numbs my skin, relaxes my mind, and causes a sense of stability.

"Sit back and relax. The drive is long," Rocco shares, taking care of me.

"Two black Lincolns are following us," I say, studying my side view mirror.

"Joey and Yorkie are looking out for your best interest."

"Jesus," I whisper. "Please tell me they won't shoot anybody during the service."

"Of course not," Rocco confirms. "They'll be on their best behavior."

I try to relax, lean my head back, and close my eyes. I think of Felicia and the last time I saw her. I say to Rocco, "I was supposed to buy an Italian stripper to enjoy. He was going to jerk off for me. She liked knowing that my sexual fantasies were tended to. She made me retrieve four hundred dollars from her dresser to pay for the guy. I never did get a chance to go to Pallyo and search the guy out. Her four hundred dollars is in my apartment."

I tell Rocco about Felicia's movies and her days in Hollywood. I tell him about Alex, the student from Prague who stripped for us. I tell Rocco about ...

He just listens to me, driving. His hands never leave the steering wheel. Rocco doesn't turn his attention to me, asking questions. Sometimes he blinks. So quiet and still. Unmoving. Listening.

It's raining out, which Felicia would have liked. She said the rain brought her luck; I tell Rocco this, too. The rain falls in sheets, hurricane Melvin is in the Gulf, pissed out of his mind. It's a good day for a funeral, I imagine. Rain. Gloom. Death. They all seem to go well together; I tell Rocco this, too.

"Fisk was invited to the funeral, but we still can't find him," Rocco eventually says.

"Did you check with Walter Landing? Maybe he knows where Fisk is."

"Who is Walter Landing?"

I turn my head to the left and look at Rocco. "You don't know who Walter Landing is?"

"I wouldn't have asked if I knew."

"Flamingo Cove's best-selling author. He writes queer mysteries. Walter took a liking to Fisk and is probably hiding him out."

"Where does Walter live?"

"Coconut Key."

"That's pretty ritzy."

"Walter can afford it."

"How close is Walter to Fisk?"

"Let's just say they make a good daddy and son couple."

"That close, huh?"

"Walter was in love at first sight when he met Fisk."

"That's not typical in the gay world."

"Nothing is typical these days. Everything's crazy now."

Rocco finds his cell phone inside his shirt pocket, flips it open, and punches in a number. He waits a few seconds for the person on the other end of the line to answer and says, "Keen, its Rocco. I need you to do a check on someone for me ... Yes, as soon as possible ... The name is Walter Landing ... Yes, the writer. I didn't know you read him ... I'll pick *Death to Boys* up and give it a try ... Do some homework on Landing and see if he has Fisk ... I need to hear back from you as soon as possible ... Yes, I have the funeral to attend ... I'll be reachable after two ... Thanks and so long." Rocco closes the cell phone and returns the device to his shirt pocket. He turns to me for just a second and says, "Keen's a good guy. He looks like Ken Ryker."

"The porn star?"

"Yes. They could pass for twins."

"Does Keen have a boner the size of Ryker's?"

"Wouldn't know. It's all business between us."

I'm sort of glad. I really don't want to hear about the sexual escapades in Rocco's life before I came into the picture. It seems wrong to learn that he was a man-slut, just like me. Some things are better left unknown and unsaid. Instead of inquiring about his sexual romps as a Mafia boss's son, I decide to rest, keep quiet, and just enjoy the ride.

Silence. A few bumps. Blackness behind my closed lids. I take it all in, nervous about attending Felicia's funeral. Half of me wants to tell Rocco to stop the Hummer and turn around. I can grieve at Castlegate, alone. There's really no reason to share a last goodbye with Felicia, is there?

"Derek, you okay?"

"The pill's working," I chant.

"Any side effects?"

"A little numbness. We both know it's not going to take away the inside pain."

"You're right. It won't."

"I need a nap," I confess.

Rocco places his right hand on my thigh and begins to pat it. "It's a forty-minute drive. I'll wake you when we get there."

Twelve grievers sit in uncomfortable chairs in a room no bigger than a bathroom. We listen to Pastor Reynolds pray out loud. Some of us have our heads bowed. Others take in the baskets of gladiolas, carnations, geraniums and daylilies, which are scattered throughout the room. Felicia Horodowski forever sleeps in an ash coffin lined in maroon-colored satin. She looks stunning in a navy-blue blouse from Bloomingdale's and Tiffany pearl-drop earrings. A light rose hue added to her lips and cheeks cause her to resemble Sleeping Beauty.

I look around the room and recognize Felicia's younger sister, Asbury Truffle, whom Felicia didn't care for much, often referring to the sibling as a cuntless snob. The woman is seated in the front row between her twin daughters, Ashley and Annabelle. The trio made the drive from Atlanta, Georgia. Ashley and Annabelle are twenty-two-year-old models, a replica of their lost aunt. Ashley gently places her head on her mother's shoulder, sobbing. In truth, Asbury looks like hell. Her flaming red hair is uncombed and her Anne Klein dress is wrinkled. I catch a glimpse of her profile, which is ghost-like and red-eyed. The poor thing looks as bad as I feel, which I will never hold against her.

Emil Cojure is present, Felicia's agent. The guy is about one hundred years old and walks with a cane. The man is asleep, I think, with his head bowed and his eyes closed. He has flown in from Hollywood for two days, just for this sad occasion.

Sylvia Ryer sits behind me. After many years without seeing her, she is still blonde, thin and beautiful. Before Felicia was diagnosed with stomach cancer, Sylvia was Felicia's lover for three years. The handbag designer became scared of Felicia's condition and left for Texas. I haven't seen her since, until today. Upon entering Sinclair's Funeral Home, Sylvia made eye contact with me. It wasn't icy or warm. The look was neutral and expected; I guess we'll never be friends again.

An empty seat for Fisk is saved on Sylvia's right. It's a shame he is not present for the funeral because Felicia would really want him to be here. Fisk helped Felicia on many days, no matter what his questionable profession entails. He took away a portion of the pain when it was too much for my friend to handle.

Rocco sits to my right. He leans into me and asks, "You hanging in there?"

I whisper, "I've had better days."

Pastor Reynolds talks about heaven and angels. He reads verses from the *Bible* about life and death, and the almighty presence of God in our lives.

Asbury whispers something to Annabelle. Seconds later, the daughter passes a handkerchief to her mother.

Emil wakes from his slumberous sleep. He coughs, clears his throat, and continues to doze.

For the very first time, I see Ten Faulkner to the far right in the second row. The actor is dressed in an expensive suit from Italy and wears his three hundred dollar pair of sunglasses on top of his head. Ten sits up straight and is golden with his tan. In the movies, he was Felicia's chemical romance. Sort of like what Rock Hudson was to Doris Day. America fell in love with the pair. The two did a dozen comedies together: *Fire in the Home*, *Robust Flavor*, *Yellow Parachute in Kansas*, and *Beth after the Affair*.

Felicia talked about Ten all the time: He is in love with a model named Felix Bender; Ten's traveling through Spain; he just sent me a postcard from Milan; Ten is falling for a watercolorist with the longest dick.

I sort of smile now, remembering Felicia's confession to Ten: "You'd be my lover if I weren't queer. We would have fallen in love and had six kids together."

Silence. A period of meditation. No shorter than three minutes.

Pastor Reynolds shares another prayer; this time it's about the dearly departed. Once the prayer is finished, he says to the grievers, "Would anyone like to say a few words?"

Asbury cries and can't muster the embarrassment. Emil is asleep again. Sylvia wouldn't dare. It's Ten who stands and walks to the small pulpit. Once the actor is positioned in front of the audience, he clears his throat. Ten looks confident and strong in front of the grievers, noble and prestigious. He says, "I'd like to tell a story about Felicia that happened over twenty years ago."

I've heard the story a dozen or more times before from Felicia. She and Ten were traveling in Durango, Mexico, lost and without a map. Like being lost wasn't enough, the rented Ford they were driving was out of gas, and they ended up stranded at a brothel for the night. Both were paid to sleep with adorable dark-skinned Mexican boys. Ten brought his Durango lover home and lived with Juan Comples for three years. Felicia purchased a new handbag with her money from the night's straight exploit.

By the end of Ten's story, everyone is laughing, including Rocco. Ten accepts the laughter like applause, tells the group that he will always love Felicia, and returns to his seat with a pleasurable smile on his handsome face and tears in his eyes.

Pastor Reynolds takes the pulpit and inquires, "Would someone else like to say something?"

Rocco looks over at me. I shake my head, unable to stand at the moment, let alone tell a story like Ten's. Rocco understands and doesn't push me into something I would rather not like to carry out.

Behind the grievers, the door to the room opens. Most of us turn around to see who the tardy guest is. Two guests arrive instead of one. And both surprise me with their attendance.

Rocco whispers, "Oh my god," beside me.

My heart falls to my stomach and I whisper, "Unbelievable." Are my eyes playing tricks on me? Rocco's little pill must be causing hallucinations.

At the back of the small room stand Walter Landing and Fisk, holding hands.

The mystery writer and his lover are dressed in *GQ* suits and expensive looking shoes. Fisk takes a seat in the empty chair beside Sylvia. Walter stands at the back of the room. He leans against the wall and crosses his arms over his chest. Fisk makes eye contact with me, and I smile. Walter shares a proper smile and nods his head at me; I do the same to him.

Again, Pastor Reynolds asks if anyone would like to say something to the gatherers, a light and airy speech or warm and fuzzy memory about Felicia.

Fisk chooses not to, just like me. Walter really didn't know Felicia, is more or less present as Fisk's companion and emotional support; he avoids the pulpit, unwilling to share something cozy and dramatic regarding Felicia.

"I have to pee," I lean into Rocco and whisper.

"Do you want me to go with you?"

"I'm good," I clarify, stand up and ...

Pastor Reynolds thinks I want to say something to the group. He steps away from the pulpit for me to take over.

I ignore him, heading in the opposite direction, out of the room. Quietly I close the door to the room behind me and stand in a hallway. A red-and-white EXIT sign hangs from the ceiling to the right, above a steel door. Three closed wooden doors are to my left; one says RESTROOM on it. I head to the labeled door and escape inside.

How long am I standing at the middle urinal, unable to piss? It feels like twenty minutes. I stare at the white tile wall, down into the urinal, and then at the wall again. It feels like ten more minutes tick by. Then, my hose works. Once my urine flows, I can't stop it.

Behind me, the bathroom door opens. I believe it to be Rocco, checking up on me. Maybe he thinks I'm having a sobbing episode and need some comforting. It's not Rocco, though. Fisk steps up behind me, grinds his pelvic area into my backside, wraps his hands around my sides, and says, "You're right where I want you, Derek. Long time no cock."

Urine backs up into my rod. I shake it, zip up, and spin around. Fisk is in my face. I say, "Rocco's men have been looking for you for a month, ever since the night in the Gulf."

"Walter Landing adores me. He's turned into my sugar daddy."

"Have you been staying at Coconut Key with him?" I gently push him aside, walk across the bathroom, and step up to the sink to wash my hands. Fisk's image hangs behind me in the mirror.

He nods his head. "The place is amazing. Think *Dynasty* all over again. Walter has been so nice to me. I'm his pampered pet, which beats the hell out of Flamingo Cove."

"Any signs of the Baskin bad guys?"

"Coconut Key is sealed off from the public. Walter has made millions from his books. Making lots of money is his number one priority."

"What about the two hundred grand? Any idea where it's at?"

Fisk shakes his head. "Doesn't matter anymore. Walter is writing Rocco's dad out a check. My debt is clear."

"What about the cocaine?"

"The Baskin guys have had it all along. Boss Malonni knows it, too."

"You're doing well for yourself. Felicia would be proud of you."

"I didn't think I was going to make it today. Walter was having chest pains and ..."

"Felicia's waiting for us. We should get back," I cut him off, finished washing and drying my hands. I spin around and Fisk clamps my arms at my sides. He's quick about kissing me, open-mouthed and with his tongue.

The bathroom door opens and Rocco steps inside. He sees Fisk kissing me. Rocco asks with anger in his voice, "What the fuck's going on in here?"

I push Fisk away and yell at him, "What did you do that for?"

Rocco rushes up to Fisk with a balled right fist. He swings the fist into Fisk's jaw. Fisk falls to the tile floor. Blood drips out of his mouth. Rocco now turns and looks at me with a set of puppy dog eyes, obviously stung by what he has just witnessed. He says, "I thought we had something going on. I thought you loved me."

I'm aghast, disbelieving what has just transpired. I point down at Fisk and reply, "I spun around and he grabbed me. I couldn't move and ..."

Rocco yells, "Whatever!" and bolts out of the bathroom, rushing away from me.

I feel tears ebbing in my eyes. Unable to stand, I lean into the sink. Everything begins to twirl, vibrating inside my head. The Earth falls off its axis. The planets plummet out of the galaxy. Bombs explode in my ears. Rocco is gone, done with me. I fall to the floor, close my eyes, and faint, all in a matter of seconds.

Part Four – Paragon Island

Chapter 18 – The Horndog Houseboy

Fisk and Walter drive me to Flamingo Cove after I come to. Quinn meets me in the lobby of our apartment building and rescues me. He is all big-eyed and filled with concern. "What's going on? What happened? Where the hell have you been for the last month?" So I spend the next hour with a bottle of whiskey and a shot glass, and explain every detail to him regarding my captivity at Castlegate, up through Felicia's funeral.

After hugs and light kissing, Quinn has a few shots with me in his bedroom. "I knew Tank was a badass. I can't pick men for the life of me."

"Let's forget about Tank and move onto the next topic." I've missed him and our sexy roommate times together. The man seems honest. One who just happens to be easy on the eyes, and always listens to me. Anyone would want him as a roommate.

Quinn says, "Fair enough," and hands me a dozen or more scraps of paper. Each has a date, time, and Mr. Chaz's name and cell number on it. He adds, "The guy is driving me crazy. All he wants to do is hook up with you. I didn't know where you were, so I couldn't tell him anything."

Mr. Chaz is into Worthington Philip Lewis, the porn industry kingpin, according to Walter Landing's confession a month before. I pass the scraps of paper back to Quinn and say, "Sorry, I'm not interested."

"He says he wants to continue a game you two were playing. What kind of game is he talking about?"

I shake my head, take another shot of whiskey, and respond, "Don't worry about it. Our game is over. If he calls again, tell him I'm not interested."

"Tell me what kind of game it was."

I'm quiet for a second or two. I take Quinn in: solid pecs and shoulders, thin waist, handsome face. The guy has a nice personality and comes across as being sweet. Why doesn't he have a steady boyfriend? Why does he date guys like Tank? Finally, I answer him, "The game is about role playing and sex. We were fucking until the night of my abduction by the Baskin guys."

"Does Rocco know about your game with Mr. Chaz?"

"No. Not that it matters now. Rocco swears I was putting the moves on Fisk in the men's room at Felicia's funeral. What a bunch of chaos that was. Now Rocco is out of the picture and I'm ... confused."

Quinn moves up to my side and places his head on my shoulder. He says, "Get back into your normal groove. Do some errands tomorrow. You've been gone for weeks. It's time for you to try and find yourself again."

"I miss Rocco, and it's only been a couple of hours without him," I whisper, drunk and blurry-eyed. The whiskey numbs me. I take another shot, downing it in a matter of seconds. The stuff feels like fire water against the back of my throat, but I really don't care.

Quinn snuggles against me as if we're lovers. "You love him, don't you?"

"I do ... Or, I think I do ... I don't know."

He smells clean, of vetiver and coriander. His shoulder rests next to my left cheek. I feel comfortable beside him, safe from any bad guys.

He pours us one last shot of whiskey. We drink the shots together. Quinn confirms, "Love has kicked you in the ass, my friend."

"It has," I admit.

"But it doesn't mean your life is over. Things can only go up from here. You can count on it."

We go to bed. Quinn decides to sleep with me, cuddling me throughout the night. We dream and snore together, side by side. In the middle of the night I have to pee. He checks on me to see if I'm safe.

And by dawn, I'm practically underneath him in the bed, but he doesn't take advantage of me. Friends are like this, I guess. They are always available when you need them, present in the worst conditions, permanent.

The next morning, I try to reach Rocco on his cell phone. His voicemail answers, and I leave the message: "This is a total misunderstanding. Fisk caught me off guard. He jumped me. You have to get that. I wasn't messing around on you. I wouldn't do that. Please, call me. I want to talk to you about this."

Rocco doesn't return my call.

Fuck!

I e-mail him and wait an hour for his response. It's a hopeless cause on my part, but at least I try. After checking my new mail a dozen or more times, Rocco doesn't respond. I surmise he completely dumps me because of Fisk.

Fuck again!

Quinn drives a 1998 Toyota truck with a few dings, many scratches, and a missing windshield wiper. I beg to borrow it, which he doesn't have a problem with, but inquires. "What are you up to, Derek? You never want to use my truck."

He is still in bed, naked and looking well-rested, and well-hung if I may say so. It's a face and body anyone would want to wake up to every morning; this is how handsome Quinn is. I don't know what prevents me from kissing him every minute of the day, honestly. Wrong. I do know what prevents me. This is a no-brainer, something I don't even need to think about. Rocco surfaces within my mind. My life is nothing but the mobster lately, and I'm lost without him right now.

I toss on clothes, which all belong to Quinn: khaki shorts, teal-colored wife beater, booty socks and a pair of his Sketchers. "I'm going to find Rocco."

"What if he's in M?"

"M?" I ask, puzzled.

"Miami. Everyone knows that."

Quinn speaks text language again, which I ignore. "I'll drive to Miami then."

He rolls his eyes and shakes his head. "Love makes us do foolish things."

"It's only going to be foolish if I don't find him." I'm done dressing and snatch up his truck keys from the top of his five-drawer dresser. "Call me on my cell if you need me."

"Will do, Nancy Drew … And good luck."

I'm out the door in a flash. Before I know it, I'm sitting inside the cab of his Toyota, which smells like dried semen lined briefs. I start the truck's engine, pull out of the building's parking area, and head south, toward Rocco's beach house.

Farrell greets me at the beach house's front door. His face blooms with an intoxicating smile and he says, "Back for another fuck, buddy?"

I shake my head and reply, "I'm not your buddy. Our fuck session was a one-time thing."

"Come on," Farrell begs, touching fingers to my wife beater, grazing a nipple. "We had a good time together. Let's give it another try."

I ignore his suggestion, peer over his right shoulder, left shoulder, and ask, "Is Rocco here?"

Farrell unbuttons his sleeveless cotton shirt, takes it off, and drops it to the foyer's marble floor. He informs, "You've got to go through me to get to Rocco."

He's kidding me, right? This is a joke. Farrell cannot be serious. What a horndog houseboy he is. I can't believe I actually fucked around with him. Shame on me. I shake my head in a persistent and angry manner, and share, "Listen, I'm not here to fuck you. I need to see Rocco."

Farrell unbuttons his Levi's and shows off his porn-goods. He pulls out his already-firm yanker from his denim and suggests, "We can enjoy a quickie. Rocco doesn't even have to know about it."

I watch him stroke his beef up and down with two palms. Granted, it's hot. But seriously, I'm not into him. Once Rocco saved me from the Baskin bad boys, I was all his for the taking. I try to look over Farrell's left shoulder, right shoulder, back over his left shoulder, but he keeps bobbing and weaving like a skilled boxer, blocking my view. Eventually I hold my ground, keep a stern face, and ask, "Will you just let me in?"

Farrell cannot be human, I decide. He spanks his own ass with his left hand and says, "Fuck me, and I'll let you in to see Rocco."

I shake my head and call over his right shoulder, "Rocco!? ... Rocco!?"

It gives Farrell a sufficient amount of time to grab my waist and pull me toward him. His fingers clamp against the front of my khaki shorts and their top button. He now slips one hand down into my boxer-briefs, finds exactly what he's looking for, grazes my cock, and supplies, "You know you want to fuck me."

I try to be a gentleman and pull away from him. The last thing I want to do right now is fuck him. Farrell starts to get rough, though, and the gentleman in me soon vanishes. When he tugs down on my khakis, trying to remove the cotton from my skin without unbuttoning them, I begin to go nutso and inquire, "What the fuck are you doing to me?"

Chest to chest, Farrell growls, "Don't make me do something you might regret." He tries to kiss me open-mouthed, obviously hungry.

I'm over him. Enough is enough. I pull my mouth away from his and slap him across the face with an open palm. I ask, "Rocco's not even here, is he?"

Farrell chooses not to answer me, pissed. He pulls his hand out of my shorts and touches his stinging cheek. He balls up his other hand and attempts to pop a quick punch at my face.

I dunk and weave; now the boxer.

He carries out two more air-jabs, missing me.

I nail him in the gut with a tight left fist.

Farrell makes an ughh sound and clutches his stomach, doubling over. He complains, "You motherfucker, you nailed me."

"Think of it as beginner's luck. I'm going to look for Rocco." In horrible pain, I walk past the houseboy and down the foyer.

"Rocco is not here! He wanted to be alone and went to Castlegate." Farrell can barely get the words out, but he manages.

I turn around and hiss at him, "You could have told me that from the start."

He is quiet, still doubled-over. In passing, I want to do some crazy-shit things to him. Removing his testicles is not out of the equation. I'm a gentleman, though, and head out of the beach house, down the steps, and back to Quinn's Toyota, which is parked in the driveway, waiting for me.

I witness Tiempo and Carlos at work in the East Garden when I arrive at Castlegate. Tiempo waves, sharing a bright smile with me. I drive past the duo in love and park Quinn's truck next to the front verandah.

As usual, the day is all sunshine. Not a single cloud waves by in the sky. It's a hot ninety-three degrees out with thirty percent humidity. I walk up to the double doors between life-size cement lions and ring the doorbell, waiting to be met by Rocco.

Miguel answers the door in a cherry red, lace up trunk. A scolding yellow cotton towel is draped over his bare right shoulder. Once he sees it's me, Miguel says, "Derek, I was just getting in the pool. You should join me."

Miguel still looks good. No, he looks extraordinarily yummy. I'm sure he's dating the most beautiful woman right now. I try not to drool over his packed pecs and neck-size biceps. My stare tends to stray to his plump privates in the nylon suit and succulent looking thighs. I think: Stop, Derek! You're into Rocco, not Miguel. Shame on you. I steer my view back up to his Instinct face and reply, "Honestly, I need to speak to Rocco."

"Of course. Why don't you come in and I'll tell him you're here."

I follow Miguel into the extravagant foyer and feel like a stranger. Did I really spend a month here? It certainly doesn't feel like it. The satin settees and gold-trimmed mirrors lining the walls look foreign to me. The all-white marble floor is unfamiliar, as well as the crystal chandelier hanging overhead with its three tiers of gold and sparkling glass. I feel like an intruder of sorts, unwelcomed and trespassing, even if Miguel is being cordial to me.

"Derek, don't be shy to make yourself at home. Follow me into the library."

I listen to Miguel, following him through a wide passageway with two mahogany doors, which just happen to be open.

Miguel tells me, "Get comfortable while I fetch Rocco from the pool."

Hours have been spent in this library reading Alice Walker, William Faulkner, Tennessee Williams, John Irving, Christopher Rice, Shirley Jackson, Patricia Highsmith, Edmund White, David Sadaris and Peter Cameron, just to name a few of the authors I've enjoyed. The library is one of my favorite rooms in the palatial mansion. I like its slate-gray floor and rustic-style high back chairs. I have fingered the twenty thousand tomes inside the room with their leather bindings and gold-gilded pages. Rocco's personal library is serene and comfortable, a room with enchanted spirits and a secret passageway leading to his private bedroom on the second floor, which I have followed a few times, taking naps in his queen-sized bed on heated afternoons.

During the short period of time Miguel leaves me to myself, I find a battered copy of *Giovanni's Room*, one of my absolute favorites. I sit in one of the available chairs near an east window and begin to thumb through the book, reading numerous passages.

Approximately six minutes later, Rocco enters the library without Miguel, which causes me to place Baldwin's masterpiece on my lap. He sports a maroon-colored windsurfer trunk with white strings and an elastic band at the waist. He has just escaped the outside pool and drips all over the massive Oriental rug.

He is beautiful, I conclude. He will always be beautiful. Rocco's golden suntan perfectly fits his skin, particularly against his plated chest and delicious looking treasure trail. He is porn star material all the way, minus the dirty. Something to make you drool. A head-turner. My once-boyfriend.

I really want to hug and kiss him, but we are separated by twenty paces. Rocco chooses to keep his distance, which I respect. Of course he is icy with me. Who wouldn't be after being caught with Fisk Deveraux in a provocative (and unexpectedly shocking) position? Rocco appears pissed at me, unable to look me in the eyes. Instead, he stares at the slate-grey floor beyond the Oriental rug, licks his lips, and fails to verbalize anything.

To break the ice I say, "Look, Rocco, I know you don't want me here. I understand where you're coming from. What I don't understand is less simple: Why don't you believe me when I say Fisk caught me off guard and totally crossed a line with me? In short, I didn't see his kiss coming. It happened ... out of the blue. I can't take that back."

"I didn't see you push him away." It's a good comeback, a remarkable comment made. Kudos to Rocco. One point for him. Zero for me.

"I didn't have time. You walked in the room right when he jumped me."

"You didn't look like you weren't enjoying it."

I heavily sigh, growing perturbed. Pleading is not beneath me. In fact, I pride myself in a good defense with much beseeching. Come on, it's the only thing some guys have to protect themselves with, just like me. "I wasn't feeling anything for him. I never have. Fisk has always wanted in my pants. He's been trying to boink me for the past year. His kiss is all a misunderstanding. It was totally one-sided. I was a victim."

Rocco lifts his view from the floor and stares at me. He looks hurt. No, he looks badly stung. His eyes are swollen a bit, and I can tell he's been crying. Shit, this is horrible to see. Damaging. The worst.

He says, "You shouldn't be here. What we shared doesn't exist now. What I saw between Fisk and you was real."

"That's not true, Rocco. We have nothing. It wasn't real. He attacked me."

"I didn't see that. I just saw the two of you kissing."

Still sitting in the high-back chair, I slap a palm against my forehead and confess, "This is hard to explain. How can I defend myself when there's nothing to defend?" I shake my head, drop my hand from my forehead, and share, "Rocco, you are not being fair with me. I'm being totally honest with you, and you're not even trying to absorb what I'm attempting to get across to you."

My heart races, and my temperature climbs. Obviously this unannounced visit is a mistake today. In truth, he has already made up his mind about dumping me over a bogus kiss. Now I feel like a victim twice. Once with Fisk, and now with Rocco. I try one last attempt to defend myself and whisper, "Rocco, I thought you loved me."

"I'm not sure what I feel for you now."

Tears form at the corners of my eyes. I want to faint, but hold my ground. I whisper, "Give me a chance here. I'm telling you the truth. Fisk is nothing to me. I was a victim. I was ..."

"Stop!" Rocco barks at me, cutting me off. He lifts his right index finger and points it at me in a direct manner, and rattles off, "I'm done with this, and I'm done with you, Derek. It's over. It was a good time while it lasted, but now it's over."

Before I can express my concern, contempt, love and upset, Rocco is gone. He vanishes from the library, bolting away in his skin-tight trunk. I'm left behind, sobbing with my bare heart in my palms. I accidentally drop *Giovanni's Room* to the library's floor, next to my feet. I'm numb all over. Breathless. I think this isn't fair. Rocco's being stubborn. He has to believe me. He must. I was a victim ... I was a victim ... a victim.

During the long, tedious and teary drive back to Flamingo Cove, I receive two calls on my cell phone. The first is from Quinn. He asks, "When are you getting back with my truck?"

"I don't know. Why?"

"Because you shouldn't come back."

"What are you talking about?"

"Tank just paid me a visit here at the apartment, and he's looking for your ass."

I'm stunned by this news and ask, "Why me? "

Quinn clears his throat and replies, "He said something about finding you and ripping you apart."

"He is not very good with men," I say, not intentionally making a joke. In truth, I'm a mess. Blaring horns are heard all around me because I accidentally swerve into oncoming traffic. The horns bring me back to reality and I steer the truck into the proper lane.

Quinn asks, "Are you driving like an asshole?"

"No! ... Never!"

"You'd better not be, or I will rip you apart."

"Why does Tank want to rip me apart?"

"It's all about that shit you caused on the Baskin fish boat a month ago."

"Crap," I whisper.

"He obviously has his bad moments. Someone will set him straight one of these days. It doesn't mean I don't care for him, though," Quinn provides. "So don't come home. That's why I'm calling you."

"Where can I go?"

"I don't know."

"What about Push-ups?"

"Pete doesn't like stayovers. He says it's bad for the gym's business."

"Fuck!" I scream into the cell phone. "Where am I supposed to go?"

"Think about it. Something will come up. Keep the truck for a few days. If you need me, call."

"I'll do that. Thanks, Quinn."

"Hey, buddy, what are friends for?"

The second call is not from Quinn, although I think he's calling me back to tell me something he forgot to say in our first conversation. Because I'm driving, trying to be as careful as possible, I don't look at the cellular's call screen and study the incoming number. Instead, I flip the phone open, slip it up to my right ear, and carry out my normal spill, "This is Derek."

To my utter surprise, Walter Landing is on the other end of the line. He says, "Derek, Fisk is missing and I need your help."

"I'm not looking for Fisk," I provide. "He's done a doozey on me, and I'd rather not be involved with him anymore than I already am."

Walter says, "Listen to me. I don't want to find him. In truth, Fisk is always missing. Last week he went to Aruba. The week before that it was Puerto Rico. Sometimes the boy needs to be on a leash."

"How do I fit into this? What kind of help do you need from me?"

"The commitment ceremony between Andrew Chaz and Worth Lewis is tomorrow, and I need you to fill in for Fisk. Originally you were supposed to go, but you've been missing for thirty-some days, so I wanted Fisk to attend the function with me ..."

"But now, Fisk is missing, and you want me to attend, right?"

"Exactly." Walter takes a deep breath and continues, "Of course I will pay you well. All expenses included. The works. Whatever you need. I want to be seen with somebody young and healthy, with your build, if you know what I mean."

Tears stop falling from my eyes. I can breathe again. A little smile forms on my face. Talk about good timing. Walter couldn't have called at a more opportune moment. I inquire, "Do you have a suit for me?"

"Are you the same size as Fisk?"

"Pretty much."

"Then you have a suit."

My smile grows wide. "I'm on the road right now. I'm about two hours away from Coconut Key. Have a blue gin and tonic ready for me. Plus, I'm hungry."

Walter replies, "Will do. Drive safe. And thanks for helping me out."

Chapter 19 – Beware of Daddy

Gulf Bay Stables is twice the size of Castlegate. Three floors of marble, stucco and granite peer over the ocean. Palm trees add refreshing shade, and Spanish moss drapes over laurel bushes, which offers a romantic touch and a serene landscape. The property is a playground for fairies or young men, a palatial resort for visiting guests, family, and those considered "close friends." Three massive gardens surround the mansion: Lulabelle, Geniveve and Marpessa. Between the gardens are freshly manicured greens and slate walkways. The commitment ceremony is being held between the Lulabelle and Marpessa gardens at the rear of the property, next to the ocean.

Walter sits to my right. He looks dapper in his khaki-colored chinos and pale green shirt. Something is bothering him, but I'm not sure. He jostles in his seat too much, fidgety like a child.

"What's wrong with you?" I inquire.

"You honestly don't want to know," he whispers.

"Tell me. Maybe I can help."

"Let's just say that my Chris Wide dildo was very big and quite frisky last night. I'm paying for it today."

I'm wrong. I can't help him. Enough said. I merely turn around and take the setting in, quiet as a church mouse.

The setting is an outside ceremony next to the Gulf. Approximately fifty-plus guests garnish the lawn in white chairs. All of Worth's family and friends sit to the right. I see familiar porn stars from his company Gladiator Media Limited: Branch Murdock, Danny Brass, Luke Darling and Franky DeForri. The skin stars all sit in one group, dressed to the nines and on their best behavior.

Mr. Chaz's family consists of his son, Corey, and his younger brother, Daniel, who sit on the left side. His friends are scattered around me, strangers' faces.

Between the two groups is a narrow aisle of maroon satin carpet that stretches to the front of the coexisting groups. A trellis decorated with maroon and white roses stands at the end of the carpet.

Beyond the trellis stand Pastor Roberts, Mr. Chaz and Worth. To the right of the trio is a male cellist, who looks to be nineteen and spanking young out of the pages of *Freshmen.*

The male couple looks dashing in black tuxedos, white shirts and maroon ties. Mr. Chaz makes eye contact with me and winks. I make it quite clear I'm attached to Walter, lean into the mystery author, and dab a kiss to his cheek.

Walter leans into me after my suggestive peck and whispers, "Dear Lord, look at that tasty pastor. I can think of a dozen or more ways to sin with him."

I cordially and quietly reply, "You're naughty, Walter. I like this side of you."

Ordained Pastor Roberts stands perpendicular to the blissful couple. He looks absolutely adorable in his black and white garb, the golden cross around his neck accessorizing with appeal. Pastor Roberts is five-foot-ten with cherry-colored cheeks and lips, and sports fall-into amber-yellow tiger eyes. His hair is blond, wavy and model-mussed, presenting a sexy side to God's distinctive work and religion as a whole.

Following my comment, the service begins. Pastor Roberts informs, "Let us bow our heads for a moment of prayer."

Walter and other guests bow their heads. I choose to take in the Gulf with all its splendor and spectacular glory. The day turns out to be quite striking: a bright sun and cloudless sky unite the two men, however long they wish to be together; the wind is ever so lightly tainted with the scents of honeysuckle and oranges; and Pastor Roberts has shared a one on one with Jesus, asking for (and receiving) low humidity and a balmy eighty-two degrees.

I'm happy for Mr. Chaz, yet extremely bitter. One description bounces to and fro within my mind: player. Mr. Chaz will not be able to keep his cock in its pants, and Worth will inevitably have his heart forever broken. Unless both husbands agree to "playtime with others," Mr. Chaz is destined to fail at his second long-term relationship, dangerously playing the field of unlimited gays.

I'm bitter with him because our sex game is over, and he has kept Worth a secret from me. I'm bitter because I really liked Mr. Chaz. Not only did he bring out the naughty in me, he also showed me that a Daddy/boy relationship can have all kinds of fun together. I have to get over it, though. Life will inevitably move forward, with or without me. Perhaps it's better to label my past with Mr. Chaz as a bygone, and move ahead, briskly.

Both Mr. Chaz and Worth share memorized vows with each other, and the gatherers. Worth cries, which makes Mr. Chaz cry, which then in turn causes most of the guests to cry, including Walter.

Pastor Roberts keeps it together, though. He says, "With the power invested in me, I now pronounce you husband and husband. You may kiss the groom."

The kiss is sloppy and unattractive. Granted, Mr. Chaz is primo-hot, but his partner is rather hard on the eyes.

"Yuck," Walter leans into me and whispers.

"Double yuck," I respond, ready for a drink to numb my eyes from the visual pain.

The reception is held next to the Marpessa Garden with a white tent, chairs and tables. Twenty-something waiters, which just happen to be yummy looking, move about the guests, serving hors d'oeuvres, golden champagne and chocolates. A tent is set up for people who need to hide from the sun. The rear of the tent is made up of a wooden floor and a group of four cellists called Breeze. Some of the guests gather around the two bar areas. Others mingle from table to table, enjoying gossip and company.

Walter and I have martinis at one of the bars. We admire some of the male porn stars and their delicious looking bodies.

Luke Darling, a very butch, all-muscle top with an eleven-inch wanger shares suggestive eye contact with Walter. He finds his way up to our twosome and introduces himself. Luke drinks a fruity cocktail, seems semi-buzzed, and is all smiles. He turns his full attention to Walter and says, "I know you."

"Of course not," Walter replies, shaking his head.

"I do know you. You interviewed me a few years ago regarding your novel, *The Houseboy Murder*."

"I don't recall," Walter politely says.

"Before I was in the adult industry, I answered your ad in the *Sunday Current*. You interviewed approximately eight houseboys for your book. I happened to be one of them." Luke lights up with a blistering smile. He is thrilled to see Walter again, even if Walter doesn't remember.

"I'm sorry," Walter responds. "My memory isn't what it used to be. In truth, I saw your performance in *Bronco Boys* and absolutely loved it. I was particularly fond of what you did with those naughty twins in the barn."

Luke blushes. He is rugged-cute with just a pint of charm mixed in. "I'll be working with the Romeo twins in two weeks. We're all flying to a remote spot in Cancun and filming. I can't wait."

"I'm jealous," Walter says. He dabs the tip of his right index finger to the porn star's nose like a grandmother winning over her grandson. "You wouldn't happen to know that remote location, would you? Derek and I would love to see you in action."

Luke laughs and shakes his head. "You're entertaining, Mr. Landing. I like you."

"Not as entertaining as you," Walter adds, downing his cocktail.

The star of *Bronco Boys* is soon whisked away by one of his cheeky coworkers. The two young men float away like butterflies in search of fresh drinks and other guests to mingle with.

"Luke is breathtaking, both in his clothes and out," Walter says, rescuing a fresh martini from the bar located behind us.

"He is rather soft on the eyes."

"And hard between his legs."

"I didn't notice."

"Shame on you, Derek. The boy was like steel in his slacks."

I ignore his comment about Luke Darling and ask, "Will you dance with me, Walter?"

"I'd love to, chap."

Off we go to the dance floor with drinks in hand, passing threesomes at talk. Once near the stage, where the cellists play, Walter finds a home for our empty martini glasses. He pulls me into his arms and saunters me to the middle of the floor where we become Fred Astaire and Ginger Rogers.

Walter can dance; a champion of the waltz and foxtrot from his academic days in private school. He proves his skill with a half turn, two aerobatic spins, and a gentle dip. Our lips touch, fall apart, and I am dipped again. He is a master on the wood, twirling me at one point, catching me, and kissing me again. We become a spectacle on the dance floor, which clears of other dancers. Guests are enlightened with Walter's leading and my graceful following. Everyone becomes wide-eyed and fully entertained by our cohesive movement. They applaud and cheer following our performance.

Being a gentleman, he escorts me back to the bar. Side by side, we have martinis, surrounded by congratulatory guests. He pats me on the back numerous times, so very proud of my work on the wood. I'm kissed several times on the cheeks by strangers. The moment becomes fairy tale perfect and breathtaking, or maybe I have just had too much alcohol to drink.

Worth Lewis steps up to our twosome and shares a hug with Walter. He shadows Walter by a couple inches. His middle is thinner, and he has more hair. Worth looks like Oscar the Grouch, eccentric and very low-brow, but wealthy as all hell.

Walter introduces me, and I shake Worth's hand. His grip is strong, manly and offers an unexpected kick. After our handshake, Worth says, "You two were smashing out there."

"Honestly," Walter provides, "we didn't intend to steal the grooms' thunder."

Worth waves a hand forward, bending it at the wrist, and clarifies, "You didn't. The guests were loving it. The two of you looked as if you were having all the fun in the world."

"We were. Walter is a natural."

"I'm not." Walter blushes, turning a light shade of pink.

Mr. Chaz's new partner steps back and eyes me up and down. A furrowed brow and inquisitive smile are shared. He politely asks me, "Are you currently employed?"

If one could call running errands for tenants at Flamingo Cove a job, then I am employed. I nod my head and respond, "Yes, I am."

"That's too bad. You'd be absolutely sparkling in my new movie. You have an amazing body and would look good naked." Worth finds a card in his tuxedo and passes it to me. "If you ever need employment, feel free to buzz me. I would personally take your call."

Something tells me that Worth Lewis would like to take more than my call. I don't share this with him, though, nor Walter. I merely take the card from Worth, slip it into my back pocket, and respond like a gentleman, "Thank you."

Mr. Chaz pulls Worth away; it happens so abruptly I don't even know what's going on. Again, we make eye contact. He smiles. I smile. And Worth and Mr. Chaz vanish into the crowd of guests.

Corey Chaz finds me among the many drinkers at the bar. The kid is totally blitzed. He swaggers up to our twosome, discovers Walter's shoulder, and leans into the writer, so he doesn't fall over and drop to the manicured grass. What a little fucker.

I ask, "Are you old enough to drink, Corey?"

He laughs. It's a handsome laugh, kind of innocent and fun, but obnoxious at the same time. "Are you old enough to fuck my dad in his apartment?"

Corey is out of control, evidently intoxicated to his fullest potential. His smile broadens in an animated manner.

"Who is this?" Walter asks, holding the boy up.

"Mr. Chaz's son," I respond.

"He's quite fine looking, and beefy in all the right places."

"He's drunk and underage," I share.

"How many times did you fuck my father, anyway?" Corey questions in a loud tone, totally misbehaving and overly inebriated.

Guests turn to view the excitement.

Walter whispers to the boy, "People are starting to stare."

"You're a fucking slut!" Mr. Chaz's son points a finger at my chest, pressing hard. "You're a whore!"

Fuck! What's happening? Corey is embarrassing me.

Walter whispers in the boy's ear, "That's rude."

"You suck cock, and you like it up the ass!" Corey yells for all to hear.

I turn an embarrassing shade of red in the color wheel. Quickly, I do a tiny spin, place my martini down on the bar, and excuse myself from the scene. I head to the house for some privacy and to calm down.

Behind me, Mr. Chaz calls out to his son. I imagine he runs after the boy and rescues him from the gawking guests. I believe Mr. Chaz takes Corey into his arms, walks him to the driveway for some time to sober up, and ...

I find the bathroom on the second floor for escape. It looks like a giant seashell. I think of that famous painting with the naked chick in the overly decorated oyster, but I don't like chicks, so the thought passes quickly. Christ! Everything is fucking seashells! The hand towels are shaped like seashells. Shadow boxes are showcase an arrangement of seashells. The toilet seat is shaped like a seashell. There are seashell soaps, a cup, and two rugs on the seashell-colored marble floor. The bathtub and sinks are shaped like seashells!

I dab some water on my face at the sink and use one of the seashell-shaped hand towels to dry off. I place the towel aside, wash my hands for two minutes, find the towel again, and begin to dry my hands off.

The bathroom door opens and my head lifts to the mirror. I see Mr. Chaz walking toward me. "We meet again, young man. I feel like you've been hiding from me," he says. His palms collide to my hips and he casually spins me around like we're on Dancing with the Stars.

"You're still sexy after all these weeks. Do you know how hard I get when I think about you?"

I drop the seashell-shaped towel to the bathroom floor, finished with the task of drying my hands. Half of me regrets not locking the door. The other half is glad to see him. My heart shutters within my chest, my cock bounces in my suit pants, and I begin to perspire. I ask, "Shouldn't you be with Worth?"

"Don't worry about him." Mr. Chaz begins to unbutton my shirt. A blistering smile spreads across his masculine face. "Daddy has missed you, Derek. Why don't you kiss Daddy's cock?"

I shake my head, disbelieving this is happening. Today is Mr. Chaz's commitment ceremony day, and he has given his heart to a special man, sharing his vow of love in front of a crowd of fifty or more. I try to pull away from him and reply, "I can't do this. I'm taken."

"It's that Mafia guy, isn't it?" He tries to push a hand into my slacks, but I pull away, backing into the sink.

I nod my head. "How did you know?"

"Word travels fast in small circles of friends. I was told he dumped you."

I don't respond. I shake in front of him and wonder how I can get past him. I'm trapped, his prey and find. There is nowhere to go – no escape.

"You're single, right?"

"You're not. This is your reception. You should be all over Worth."

Mr. Chaz laughs, "He's probably with a boy like you right now. We have an understanding. It's a mega-alternative relationship. Later, when we're cuddling together in bed, we'll share all the details regarding our sexual adventures with boys like you."

"I can't do this," I repeat, attempting to pass by him, giving my great escape a try.

He is quick and strong, a bull of sorts with a temper. "You're not going anywhere," Mr. Chaz explains, grabbing my waist at the belt buckle. His other hand clamps down on a shoulder, preventing my escape. He leans into me and drags his tongue along my neck. He kisses my left cheek and goes for my mouth, but I fight him off and turn away.

"You can't do this to me. We're not playing the game anymore," I whisper.

"Who said anything about a game? This is real. The here and now."

I shake my head. "No, it's not."

"The fuck it isn't!" Mr. Chaz proclaims, raising his right hand to slap me across my face.

The knob on the bathroom door turns and the door pushes open. Thank God it's Walter rescuing me from the architect.

Mr. Chaz drops his hand and releases my belt buckle.

Walter inquires, "What's going on in here?" A quizzical look surfaces on his mature face with crinkled eyebrows and pursed lips. Walter stares at me, questioning my situation.

"You're ready to leave, right?" I ask Walter.

"Of course," Walter supplies. Quickly, he pulls me away from the sink. Walter is not very pleased with the encountered scene. He huffs while walking me out of the bathroom, "No one should be left alone with that fox. He'll eat anyone up and spit them out." He tugs me to the right, down the hallway, and ...

Two male figures dressed like caterers leap out of a semi-dark bedroom. The larger of the two slips a white cloth against Walter's mouth as the shorter one jumps behind me and places a knife to my neck.

Walter becomes unconscious and falls to the floor, temporarily poisoned from the contents in the white rag.

Shorty says behind me, "Don't make a fuss," and slips a ski mask without holes over my head. I feel a prick in my right arm, become dizzy in this new black world, and my legs grow weak. Shorty mumbles something I don't comprehend. My arms and neck feel drained. My eyes close, and my mouth begins to feel tingly. Like Dorothy in Oz. Like Alice in Wonderland. Again, I pass out and plunge into a state of nothingness.

Chapter 20 – Hurricane Brass

"Welcome to Turtle Island, Mr. Reed," Boss Malonni says to me when I come to. "It's private, serene, and one of the most beautiful places in Florida."

I sit up on a bamboo bed, rub my eyes, and begin to look around. Mr. Malonni and I are outside, among palm trees, a one hundred foot waterfall, and boulder-size rocks. Thick jungle surrounds us. I hear lapwings and plovers, Junkos and pipits. The waterfall is loud, too, a tumbling of water into a crystal blue pool at its base.

As I take in the scenery, my mind fills with questions: Where did I leave my martini? Where is Walter? Is the reception over? Did Corey pass out from consuming too much alcohol? Is Worth really serious about me starring in one of his XXX movies? What happened in the hallway outside the bathroom at the Gulf Bay Stables?

More questions stir within my mind, all regarding my current position: Where is Turtle Island? What is Rocco's father doing here? How did I get here? What's going on?

Boss is dressed in khaki shorts, Italian sandals, and a tacky shirt covered in rainbow bright toucans. Sunglasses cover his eyes. He sips an aqua-colored drink with a paper umbrella and too much fruit. On a bamboo table to his right sits an ashtray, Cuban cigar, Zippo lighter and a .45 Magnum.

I say, "If you're going to kill me, Mr. Malonni, please just get it over with."

A barefoot Mexican boy exits a narrow path in the jungle. He wears a hemp cloth around his middle and carries a bamboo tray in both hands.

Boss says, "Mika, please put the tray beside Mr. Reed."

Mika does as he is told. The tray is filled with fruits, nuts and a coconut drink in a half shell. He places the tray down on the ground near the bamboo bed, and passes me the available beverage. Once Mika returns to the jungle, I take a long sip of rum and pineapple juice from the coconut shell, consuming its strong and refreshing flavor. I think this just might be my last drink, considering the gun at Boss's side. Eventually, I say, "Please, don't kill me. I didn't mean to hurt Rocco."

Rocco's father tilts his head back and provides a hearty laugh. "What gives you the idea that I'm going to kill you, Derek?"

I point to his table and say, "The gun is pretty convincing."

"It's only for protection," he clarifies with a raised smile. "These parts of Florida are known for their gators. You can never be too careful."

Butterflies circle me, floating away. I stare at the gun, then Boss, and back at the gun.

Rocco's daddy asks, "Do you know why you're here?"

"I really don't know," I lie. I have reasons, I guess: Fisk kissed me, and I accidentally betrayed Rocco. These are good enough reasons, I assume. One never really can justify such a question when confronted by a mob leader and his .45 Magnum, right?

"Walk me through this kiss with Fisk, if you don't mind."

Fags in thongs! Do I have to? It's embarrassing and dirty and ...

"I already know what happened, Derek. I just want to hear your side of the story. My son is a very hard-headed young man. Listening has never been one of his key strengths. I'm sure there was a very a good explanation why you broke his heart."

Does he really just say this? Come on. The guilt is overwhelming, even when I shouldn't have guilt. I blurt out, "Fisk attacked me in the bathroom at Felicia's funeral and ..." I walk Mr. Malonni through the entire day: from climbing into Rocco's Hummer to taking a piss in the second floor bathroom. "Fisk literally jumped me," I confess.

"Yes," Boss agrees, "that's what the video coverage clarifies."

"What video coverage?" I inquire.

"You know you're constantly being watched by my men, right?"

I shake my head while grabbing a few whole cashews from the bamboo tray. "I didn't."

"Of course you are. The Baskin group is still after you. They mean business. They claim you have the two hundred grand, and the cocaine. Murder is not out of the question when it comes to bad guys, Mr. Reed." He takes a sip of his fruity drink, places it on the table by his handgun, and finds the cigar and Zippo. He slips the cigar in his mouth, lights it, inhales, exhales and adds, "My men have been watching you ever since you left Castlegate."

Shit! Is this for real? Is Rocco's daddy telling me the truth? "This isn't about the kiss with Fisk?"

"Of course not," Boss responds, puffing on his cigar.

"This isn't about Rocco being pissed at me, either?"

"Rocco will come around. The kiss between Fisk and you was harmless. The video footage proves that," Boss shares. "Listen, one of Baskin's men was at the Gulf Bay Stables. His name is Luciano 'Weasel' Spada, and he was going to mutilate you. My men had to step in and save you from being hurt or killed."

I roll my eyes and ask, "The caterers were your men?"

Mr. Malonni takes another puff of his cigar, blows out a plume of smoke into the beautiful day, and responds, "Some of them. They were there to watch you."

What transpires next causes me to jump where I'm sitting on the bamboo bed. Following his informative confession, biting the end of his cigar, he immediately retrieves the gun from the table, aims it at me, and fires off a shot.

Holy fuck! A horrendous echo bursts through the jungle. Birds scatter. Butterflies become extinct. The waterfall is the only thing that feels real around me, almost soothing.

Holding the smoking gun, Boss confirms, "A gator was creeping too close to you, Derek. He was going to have you for breakfast, and I had to scare him away."

I look to my left and right and see that the gator is gone, retreating into the jungle behind me. Half of me believes that Boss purposely devised the gator story just to fire his gun and scare the queer out of me. The sane part of my brain understands that he was only looking out for my best interest, protecting me from danger, just like his son.

"You can never be too careful out here," Mr. Malonni explains. "It's not Flamingo Cove, of course."

My heart races within my chest, and my hands shake. I have to put down my beverage before I spill it. I confess, "I didn't even hear it next to me."

"Why would you? You're a city boy. You've probably never read *The Jungle Book*, have you?"

I shake my head, embarrassed.

"Never fear, though. I always carry protection." Boss places the gun down on the table next to him. "I never kill them. That's too violent for me." A sneer rises on his handsome face. "It's all about the survival of the fittest, which doesn't always have to entail murder. In fact, I adore the gators. They're very much like men in battle: brutish, confident and overpowering." He takes a sip of his drink, relishing its soothing flavor. Next, he puffs on the cigar, relaxing and being refined. "Mr. Reed, may I be frank?"

It's a catch twenty-two question. He'll murder me if I say no. Do I want to live another day? I nod my head, feeling edgy regarding the dangerous jungle and the wicked man across from me.

"How much do you like Rocco?"

I swallow saliva down the back of my throat. Talk about being nervous. What is the right answer to his question? Of course I like Rocco, but is this what his father wants to hear? I sigh heavily, attempt to relax, and respond, "Extremely. Rocco's a nice guy. I could easily fall for him."

"This is very good news. Do you miss him?"

I do. Rocco has been good to me. The whole thing about Fisk and the kiss is a total misunderstanding, bogus shit that I want over and done with. Rocco has not only made me the happiest guy in the world, but he has also saved my life. I tell Mr. Malonni, "Of course I miss him. Rocco is my boyfriend. If memory serves me right, you've bequeathed me that title. I just don't know if he wants me as his boyfriend anymore. Something tells me he doesn't want anything to do with me."

"Let me handle that. Rocco needs some time. As I've said, he's very hard-headed. In truth, he's not the easiest of my boys to raise and love. To no avail though, I give it my best. I'm just quite pleased that you still have an interest in him."

"Why me?" I ask. "There are thousands of queer guys in Florida that could be with your son. Why do you want me to be with Rocco?" The question just kind of slips out. I can't believe I have the balls to ask this. Kudos to me.

"What's not to like about you? You're honest, practical, humble, adventurous, brave and perfect for Rocco. You two have more in common than you're aware of. I know how to read people, and I have easily determined that Rocco needs you in his life. A parent is always looking for a good mate for their child. I see all good qualities in you. Rocco belongs with you."

I'm confused, trying to take all of his wisdom in.

"I like you. One of my duties as a father is to create a better life for his sons. This is what I'm doing for Rocco, and you."

Movement stirs in the jungle to my left. I think it's another gator. I expect Boss to retrieve his pistol and fire it again. To no avail, he stays calm, cool and collected.

Foliage continues to rustle and welcomes a brawny, dark-skinned hunk in his early thirties instead of a hungry and frightening gator. The stranger's six-three frame sports a bright yellow swim trunk and nipples the size of Madagascar beetles. His legs are steel plates, and his biceps gleam with fresh coconut oil. He has a military cut, azure-colored eyes, and a USMC tattoo on his right bicep. The hunk walks up to Mr. Malonni's left side, stands straight, hands locked over his crotch, and shares a debonair smile that is simply irresistible.

Rocco's father rises from his seat and shakes the marine's hand. He says, "Thanks for joining us." Boss turns to me, which prompts me to jump off the bamboo bed and stand at attention. "Derek, this is Hurricane Brass. He will be your personal bodyguard for the next few weeks."

I do an up-down on Hurricane.

He does one on me.

We shake hands.

Hurricane's voice sounds rough and tumbly. He says, "Nice to meet you, sir." His grip is mighty and can take down King Kong.

My natural instinct to study his rock-hard core is almost embarrassing: his lips are buttercup smooth, his neck is lined with thick cords, and he is all-beef from head to toe. I ramble, "My pleasure," and tell him to please call me Derek.

Hurricane nods his head, shares a twinkling all-white smile, and clarifies, "Of course."

A jazzy ring-tone goes off in Mr. Malonni's front pocket. As he retrieves the cellular, he says, "I need to take this in private. You young men become acquainted with each other." He walks away, taking the jungle pathway that Mika used only minutes before, vanishing.

"You Rocco's man?" Hurricane asks, stern and beautiful.

"I'd like to think I am." I sit back down on the bamboo bed, trying to relax.

Hurricane flashes a gold band on his left hand and shares, "My guy's name is Cole. We've been married for two years."

"You're gay?" I ask, blown away that he plays for the same team as me.

"What, you never saw a queer marine before? Trust me," he chuckles, "they're a dime a dozen."

"No way?"

"Cole is a marine, too. He's gorgeous. Think of an older Zac Ephron on steroids. One hundred percent huggable and all mine. I just love him." Hurricane sounds excited, flicking a winged bug off one of his plated abs. "Do you love Rocco?"

"Not yet, but I could."

"Trust me, one minute the two of you are having an earthquake of a fight, and the next minute you're in love. Give it time. It happens with lightening speed."

"Thanks for the suggestion." I'm really not sure how to take this beefy Dr. Phil's advice. He seems smart and easy to talk to. Maybe it's meant to be that we meet like this.

Hurricane says, "Relationships are all about understanding. That's one of the first steps to a successful balance. Be honest and be understanding. The rest sort of slips into place."

I open up to Hurricane, spilling my guts about Felicia's funeral, Fisk's advancement in the upstairs bathroom, and Rocco's horrible and unpredictable response.

Hurricane talks me through my ugly situation and advises me to be patient, caring, and open to a new beginning. He adds, "Men never like to lose things. Rocco will be returning to your world before you know it."

"How are you so sure?"

Hurricane flashes his wedding ring at me again and replies, "Trust me, guy ... I know ... And I'm sure."

Being a sharp bodyguard, Hurricane watches my every move, following me ubiquitously. Boss says I have full access to the bungalow and its twenty rooms. Hurricane follows me to the sunroom, my private bedroom, the sauna room, the exercise room, and the bathroom. A screened-in patio is located on the west side of the property where I find it cozy to read. I plunge through the latest John Patrick collection of erotic short stories when Hurricane enters the room and finds me.

He wears a skimpy trunk and nothing more, showing off every toned muscle on his molten steel body. Hurricane finds a home for his icy bottle of light beer on a nearby table.

I close the book and place it on my lap. "You're very good at your job, aren't you, Mr. Brass?"

He has a seat next to me, crosses his ankles, and says, "I'd like to think I am."

"And you don't like to wear clothes, do you?"

"You're very observant."

I share a brief smile. Men are such dogs and always make me smile. "Cole must love your body."

"Among other men," he says, but not arrogantly.

I miss Rocco's body. Hurricane reminds me of him. Not that they are of the same size and definition, but because both are chiseled and quite handsome.

"Am I disturbing you, Derek?"

"A little."

"I'll keep my distance."

"Something tells me you won't."

"You're very bright," Hurricane says, rising from his seat. He snatches up his bottle of beer and escapes the room, leaving me to my short stories.

Hurricane checks on me one last time before Turtle Island falls asleep. He taps on my bedroom door three times with knuckles. "You okay in there?" he asks through the bamboo.

"I'm good."

"I'll be in the room next door if you need me. Good-night, Derek."

Before he walks away, I call out his name, "Hurricane?"

Pause. Listening. He calls through the door, "Yes?"

"Come in here for a second."

The door opens and he steps into the dim light created by a kerosene lamp. He sports a tiny pair of white boxer-briefs, which accentuate his thighs and rippled stomach. It's the first time I see the tiny sprigs of hair beneath his navel, which I find totally arousing. "How can I help you?" he questions.

I lie in bed, wide awake, unable to sleep. The John Patrick collection awaits a long night with me. "I just wanted to thank you for all your help. I didn't want to come across as being rude this afternoon on the patio while reading. I just wanted you to know that I appreciate you being around."

"Of course," he whispers. "It's my pleasure."

After he leaves, closing the bungalow's door behind him, I snuggle up with John Patrick in my hands and begin to read. Unfortunately the words aren't making any sense to me, and I put the tome down. I turn out the kerosene lamp and stare at the shadows on the circular ceiling. Here, I collect warm and fuzzy thoughts of Rocco within my mind: dancing at Pallyo; walking hand in hand along the Gulf; him rescuing me from the Baskin bad boys; his stringent breath against the nape of my neck; the way his elongated fingers graze my solid chest.

Eventually, my eyes begin to close and I drift away, falling into a dream, a distant place called Nowhereland, meeting Rocco again, finding his open arms.

Chapter 21 – The Brazen Bodyguard & Guests

The next morning, just before noontime, I'm hidden behind palms and hip-high ferns, approximately fifty feet from the waterfall. The day is glorious with an effervescent light wind. Darters and plovers fly from one tree to the next, calling from the Spanish moss and peeping at my side. Cicadas the size of taxi cabs perform unpleasant concerts in the trees. Tiny, green anole lizards scamper in zigzag formations throughout the jungle, busy playing or searching for lovers.

My spying is an impromptu act of curiosity. Upon walking away from the bungalow after a good night's sleep, through the waking jungle, and to the waterfall for an energetic swim, I see Hurricane in his glorious buff, sitting on one of the boulders. The waterfall's mist sprinkles across his to-die-for body. To my surprise (and satisfaction), he sports an upright log between his sculpted legs, taking enjoyment in an AM tug-fest.

Because I am crouched and hidden behind a line of waist-high ferns and other jungle foliage, Hurricane doesn't see me. Nor does he see the sandals on my feet or the lime-green trunk that covers my bottom and privates. Here, among the Florida plants and animals, I secretly spy on his naughty self-exploration.

The scene at the waterfall is ten minutes long and material that can be viewed in an adult film starring one of the Colt models:

Minute one: Hurricane uses both palms on his ten inches of solid beef. His strokes are meticulous, smooth and rather slow. Fingers strum the stiff wanker while stroking the flesh in a north and south current. He arches his neck back, consuming the sun's brilliant rays and the waterfall's soothing mist.

Although I'm quite attracted to Hurricane, missing Rocco to the fullest, I cannot prevent a stone cylinder from forming in my borrowed square trunk. The sphincter grows and grows, swelling like a tubular balloon filling with cream. My mouth waters and bubbles of perspiration pop against my navel. I think: Rocco, where are you? I miss you. Let's get over this bullshit and make up.

Minute two: Hurricane removes his left hand from his spike and rolls three fingertips up and over the center of his chest, collecting droplets of perspiration between his pumped plates. The fingertips find his mouth, and he begins to lap at each with his extended tongue. A look of sheer happiness rises on his face from the liquid-meal.

I won't touch my pulsing rod in its trunk, saving it for Rocco's kiss, tongue, throat – whatever he decides to share with me when, and if, we get back together. The tool presses uncomfortably against the lower portion of my torso, which is on fire inside the nylon suit. Indisputably the shaft needs to be touched, licked or sucked – whatever it will take to burst a sticky load. But, I won't manipulate its movable skin in any way, holding out for Rocco's attention, faithfully.

Minute three: What transpires on the boulder is top of the line pornography. Hurricane uses his marigold-colored swimsuit as a pillow, resting his head. In a matter of seconds his legs separate and his happy hairless hole gawks in my direction. The bodyguard removes his left set of fingers from his mouth and begins to tease his bottom with airy and swift strokes.

How many men and boys have invaded that tight tunnel of love with tongues, fingers and cocks, among other toys in a queer's closet? Has Hurricane Brass ever taken on a train of men, using that soft and clean looking backside for fun? Does he do films, moonlighting as a professional skin-flick artist when his bodyguard job isn't paying the bills? I wonder.

Minute four: Just the tip of his index finger on his left hand gently grazes the circle of pink passage. Hurricane lets out a muffled moan, which is absorbed in the waterfall's poetic resonance. Continuously, he works his right palm on his solid stick, up/down, up/down, up/down. A second fingertip finds his hungry hole and caresses it with the first. The two mingle together, working overtime in a playful and robust action.

What a man does with his fingers is his own business. I'm not the type of queer to intervene, of course. I would rather eradicate Rocco from my mind, heart and soul, using my fingers on the bodyguard's delicious looking skin. In truth, I am not into cheating and boldly decide to keep my distance, and appendages, to myself. I find it necessary to ball my hands into fists, containing them from straying and finding my own body parts.

Minute five: Hurricane's right hand is removed from his pole. He places the palm near his mouth and spits upwards, into it. Saliva is cupped and carried down to his private part, which he uses as a lubricant for a painless ride, comfortable friction, and the means to blow his load, soon.

I'm going to explode in my trunk, even without touching myself. Spew is going to automatically ejaculate from my beef and decorate the V-area between my legs. The boulder event is irresistible. The vibrations that skirt through my system are overwhelming, filling me with an electric current of lust. I can feel the build-up of cream inside my tool. I can ...

Minute six: His hands move together in a fluent and speedy manner. One tugs on his protein stick while the other continues to tease and finger his taut bottom. His hands are very busy, synchronized with their play, prepping the bodyguard to blow his hot and fiery shoot everywhere.

I'm a very weak man; shame on me. I shouldn't invade Hurricane's private moment. A man sometimes has to do what a man needs to do on his own, without interferences. A watcher is never always welcomed. But Hurricane Brass doesn't see me in the thick foliage. I'm an animal with its own needs, the voyeur hunting, hidden very well.

Minute seven: The sound of Hurricane's gritting teeth and hearty murmurs are unheard, neutralized by the waterfall's rush. Hips rise and fall. Fingers prick his bottom, pull out, and prick again. His right hand goes wild on his boner, thrusting the meat chaotically, north/south.

My vision blurs for a second, two seconds, three seconds. I lose consciousness, come to, and feel breathless. As Hurricane continues his pole-tugging, I can't help myself and purposely graze my right hand against the trunk-covered cock between my throbbing legs. Windblown, I immediately pull the hand away, thinking of Rocco.

Minute eight: It happens just the way I expect it to happen. Hurricane's motion continues as his solo-passion is found. Red-cheeked, chest heaving on the boulder, fingers pushing into his rump, more fingers working his shaft ... he blows an arc of creamy-white sap against his chest plates.

My cock vibrates on its own accord, finding pleasure. The untouched mass leaks into its lime-colored trunk, glazing my right inner thigh. Elation is found as bubbles of cock-spit exit its mushroom-capped head. My entire body shutters with enjoyment, finding bliss. My taste buds crave the gooey food, and I slip my right hand into the trunk, using three fingers to gather up some yummy man-sap to enjoy.

Minute nine: Fingers are removed from his drained cock. Hurricane is winded, out of breath. Three fingers find the shallow puddles of man-liquid on his Olympian-built chest. They remove the goo away with the finest strokes. A morning treat is tasted as the brazen bodyguard opens his mouth and places the fingers inside. He sucks on the appendages for the longest time, enjoying himself, satisfied with the taste of his shoot, enthralled.

The jizm tastes bittersweet in my mouth, along my tongue, and at the rear of my throat. Some of the juice sticks to my lips and chin from a sloppy feeding. I push the three fingers deep into my mouth and collapse my goo-glistening lips around them. Second knuckles and fingernails coated in ooze are tasted. I think of them as the width of Rocco's cock, forbidding myself from this unexpected meal.

Minute ten: Spent. Exhausted. Clean of his spew. Hurricane stands, showing off his bulbous buttocks, sweat-slicked thighs, and muscled back. Leaving his trunk/pillow behind, he walks to the edge of the boulder and dives into the aqua-blue water, vanishing from my view.

I wipe the residue of pre-come away from my lips with the back of my right hand. Disappointment seizes me that Hurricane disappears in the water, ending his tug-fest on the boulder. Following another minute of spying, I see his head push up and through the water. He climbs the boulders and stands underneath the waterfall. Here he showers, rolling both palms up and down his sticky chest, cleaning his flesh from his explosion of man-splashing fun.

I rise from my position behind the high ferns, ready to join him for a quick swim beneath the aqua-blue waterfall. I lift my right foot to make one step forward when – out of nowhere, catching me completely off guard – a strip of cotton is looped over my mouth and promptly pulled against my lips and teeth, preventing me from yelling for Hurricane's help. My arms are pulled behind my back and immediately tied with rope.

I want to lunge backwards, but can't. A shot scares the hell out of me, ringing out from behind me, echoing in the jungle. I think I'm being executed, but I'm not the one in the shooter's crosshairs.

In the distance, still showering in the waterfall's spray, Hurricane takes a hit in his right thigh. The shot drops him to the boulder, and he rolls forward into the pool of water.

Before I can react, I'm knocked to the jungle's floor and see two dark chocolate muscleheads standing over me. The taller of the two is pivoted above my head and aims a Smith and Wesson at my skull. The shorter one ties my knees and ankles together with bull rope, which causes my skin to burn. Mr. Tall yells out to his friend, "Get the pole!"

Shorty vanishes from the scene for just a second or two. He returns with an eight-foot long bamboo pole, placing it on the ground, perpendicular to my feet.

Mr. Tall instructs, "Roll him over on his stomach."

Shorty does as he's told. I eat dirt, sniff a beetle, and ...

"Let's get rid of him," Mr. Tall says, retrieving the pole from the ground, slipping it through the rope loops at my ankles, knees and hands. Mr. Tall takes position at the front of the pole while Shorty mans my rear. Together they lift either end of the pole, placing my weight on their bare shoulders.

Swinging left and right on the middle of the pole, I'm carried through the jungle like an animal on a spit. Mr. Tall says something to Shorty in Spanish. Shorty laughs. Mr. Tall returns a laugh. I don't know what they're saying, suffering from the language barrier.

How large is Turtle Island? Where is the dark chocolate duo carrying me? I swing to and fro on the eight-foot pole for what feels like an hour or more. Fiery pain burns my wrists and ankles, rubbing against the bound rope. Tops of ferns brush against my stomach and crotch as I am carried through the jungle. My mind drifts to dark places from scenes on CSI or some horror film. I think: The Baskin bad boys are at work again. They're up to some serious shit now. I'm in deep trouble and ...

A *Mission Impossible* move is out of the question. The bull rope is tied too tight around my limbs. Loops hang from the bamboo pole, proving their strength by my weight. It's unfeasible to escape this ugly situation. The duo has me right where they want me; a prisoner without options.

The jungle opens up to a sandy white beach, a Bluenose sloop boat with its masts down, and a third dark chocolate bad boy. The addition to our party stands by the beached sloop boat, patiently waiting for his buddies' arrivals.

I'm carried over the sand and to the sloop boat. The third villain instructs his cohorts, "Don't waste anymore time. Get him in the boat."

Mr. Tall and Shorty take commands well, faithful employees. With my body still attached to the bamboo pole, I'm tossed into the boat between the seats. My right hip and temple strike the hull. A dizzy spell surfaces in my skull, behind my eyes. Pain arcs through my center from the force. I swear under my breath, calling the trio motherfuckers because of their inappropriate man-handling.

Shorty pushes the sloop boat into the Gulf, jumping inside thereafter. All three goons are in the boat with me. Number 3 starts the engine at the stern. A purring ensues, and the boat moves over and through the choppy water, escaping Turtle Island, Mr. Malonni's bungalow and Hurricane Brass.

The trio talks:

Number 3: "Mr. Drago is going to put you bastards on your backs for being late."

Shorty: "We had to take care of his bodyguard from drowning. Mr. Drago will understand."

Mr. Tall: "I'm working to be the employee of the month."

The three laugh at Mr. Tall's comment, keeping me a prisoner inside the hull. Shorty kneels next to me, aiming a revolver at my head. He says, "You ever eat lead, faggot?"

Number 3 chuckles at the question.

Shorty continues, "You look hungry for some lead, queer. How about I shove this muzzle into your cock-eating mouth?"

He doesn't, though. Shorty is just showing off, being an asshole in front of his tough buddies at my expense.

The boat continues to bounce across the Gulf for hours. How many miles are we from Turtle Island? Where am I being taken? Who is Mr. Drago? Will I be beaten again by the Baskin group? Will I be tortured and eventually murdered? Will I ...

Mr. Tall coaches Number 3, "Bring us in slowly. You're about thirty yards from shore."

"I got it," Number 3 responds. "Who the fuck has the yacht, anyway?"

Shorty snickers, "Mr. Drago, asshole."

"Fuck off!" Number 3 yells, sounding like a venomous demon.

If the sloop boat were not meeting shore, the three goons would charge into a fistfight to the fullest degree. Mr. Tall breaks up the chaos and says, "Mr. Drago wants us at the sight in two hours."

"We can do that," Number 3 confirms. "The faggot has to walk on his own, though."

Shorty presses the revolver's muzzle to my forehead and says, "Welcome to Paragon Island, Mr. Reed. It's time for you to kiss your ass goodbye."

Chapter 22 – Crime on Paragon Island

Paragon Island is not a tourist attraction. The terrain is all rock and jungle. There are no sprawling white beaches or comfortable bungalows. There are no hotels, casinos or cafes. There are no elegant hidden hideaways. The island is eerie, overtaken by jungle and animals. It resembles something like in a horror flick, creepy and dark.

Before climbing an incline of rocks, the rope securing my wrists, knees and ankles is cut free from the bamboo pole. Shorty plants his revolver's muzzle into my back and coaches, "Move, dick-eater. No breaks. No games. Just move."

I'm exhausted, hungry and thirsty. I can't believe this is happening to me, again. Every time I turn my back, I'm abducted. Whether it's by the Baskin bad boys or Rocco's father; it never fails. Physically, I'm drained. My back and muscles sting. My shoulders and legs kill me. I need a day at the spa just to pull myself together again. I need pampered and treated like a princess. Where the hell is Rocco when I need him to save me? How much more of this shit can I take before I pass out?

Number 3 climbs the steep grade first. Mr. Tall is second, whom I follow. And Shorty brings up the rear, his revolver still positioned against my back. The rocky incline is almost two hundred feet high. A narrow pathway of rock that resembles something Biblical becomes narrow at its apex. Once at the top, we make a sudden decline through a foliage-covered slope of thick brush, deep into the jungle. We cross a stream and tour more jungle. A slender cave with minimal light welcomes our foursome. Bats of various sizes become pissed at our intrusion and fly to their escape. A chilly wind blows through the cave, grazing my body. More bats obnoxiously exit, brushing my shoulders. At one point, I stop walking, but Shorty pushes me forward with his revolver and says something in Spanish that I don't comprehend. I listen to water run down and between layers of rock inside the cave. The smell is stagnant, mossy and not at all pleasant.

At the opposite end of the cave, white-blue light meanders into the deep jungle, illuminating our exit. Dense vines mix with thick bamboo and high grass. The untamable grass becomes a giant wall in front of us. I hear a hundred or more birds and monkeys, but the sound of the ocean is forever lost in front of me, somewhere.

Mr. Tall and Number 3 remove machetes from their backs and begin to clear an entrance through the solid wall of jungle.

"Move it," Shorty exclaims. Once a pathway opens, he pushes me forward, his hardcore brutality continuing.

I realize I can't take all three men in a brawl, let alone one. Rocco could without even breaking a sweat. I'm not Rocco, though. Instead, I follow Shorty's instruction, step forward, and follow Number 3 and Mr. Tall into the deep confines of the hungry jungle.

We walk for almost two hours through the thick foliage before a clearing opens, and I see a collection of bamboo huts, but no inhabitants.

The huts are designed by approximately ten square feet by twelve square feet of bamboo poles with straw roofs. Each has a single window and doorway to enter/exit. I still see no inhabitants. The huts are used for storage, bunking and provisions. One hut has a white powder on the ground in front of its bamboo door, which obviously stores a portion of the smuggled cocaine. I put two and two together and realize that Paragon Island is a safe haven for the illegal drugs once they reach the United States from Columbia. And from here, I believe the cocaine is shipped inland by Baskin, flooding Miami, Tampa Bay and Jacksonville.

Shorty continues to push me forward, passing three of the ten huts. He directs me to the rear of the fourth hut and ...

Three refrigerator-sized bamboo cages stand behind the hut. A rusty lock hangs from each bamboo door. One of the cages just happens to house a prisoner – Fisk Deveraux.

My heart races at the sight of Fisk and I immediately ask, "What's going on? What are we doing here?"

Shorty doesn't like it that I'm speaking and decides to punch me in the back of my neck. Again, he yells something in Spanish to me.

I fall to the ground, unable to go anymore. Pain skies through my neck, back, and shoulders. It feels like fag-bashing all over again, something I went through outside Pallyo when I was eighteen.

Shorty attempts to pick me up by a handful of hair and says in a bitter manner, "No talk."

Fisk peers through two of the bamboo bars. He says, "Run, Derek. Get away from them if you can."

Number 3 bashes his fist to Fisk's face, bloodying his nose. Fisk falls backward, sliding down the cage's rear wall, silent again.

Shorty is all over my ass, preventing my escape. He pins his whole body against my back and wraps his right arm around my right side, aiming the revolver at my temple. He says, "Save yourself the struggle. You're not going anywhere."

Number 3 unlocks the cage next to Fisk's. He swings the door open and Shorty tosses me inside.

I fall to my knees with the force, listening to the lock click behind me.

Fisk groans in the cage next to me, "You're fucked now, dude. Welcome to hell."

A day passes. Two days. We're fed water, bread and a few raw vegetables by Shorty. Fisk tells me he's been in the cage for three days. He informs me that Mr. Drago is the drug lord behind the Baskin Fish Company. Fisk is pretty serious when he says, "When he finally arrives at Paragon Island, he'll kill us both."

"Where's the two hundred grand?" I ask.

"Drago has it."

"Where are the drugs?"

"Drago has those, too. He's going to kill us because all the shit we've caused him."

"The boat shit?"

"You got it."

"Is this place a base to store the drugs before they are delivered to dealers in the cities?"

"You know it is. If you stay long enough, you'll see Drago's men carrying bags of coke here. Weasel and Thumbs are his two top men, worker bees for the man who do all his dirty jobs."

"That's what I thought. I saw some white powder on the ground outside of a hut."

It starts to rain and Fisk shivers, soaked to the bone. He sits on the ground with his legs pulled up to his chin. "Where's Rocco, anyway?"

"He dumped me. We're over. He thinks I got it on with you at Felicia's funeral."

"But you didn't."

"I know I didn't. Try and tell Rocco that."

Fisk asks, "So, if Rocco isn't going to save us, how the fuck are we going to get out of these cages?"

"Can we dig?"

Fisk shakes his head and responds, "They check on us frequently."

"Next time one of them comes, can we knock them out and take their keys?"

Fisk shakes his head again. "Most of the time they come in twosies. Try again."

"Fuck," I whisper.

"Yeah, that's what I've been saying for days now."

Our heart to heart is a good time to ask what happened to him on the night in the Gulf, after he saved Rocco and me from the Baskin bad boys.

"I went back to my apartment. Some goons were waiting there for me. They snatched me up and took me to Jacksonville. I stayed in Jacksonville for almost three weeks under their pathetic care. Once they finally realized I didn't have their money or the coke, they beat the shit out of me and let me go. I went to Walter's place in Coconut Key and hid out there. The writer was an angel and took care of me."

The situation sounds believable; I don't even question him. Instead, I wonder how he ends up on Paragon Island.

Fisk continues to shiver, cold as a winter in the Antartic. He stinks like rotten bananas and needs a bath. My friend whispers, "I was with Walter. The Baskin guys were watching my every move; probably so I wouldn't fall off their radar. When they picked me up along the writer's private beach, I learned Mr. Drago wanted to kill me. He said I knew too much and would talk. I was then brought here, thrown in this cage."

It still rains, pouring down from the heavens. A figure steps out of the jungle approximately fifty feet away from the cages. When he becomes closer, I notice it's Tank. He drips wet from head to toe, dressed in a khaki tee, shorts, and a rugged looking pair of boots. He steps up to my cage and smiles at me in a devious manner. He says, "Long time no see, Derek. I'm glad you could make it to Paragon Island."

Tank is a pig, a piece of shit, and an animal that needs to be butchered. He's cute and sexy to the core, but oh my god is he a total asshole.

I want to blast him with vulgarities but decide to keep my mouth shut. Better to stay reserved than get the shit kicked out of me, I figure.

Tank peels his shirt off and drops it to the muddy earth. Droplets of rain ski down and over his perfectly chiseled chest. He moves up to Fisk's cage, finds a brass key in his khaki shorts, and opens the cage. He says to Fisk, "Come on out. You know what to do."

Fisk turns to me and winks. He steps out of his cage, drops to his knees in the mud, and unzips Tank's khaki shorts. Fisk pulls out Tank's semi-swollen beef and slips it into his open mouth.

Tank goes crazy above Fisk, fucking his face with his limp biscuit. In a matter of seconds though, the protein grows eleven-inches hard. Tank rams his cock into Fisk's mouth like a wild man. He calls

Fisk a little bitch and man-whore. He holds Fisk by the shoulders, plugging his hole with the solid unit of beef, jamming it inside.

The drug dealer from Flamingo Cove gags on the cock and rain; I swear he's going to choke to death while kneeling in the mud, busy on his snack. He takes all of Tank's meat into the back of his throat and hangs onto the man's hips for balance. Fisk is a little bitch and man-whore by the looks of it, hungry for the protein, overly needy, and satisfied with his reactive sucking.

A palm smacks against Fisk's head and he likes it. Tank pulls his wanker out of Fisk's throat and mouth and he starts to beat his cheeks with it; Fisk loves it, smiling with satisfaction and pleasure.

Pre-come dribbles on Fisk's nose and lips. It's no surprise to me that he uses one hand and smears the sap against his lips, lapping it up with his extended tongue. He looks up at Tank and chants with his wide-ass smile, "Fuck me up the ass … I'm ready for it."

The bad boy's uncut shaft bounces between his legs in the rain. He knocks Fisk to the muddy earth with the back of his right hand. Tank rips the denim off his captive's ass and yells down, "You fucking want it? … I'm going to give it to you!" On his knees, he pulls Fisk's head back and licks his cheek.

I watch Fisk smile with deep bliss; the guy has always liked a rough fuck according to Quinn's diary, which never lies. He calls up to Tank, "Fuck me … Treat me like a criminal. I'm ready for your cock."

In truth, I'm hard between my legs, underneath my lime-green trunk. My inflated knob pokes between two of the bamboo bars of my cage. I take in the pornographic sights, enjoying the scene in the mud and rain.

Tank slaps Fisk's ass with an open palm and swears, "Don't make me kill you with my cock, motherfucker."

Fisk wants Tank's rod badly; I can just see the happiness on his face, begging for some rough and tough action. He looks like the sexiest man-pig on his hands and knees, willing to take Tank's full-length tool up his rump.

To my surprise, Tank doesn't fuck Fisk in the mud. Instead, he pulls my friend up by the hair and tosses him against my cage, stomach and face first. He tells Fisk, "Hang onto the bars, fucker," and stands behind him. Tank adds, "Show your buddy how you can fuck," and pulls Fisk's head back by his hair, licking his right cheek.

Fisk cringes as the bouncer pushes his dog into his ass. He lets out a gruff noise, gripping two bars. His cock bounces between the bars and touches my trunk-covered one by accident. Face to face with him, he whispers, "Blow me, Derek."

I can't. I won't. I'm holding out for Rocco, even if we're not a couple anymore. I shake my head to and fro, backing away from the bars.

As Fisk's rump turns into a fuck-hole, he moans and groans, out of control. He yells at the top of his lungs, "Deeper! ... Fuck me deeper!" clinging to the bamboo bars, wide-eyed, finding both pleasure and pain.

The captor carries out his dirty deed in a violent manner. He punches his hefty prick inside Fisk and quickly pulls it out. This action persists for a dozen or more minutes. Tank presses one palm to the middle of Fisk's back. His other hand firmly grips Fisk's left hip for balance. Tank huffs and puffs, taking the ride of his life. He bucks into Fisk with all his muscle and weight, ready to get off.

"Fuck me harder!" Fisk calls out in the rain. "It's not enough! Shove it all into me!"

Tank listens. Continuous thumps pound Fisk's rump. Tank turns into a machine behind his boy toy. Rain and sweat pour down and over his body. He spanks Fisk once, twice, three times, shifting wildly in and out of him.

"Pound it!" Fisk screams, hanging on my cage. "Shove it all into me!"

Following three more consecutive and precise humps, groaning with bliss, Tank quickly pulls his solid dong from Fisk's firm ass. He strokes his beef in a wicked manner. With just a few jerks on his joint, spew drizzles over Fisk's behind, decorating his tight skin. Tank lets out an exploding roar, which is louder than the pelting rain, echoing throughout the huts and surrounding jungle.

Trembling from his post-lust, Tank slips his dog away, zips up his khakis, and man-handles Fisk back into his cage, tossing him to the earth. Tank kicks Fisk in the nuts, breaking him down, and barks, "You're a fucking animal!"

Flabbergasted, I scream, "What the fuck?" scared out of my mind, disbelieving what I have just witnessed.

It's the wrong thing to do, which alerts Tank, firing him up. He immediately locks Fisk inside the cage and shifts his attention to my cage, facing me. Tank has some pretty long arms. He balls up his right fist, thrusts it between two bamboo bars, and nails me in the face.

Pain surfaces between my eyes. It feels as if he breaks my nose. Blood drips out of my left nostril and over my upper lip. An instant headache surfaces and ...

Tank nails me a second time in the same place. He says to me, "Mind your own fucking business before I break your ass."

I lose my balance and drop to my knees. Dizzy, seeing double, everything turns to black, and I fall into mud, passing out.

When do I come to? An hour? Two hours? Dusk is purple and melancholic, and rain continues to steadily fall. Fisk is awake, sitting in his cage with his knees pulled up to his chin, shivering. We make eye contact and he says, "I never thought you'd wake up."

"How long have I been asleep?"

"Over twenty-four hours."

"I'm starving."

He gently nods his head and replies, "They'll bring you food soon."

I tell Fisk that I'm exhausted and every bone in my body hurts. I tell him I think my nose is broken, and my head is throbbing with pain from Tank's two blows. I'm death with a social security card.

Fisk is completely naked; his clothes have been removed and taken away. "Our buddy Tank came back and fucked me again. He took all my clothes." Fisk wipes a hand across his face, removing droplets of rain from his skin. "I'm not phased by it, if you want to know the truth. I've been homeless and hungry on the streets. I've been hooked on meth. This is nothing what I'm going through."

"How do we get out of here?" I whisper, curling up at the side of my cage, staring over at Fisk inside his cage.

"We wait until Tank comes back to fuck me. He'll fuck me against your cage again. You grab him and …"

Our heads turn to formless movement in the thick rain. Shorty makes an appearance. He carries a bowl of rice and bread to our cage, which he passes to me through the bamboo bars. He tells me to share the shit with Fisk and adds, "Today is your lucky day. Mr. Drago wants you two to eat before he kills you."

Shorty is gone before we know it. Fisk and I equally split the rice and bread. We stay quiet for an hour, two hours, watching it rain while digesting the food. We wait for Tank to return to the cages, willing to fuck Fisk, but he doesn't. Night comes and we fall asleep, head to head in the cages, side by side. Night passes.

Another day is lost.

Shorty feeds us.

There's no sign of Mr. Drago or Tank.

Another night vanishes.

More rain. Fuck, it won't stop raining.

I whisper to Fisk, "We're never going to get out of here. We'll die in these cages."

"Maybe that's what they want," he responds, and I believe him.

I lose count of the days and nights. Shorty continues to feed us. We smell like pigs, living in the mud, unbathed and barely cared for. Tank has not returned to bang Fisk. We drink rainwater to stay alive. We eat what Shorty brings us. We never see Mr. Tall or Number 3. We never see Mr. Drago, either. Our lives are at stake inside the cages. We'll only survive for another few days, breaking down.

Six days pass, I think. Seven days. I finally realize we're going to die out here.

Just when I think I'm going to have my last breath of oxygen, a shirtless and hairy daddy steps out of the fog and greets us with his demon-like smile. The stranger stands over six-feet tall, sports muscles out the wazoo, and carries a pistol strapped to his right hip. He moves up to our cages and introduces himself as Mr. Drago, our assailant. He says, "I'll fuck you first and kill you later." He pulls the pistol from his hip and aims it at Fisk, me, back at Fisk, and says, "This won't take long."

He stands approximately ten feet away from our cages with his legs spread. Black boots sink into the mud. He points the pistol at me and says, "Your ass is looking mighty fine for my cock." He adjusts the boner in his khakis with his free hand.

I shiver in the cold rain, sick and exhausted. I'm unable to respond, practically motionless, weather-beaten and spent.

Mr. Drago straps his pistol at his hip and moves up to my cage. He unlocks the cage, swings the door open, and pulls me out by my blond curls.

Fisk is too weak to respond, total man-mush in his mud pen. He can't move and looks like a zombie, ready to pass out for good, unable to save me.

Mr. Drago drops me to the mud and forces me on my palms and knees. He quickly removes the trunk from my body, tossing it aside.

I'm like a feather to his strength, unable to defend myself. I can't move. I can't run away. I can't ...

He slaps me on my ass with an open palm and violently fingers my hole. Behind me, he begins to laugh and say, "I've got you right where I want you."

The mud holds me in place. I'm stuck like a pig by my hands and knees. I can't go anywhere, trapped in front of Mr. Drago.

The drug lord says, "It's time to take care of some business." He rises from the place behind me, walks up to Fisk's cage, removes the pistol from his right hip, cocks it, and fires a bullet next to Fisk's head, missing his skull by inches.

Fisk starts to cry in his cage, broken in his fetal position.

From the pool of mud around me, rain blinding my eyes, I find enough strength to yell, "Leave him alone!"

Mr. Drago ignores me, pops off another shot, missing Fisk on purpose.

I cry behind Mr. Drago, "Stop! … Please, just stop!"

My outburst is enough to attract the villain's attention. He turns around, puts the pistol away, and walks up to my side. He stands above me, looks down at my stuck body, and informs, "While I'm fucking you, I'm going to shoot your boyfriend in the head."

Tears roll out of my eyes. I whimper like a baby, disbelieving what's happening to me. I'm motionless in the mud, growing hysterical.

The drug lord positions himself behind me, slams me on the ass numerous times with an open hand, and laughs. In a matter of seconds he now stands in front of me and releases his ten inches of flag from his shorts. He plays with his uncut and veined erection, stroking it up and down, ready to fuck me. He shakes the tool with his right hand and laughs down at me, "Are you ready for me to fuck you to death?"

Chapter 23 – Blood, Biceps & Bygones

Mr. Drago smacks his ten inches against my ass, ready to nail me. He continues to laugh, proud of his work, a villain in true form.

I try to move in the mud, squirming wildly, but I'm still stuck like a pig. Tears ebb out of my eyes. Am I whimpering? My body begins to shiver in the cold rain. A panic attack finds my system and I ...

As Mr. Drago slaps his beef against one of my ass cheeks, he thinks it's cute to fire off shots at Fisk in his cage, purposely missing him. The bullets fly between the bamboo bars, into the mud, making thudding noises.

Fisk cries inside his cage, scared out of his mind. I've never seen him so mentally broken. He hangs onto the bamboo bars for dear life, quivering. All the color has washed out of his face. His eyes are extremely wide, and his mouth hangs open.

Mr. Drago laughs in a hearty manner, deranged and maybe on some of the coke that he smuggles on his ships and into American cities. He yells, "Daddy's going to make this hurt!"

I try to buy some time and yell out Mr. Drago's name. It's a flawless plan for about two seconds, because he stops thwapping his erect rod against my bottom. Behind me, Mr. Drago yells, "Shut the fuck up, faggot!" and spanks me again with his palm, welting my ass.

It happens suddenly, unexpectedly. On the left side of Fisk's cage, located near the hut and behind him, a black oval object hurtles out of the dense jungle and twirls through the curtain of rain. It lands on the hut to our right, approximately one hundred feet away, crashing through its foliage-covered roof. In a matter of seconds, the object explodes the hut and a billion slivers of bamboo shoot out in every direction.

The sound is a rumbling boom in the pouring rain, popping my eardrums. My view shifts from the once-supply hut to Fisk in his cage. Fisk is open-mouthed, still trembling, and in a state of confusion due to the attack.

Mr. Drago's hit by one of the flying bamboo poles in his right thigh, which causes him to back away from my bottom and put his goods away; no damage is done to either of us. He steps to my right, taking in the debris, and says, "What the fuck?" lost in a state of uncertainty.

Another grenade flies through the rain and explodes a second hut; this one concealing a toilet and shower. I practically bury my face in the mud for protection. Once the explosion subsides, a third grenade is hurtled out of the jungle and misses one of the huts. It rolls on the ground toward us, sixty feet away. Mud and earth blows into the rainy heavens like a volcano erupting, decorating our bodies.

I lift my head and see that Fisk is still safe in his cage. To my right is Mr. Drago, pissed and confused. I see Shorty, Mr. Tall and Number 3 exit one of the unharmed huts with rifles. They separate and sneak into the jungle, in pursuit of the unknown attacker.

Silence, except for the rainstorm. Stillness. Bamboo debris is everywhere. Again, I try to escape the muddy earth, and this time it pays off. My right hand is free. I don't let Mr. Drago know this, though. Instead, I'm deceptive, holding all my weight on my left hand, patiently waiting for a timely escape.

I see a sliver of Rocco positioned where the grenades were thrown from the thick jungle. My once-boyfriend is just a mere silhouette escaping the foliage and vanishing into the stand of numerous huts. An Uzi is slung over his right shoulder and a hunting knife is strapped to his waist, complimented with a string of grenades. Anger surfaces on his face because he witnesses my current state of turmoil.

Truth is he's sexy as hell and a shiver of elation scurries through my body. My heart flutters, and a small smile forms on my face. It's the best I've felt in days, knowing that Rocco has come to save Fisk and me.

Discreetly hiding behind one of the cocaine storage huts, Rocco makes eye contact with me. Through the falling rain, I see him place a finger up to his lips, informing me to be quiet. Shirtless with his torso splotched in chamo paints, he sports thigh-tight khaki shorts, black bootie socks, and mid-ankle high boots the color of coal. My eyes stray to his erect nipples, ab-lined chest and puckered navel – I've never seen him so hot before!

Rocco pops off a shot, but misses Mr. Drago. The bullet whizzes over his head, into the jungle behind us.

Mr. Drago's pistol is out of bullets, and he vanishes into one of the huts for cover.

In superhero mode, Rocco bolts away from his hiding place and rushes to my side. He helps me out of the mud, kisses me on the lips, and holds me against his firm chest. With tears in his eyes, he quickly says, "I thought you were dead. I missed you."

There is no time for making up; this will have to come later. I rattle off, "I know of three other guys on the island besides Mr. Drago. Tank's here, too. All of them are looking for you, and they'll want to kill you."

Alert and on task, Rocco practically drags me up to Fisk's cage. He tells Fisk to stand in the corner of his cage and fires off three shots at the Yale lock, breaking it loose. He swings the door open and immediately pulls a trembling Fisk out.

Behind us, hidden in an eastern hut, Mr. Drago fires off four shots.

One of the bullets nails Fisk in his right leg. He yells out at the top of his lungs, "Fuck!" Blood runs down his mangled leg, locking him into a state of pain.

As Fisk falls against me for support, Rocco spins around with the Uzi and sprays the hut with a gazillion shots. Unsatisfied with his work, he rips a grenade off his belt, lunges it through the air at the hut, and watches the bamboo building explode into smithereens. A mushroom-shaped cloud of cocaine rises into the rain, becomes wet from the downpour, and falls to the earth, decorating the mud.

I don't see Mr. Drago anywhere. No body parts. No blood. Nothing of the sort. Apparently he has escaped the hut before Rocco's intervention.

Rocco whips back around, swings the Uzi off his shoulder, and passes it to me. "Take Fisk, go into the jungle, and hide. I'll find you. Use this if you have to."

I rescue the Uzi from his hands and rush Fisk into the jungle. We hide approximately ten feet inside a line of thick foliage. Human-size ferns camouflage us. The arrangement of huts is still in view, allowing us to see all the action unfold in the muddy clearing.

Fisk is in bad shape beside me, losing a lot of blood by the seconds. Sitting with him on the mushy ground, keeping him against me, I whisper, "You're going to get through this. I won't let you down. It's just a leg wound. We're going to survive this shit. I promise."

To our far right, Shorty exits the jungle with a shotgun and enters the clearing. I see a sliver of Rocco hiding behind one of the huts, perpendicular to Shorty. Shorty slowly spins around in a circle, two circles, three circles, just twelve feet away from where Fisk and I were caged. He looks distraught, unsure of what to do, perhaps seeking out Mr. Drago. Shorty doesn't realize it, but he ends up moving closer to Rocco's position, and his last breath.

Not having a day of military training in his life, Rocco discreetly sneaks up behind a flustered Shorty with his outstretched knife. I witness his left arm securing itself around Shorty's middle, compressing the man to his torso. Rocco's right hand slashes Shorty's neck open, causing an ear-to-ear gash in a matter of seconds. Shorty promptly drops to the muddy earth with his shotgun, bleeding in the rain, dead within moments.

A shot rings out of the jungle, fifty feet away from our position in the tall ferns. Bullets fly toward Rocco, missing him by inches.

Rocco zooms down to Shorty's body, rescues the shotgun from the ground, and bolts away, finding cover again behind a nearby hut.

I see Number 3 at the edge of the jungle, semi-hidden by dense undergrowth. He works his way along the clearing's perimeter, approximately two feet within the jungle. Fifty feet away from us turns into forty. Forty turns into thirty. Number 3 is careful and quiet, a sniper unwilling to be seen or heard. Thirty feet turns into twenty feet. Twenty feet away immediately turns into ten feet away.

Shit, he definitely is in shooting distance. I don't want to use the Uzi, though. Mr. Tall is still in the jungle and the sound of it will only draw attention to us.

Fisk shivers beside me, silent, wide-eyed and scared shitless. It's obvious to me that he's losing a lot of blood.

My heart booms within my ears. My temperature rises. I can't believe we see Number 3, but he doesn't see us. His position of ten feet away turns into eight feet. I swallow saliva down the back of my throat and fire the Uzi, pulling its smooth trigger.

Ta-ta-ta-ta-ta-ta! echoes through the jungle. Number 3 drops to the jungle's floor, his chest blown open, instantly killed by numerous hits.

Rocco appears behind us, startling the crap out of me. He holds me against him, stops me from trembling, and whispers, "I love you, don't forget that. I'm going to be a hero and get the two of you the fuck out of here." He plants a kiss on my cheek, pushes me away, and instructs, "There's a helicopter on the other side of the clearing. It's going to fly us out of this mess. We'll work our way over to it."

Mr. Tall enters the clearing, running behind one of the huts.

Rocco is totally in commando mode. He leans into me again and whispers, "Keep low. I'll be back for you two." He drops Shorty's shotgun to the ground and takes the Uzi away from me.

I watch him vanish into the jungle, heading north, toward the hut where Mr. Tall takes cover behind.

Two minutes pass. Three minutes pass. Gunfire and tossing grenades come to a standstill. Fisk becomes conjoined to me, trembling in the rain. We lie low, as requested by Rocco.

Gunfire is heard. Masculine screaming. More gunfire. I see Mr. Tall stumble into the clearing again, this time without his weapon. His chest is infested with bullet holes and blood flows from his wounds. Mr. Tall spirals to the wet earth, his face plummeting in a pool of mud, his life forever lost from this world.

Mr. Drago appears in the clearing, hunkering down by one of the huts. He carries an automatic rifle against his chest, wide-eyed and on alert. Rainwater dribbles down and over his body. His biceps flex, and his chest swells, pumping with blood. He moves around the hut, vanishes for a few seconds, and reappears.

Rocco sees him; the hero doesn't miss a trick. Mr. Drago is a moving target in the clearing. He clearly doesn't play the cat-and-mouse game very well. Being an underachiever in plain view, he's obviously ready to have his brains blown into smithereens.

Rocco is hidden, ready for a battle. My mobster man is armed and capable to fight a bloody dual with Mr. Drago.

Mr. Drago takes cover by jumping from one hut to the next, hastily and ineptly. His head moves from left to right, searching out Rocco. He tromps through the muddy puddles, carelessly.

One grenade could take Mr. Drago out, but my boyfriend has other things on his mind. Rocco is patient against his hut, unmoving and on full alert regarding his target's every movement. He has the Uzi's butt against his right hip. Both hands are ready to aim and fire, blowing Mr. Drago away. Rocco has certainly done this before, carrying out a textbook performance of sniper in action.

Beside me, Fisk whimpers, "What's going on?"

"It's silence before the storm. Mr. Drago has approximately two seconds left to run for his life before Rocco kills him."

We watch the drama unfold, keeping cover behind the massive ferns. Mr. Drago steps up to the bamboo cages, making his way around the hut.

Rocco escapes the safety of his current position and sneaks up behind Mr. Drago. The drug lord is completely unaware of my boyfriend's presence. At close range, Rocco taps Mr. Drago on his left shoulder with the Uzi's steel barrel. Mr. Drago spins around and Rocco says, "You stupid bastard!"

The drug lord tries to raise his rifle, ready to fire off a shot. It's too late, though. Rocco is quick, on task and on target. He fires off a single shot, nailing Mr. Drago between the eyes.

Mr. Drago falls to the mud, face-up and eyes wide open. Blood trickles out of his left ear and mouth, rolling down and along his left cheek, into the muddy earth.

Rocco is very much aware that Tank hasn't been dealt with as of yet. He hides against the rear of the hut, leaving Mr. Drago's remains behind. Rocco looks intense and on a mission of destruction.

I finally see Tank at the corner of one of the huts. He yells through the rain, "Show your fucking ass, Rocco! Let's do this like real men!" Tank exits the corner of the hut and enters the clearing. The man is weaponless, shirtless with his chiseled chest of pointed nipples and rock-hard abs, dripping with rainwater like a rough and tumbled supermodel; even bad guys can be sexy as hell. Tank yells, "Let's fight it out, Rocco! No bullets! No knives! Just you and me!"

Rocco steps out from behind the hut with the attached cages and drops the Uzi, his belt of grenades, and the knife clipped to his hip. He calls out to Tank, "I'm ready anytime you are, motherfucker!"

Tank is all man in the clearing. He poses as a boxer in the mud, bunching his hands into balls. He antagonizes Rocco by saying, "Come and get me."

It's a battle between the fittest in the pouring rain. Tank tries to bounce on the balls of his feet and throw the first punch, aiming for Rocco's right jaw. The mud is wet and thick beneath his weight, keeping him in place.

Rocco's defense is right on the mark and blocks the punch, though. Both know karate moves, whether by professional instruction or self-exploration, it doesn't matter. Tank accomplishes a front kick, attempting to nail Rocco in the lower torso, but Rocco's very much aware of what's coming his way and blocks the kick with an arm bar.

Tank is pissed out of his mind, grinning from ear to ear like a rabid dog, battling at his best. He nails Rocco with a groin kick. Rocco falls to the mud, grasping his nuts and cock, groaning like a little boy. Tank walks up to Rocco and attempts to strike him, meeting his heel with the man's stomach. Rocco fakes his injury and immediately reaches out with two hands, snatching onto Tank's ankle and heel, pulling him upwards, into a flip.

Tank does a backward somersault through the air. He tries to land on his feet like a gymnast, but the mud is too slick and he falls on his tailbone. Tank yells, "Fuck!" at the top of his voice, cringing.

This action gives Rocco enough time to abandon the ground and continue fist fighting with Tank. Standing over Tank, he chooses not to share any kicks or hits. He tells the brute, "Be a man and get the fuck up."

Once Tank is on his feet, he throws a punch at Rocco's face. Knuckles connect to my boyfriend's left jaw. Blood splatters over his face, spraying droplets through the air.

Rocco recovers quickly, though. He swings two tight punches at Tank. One nails his opposition in the chin, the other blackens Tank's right eye.

Both men breathe heavily. Tank attempts a bent wrist strike, but Rocco grabs the wrist and snaps it backwards, breaking it. Tank screams, his blaring voice lost in the heavy downpour.

Tank is not done with Rocco, though, no matter how many injuries he obtains. He carries out a side thrust kick, knocking the Mafia man to the wet earth. Once my boyfriend is in the mud, Tank moves up to his side and accomplishes a jump kick into his face by using his right foot.

Rocco is down for the count. Blood gushes out of both nostrils and his mouth. He lies still in the mud, limp and heavily breathing. Blood runs from his face into the earth.

Tank is a monster and rushes forward, wanting to see Rocco dead. Standing over his head, he says, "You should have given up sooner, faggot," and lifts his right foot, ready to smash the bottom of it into Rocco's face.

The dual ends instantly. Rocco springs to life and quickly reaches to his right and finds a long piece of bamboo pole, debris leftover from a hand grenade exploding one of the huts. He promptly sits up, and lunges the bamboo pole up and into Tank's left shoulder like a spear.

Tank backs away, howling. He reaches for the bamboo pole sticking out of his shoulder, but doesn't have time to pull it out.

Seconds pass and Rocco ends up on top of the bad boy bouncer within seconds. He punches Tank three times in the face. Teeth are broken, turning into shards of enamel. Blood splashes everywhere. Tank makes a ghastly sound of pain like foreign gibberish.

It's man against man to the max. Rocco punches Tank again, using both fists, one after the next. The blows are intense and driven with power. Tank flies backwards, plunging to the mud, falling unconscious.

Rocco turns into a fighting machine. His chest heaves in and out, and his breathing becomes uncontrollable. Standing over Tank, he takes out zip-ties from his back pocket, rushes down to Tank's body, and zips his wrists behind his back and his ankles together. Rocco calls over his shoulder to Fisk and me, "Let's get the fuck out of here while we can! We're taking Tank with us!"

Rocco removes the bamboo pole from Tank's chest and drags him across the clearing. Fisk and I are on his tail, following him through the jungle. Rocco removes a credit-card size cellular phone from inside his black belt at his right hip. While clipping through the jungle, he presses a button on the cellular and says, "Skin-diver here! ... Start the chopper! We're on our way!"

In the distance, approximately two minutes later, a powerful wind whips through the jungle. The sound is like a tornado. Man-size ferns and trees blow toward us. Loose foliage turns into a blizzard.

Rocco blocks the debris, still dragging Tank behind him. He escorts us through the jungle as if he were born here. Rocco looks over his shoulder to see if we're still on his tail. He quickly shares a smile with me, winks, and continues his rescue.

The chopper sits in a small clearing with its side-hatch open. Once near the chopper's mouth, Rocco tosses Tank inside. He helps Fisk jump into its opening, and then me. Before I know it, the four of us are contained by its metal belly, safe at last, unharmed.

The helicopter zooms out of the jungle and off Paragon Island. Tank is still unconscious, sitting next to a sleeping Fisk behind the pilot's seat. Bev, one of Mr. Malonni's die-hard employees, flies the helicopter to the mainland, and safety.

I sit across from Fisk and Tank, next to Rocco. My head is cocked on his right shoulder. He has me wrapped in his arms and says, "I'm sorry about not rescuing you sooner."

"Better late than never. I must admit, I was glad to see you."

"You would've died down there; which means I almost lost you."

"But you didn't," I whisper. "I'm right here. I've been with you ever since we separated."

Rocco takes my face within his palms and ... he cries. I see tears fall out of his eyes, all for me. He whimpers, "I'm sorry for being an asshole and not believing you about Fisk at Felicia's funeral. My father showed me the video. Do you forgive me?"

"Of course I forgive you. I love you, Rocco. I've loved you since the first day we met."

Rocco sniffles and wipes his tears away. He kisses me passionately, taking my breath away, melting me as our altitude increases, forever leaving Paragon Island behind.

Chapter 24 – The Million Dollar Blowjob

Forty-eight hours later, Rocco kneels between my legs, sucking on my pulsating rod at the beach house.

Night surrounds us on the expansive patio. The Gulf's breeze is enigmatic, charging our libidos. Rocco prominently drags his tongue along my pole, swallowing as much of the meat as he possibly can. He rolls fingers up and along my bare chest and tweaks my firm nipples. Coming off for air, he informs, "You can shoot your load into my mouth. I want to chow it down; this is how much I've missed you."

I whisper a reply, "We'll see what happens," and lean my head into the Adirondack chair on the patio. My mind drifts to the past two days: the helicopter ride to Turtle Island and safety; the incarceration of Tank; Antonio Malonni's men taking over Paragon Island; my trip back to Flamingo Cove; my short stay at the hospital; visiting Fisk in his apartment, just to make sure he was okay; being whisked away by Rocco to his beach house; and now this.

I roll fingers through Rocco's thick hair, moaning with pleasure. He has the full length of my inflated rod shoved down his tight throat. Fingers find my blond-fuzzy balls, and he begins to play with them in a cordial manner.

The blowjob is beyond fascinating. It's the best of the best. Rocco is definitely going out of his way to please me. Again, he tweaks my nipples. He comes off for air and wipes an arm across his wet mouth. The Mafia man begins to stroke my shaft up and down, and whispers, "Shoot it whenever you want. Just make sure you enjoy it."

I hump his hand with pleasure and roll my eyes with deep satisfaction. Groans escape my mouth because I'm fully blown away by his handy movement.

Rocco stops stroking my pole. He places his lips over its mushroom cap and starts to fall on the rod. Inch after inch enters his throat. A gagging noise escapes his mouth. He continues to tease my balls with his fingertips, petting the duo, stroking them in a gentle manner.

213

I hold his head with both hands and murmur his name in the semi-darkness. The moment is total elation with our united movement. I hump his face the way he wants me to hump it: dramatically, forcefully and ambitiously. I push his head down and over my cock, making him choke on my staff and breathe heavily; in and out motion that tends to exhaust him.

Rocco kneels on a rug in front of the patio chair. He finds a way of lifting my legs and bottom. Unexpectedly, his mouth finds my most sensitive area, and his tongue begins to tease my tight hole. At first, he makes tiny laps with his tongue against the outside area of my core. One lap turns into two laps. Two laps immediately turn into three. Three turn into a dozen. The tip of his tongue closes in on my center with each passing. Eventually the slippery appendage meets my middle and ...

"Jesus, Rocco, that feels great," I whimper on the chair, my legs reaching the moon.

He continues to lap at my hole, repeated builds up a flow. The tip of his tongue enters me, pulls out, and enters again. Rocco drives me mad and causes me to murmur his name again and again. This continues for ten minutes or more; his personal tongue-bath on my taut behind.

I can't stand it any longer and utter with complete joy and overexcitement, "Use your cock inside me. Don't hold back."

Rocco is a good listener. He comes up for air, breathing from his marathon. His cockhead teases my ass as he slaps its mass against it. He whispers down to me, "You're so bad."

"Push it into me," I reply in a dirty manner. "Don't be shy. I can't wait for it."

Unprotected, but lubed up and stiff as a rock, I feel his slab enter my middle. Approximately five inches enter without pain. Rocco breathes heavily above me and presses two more inches into my hole. The length rests inside me, unmoving, harboring in my crack.

My world rocks beneath him. I'm dizzy and in a state of euphoria. Life around me begins to spin in a haphazard and out-of-control way. Oxygen is lost, and I try to whisper his name, but can't. I try to tell him to shove his cock in deeper, but can't.

Speedily he pulls his shaft out of me. Quickly he shoves his rod back inside me; breaking me open with all of his hearty inches. Rocco begins to glide in and out of me, riding my crevice. Sweat builds on his chest and shoulders with the shifting movement. He smiles down at me and chants, "Take it all. You want it all."

The mind-reader holds my legs apart. His thumping becomes extreme and intoxicating. I can't move under him, taking in his inflated beef. Rocco is a maniac above me, using my ass in a gratifying manner.

"Jerk me off," I instruct. "Use some slow strokes."

Again, he is a good listener. While continuing to hump my ditch with his massive cock, he wraps his right hand around my firm stick and begins to stroke it up and down in a slow rhythm.

Everything about the moment is enlightening. His combined movements are systematically performed with top-notch expertise. His hips and right hand work together, methodically. He is a master at his motion, porn star material – what every man should long for when in the company of another man.

I whimper, feeling tears at the corners of my eyes. The pain is mesmerizing, blissful action that I want to last all night long. Rocco delights me to no end, working both my ass and shaft to the same beat, prosaically and emphatically, increasing both our sexual hungers.

A warning surfaces from my mouth, "I'm going to blow."

"Go for it, Derek … I want to watch you come."

Without a single breath of oxygen, I shoot juice onto my chest, and continue to hump his hand. Jizm spirals out of my cock and decorates my skin. Splotches of the gunk layers my abs and warms my flesh.

While still inside me, overly flexible, Rocco licks the spew up, consuming every drop from my chest. Once the treat is gone, he places his lips against my own and shares a compromised kiss. I taste his salvia and my bittersweet ooze on his mouth. I taste salt and sweat and …

He humps me harder, pushing into my bottom with speed. His unprotected cock jams itself into my bottom, pulls out, and pushes in again. He builds up a continuous rhythm that I ride with pleasure, delighted by his strident moves.

Rocco pulls away from my mouth and confesses, "I can't hold it in any longer. I'm going to burst."

"Do it," I whisper, pleased with his confession.

After three consecutive bolts of his pelvic bone meeting my ass, Rocco pulls out of me and begins to stroke his tool. His breathing increases in a wild manner. He huffs and puffs, ready to blow his load. He strokes his beef in a to and fro manner, quickly, rambunctiously, without stopping. He grits his teeth, losing breath, and heaves forward.

As expected, a spray of his white goo erupts from his stick. The liquid glistens my torso, forming tiny puddles, sticking to my skin.

Rocco relaxes above me, spew still shooting out of his spike. The guy is an endless vat of glue, decorating my skin. More sap clings to my shoulders and nipples. Some of it lands on my chin. The stuff washes me down like a hose, drowning my flesh.

The mobster is one steamy bad boy. Still hungry for our passion, he falls over my skin with his open mouth and laps up his squirt. Rocco tongues the pools away from my flat stomach and the dribbles on my pecs. He moans with deep satisfaction, licking his spent away, swallowing it down the back of his throat. Slowly, he pulls off and away from me, and whispers, "I love your skin and can't get enough of it." More laps remove spew from my flesh. His tour is long and tedious, but completely enjoyable. Again and again, he strokes my body with his tongue, cleaning it like a good boy, pleasuring us both.

Spent and sweaty, sitting under him in the Adirondack chair, we cuddle together in a comfortable twosome. The Florida breeze teases our flesh. A full moon stares at our closeness.

Rocco strokes my hair, kissing my neck. Eventually he pulls away and whispers, "Tomorrow's the meeting with Mr. Lusick, Felicia's executor."

"I'm a little nervous."

"There's no need to be nervous. I'm going to be right at your side."

"You promise?"

"I promise."

I cling to him, glad to be back in his arms again after everything we've been through. I say while smiling in the slivers of blue-white moonlight, "I wouldn't have it any other way."

The following afternoon, Penny, a brunette secretary with fake boobies, directs Rocco and me into Mr. Renaldo Lusick's office. Penny asks if we would like a coffee, which both of us decline. Before leaving, she informs, "Mr. Lusick will be with you in a moment."

Rocco's personal lawyer, Tanner Blue, is running late. I've hired him to work for me today. Tanner is stuck in traffic due to a fender bender on Bayside Road, making his way to Lusick's office.

The office is grey steel with white accents. Burgundy chairs line a ten-foot conference table. Steve Walker prints hang on the walls, which I admire with satisfaction and appeal.

Mr. Lusick sits across from Rocco and me. He shuffles through pages in a thick file. The lawyer is a handsome man at forty-seven: rich brown hair and matching eyes, thin jaw, narrow lips, capped teeth, one dimple on his left cheek, corded neck. He scrawls something down on one of the shuffled pages, lifts his head, shares a brief smile, and cordially says to me, "You obviously like Walker's work."

"I do. It's romantic and intense with life."

"I like that one," Mr. Lusick says, pointing the tip of his Mel Blanc pen at *Towel Boys*. "Walker did it in 2003."

The painting is rich in blues and whites. Two older boys dry off with beach towels. One sits on an expansive cement banister while the other bends over.

"Do you know Steve Walker?" I ask, naïve and simple.

"Personally? Yes ... Intimately? I'm afraid not."

"That one is my favorite." I point to a bare-chested beefcake lying on white sheets with one arm draped over his eyes and forehead.

"*Cloud Nine*. A very nice choice. Walker painted that in 2004."

Rocco points to *Wrestling* and says, "That one's not so bad." The painting showcases two naked and athletic men wrestling on what looks like brown marble tile. One man is tucked in a firm headlock and sports a bulbous ass. The other exemplifies a well-proportioned back and shoulders with a head full of coal-black hair.

"Again," Mr. Lusick proclaims, "a very fine choice. I believe Walker painted that one in 2003, from his second series."

"I love it," Rocco confesses. "It looks like Derek and me."

How uncanny a statement. But Rocco's right. The painting resembles our masculine physiques at play. How observant on his part.

The door to Mr. Lusick's office abruptly opens, startling the three of us. Tanner Blue hurries into the room with mismanaged blond hair, an askew tie, huffing for breath. He looks as if he has just been through one of Florida's worst hurricanes.

Tanner sits to my right. He opens a Kenneth Cole case, pulls out a wad of paper, and retrieves a Waterman pen from the inside pocket of his blazer. He apologizes for being late, shares a dimpled smile, and adds, "Mr. Lusick, you didn't wake me this morning, and you left the coffee pot on again."

"Mr. Blue, we'll discuss those issues in private."

Blue winks at Lusick, which makes me smile. I swear Mr. Lusick blows Tanner a kiss. Who knew they were lovers, boyfriends, something?

Mr. Lusick clears his throat and retrieves a cocoa-colored pair of spring hinge reading glasses from atop his pile of jumbled papers. He says, "As you know, Mr. Reed, I represent the deceased Felicia Horodowski."

"I do," I respond, feeling nervous.

Rocco is a saint at my side. He gently touches my leg under the table to calm me down.

"And Mr. Blue is representing you today?"

"Yes, sir." I nod my head.

Mr. Lusick shuffles through more of his papers. He scribbles something down on one of the sheets, lifts his head, and inquires, "I understand you were very close friends with Felicia."

"I was. We spent a lot of time together. I helped her on a daily basis with her cancer issues. She was like an aunt to me, and I miss her dearly."

"And you're very much aware that she wasn't at all close to her family, correct?"

"I do. Felicia kept to herself, and the movies. Her family was Hollywood, a few lesbian lovers in her day, and then me."

Mr. Lusick begins to read Felicia's four-page will. Verbatim, he mentions Felicia as a resident of Flamingo Cove, Florida. What follows is her Last Will and Testament. Minor debt is mentioned that her estate will pay off. All expenses of administration and taxes will be paid for from her estate. Blah, blah, blah. Mr. Lusick talks for the next twenty minutes, boring me to death.

He stops speaking and studies one of the Steve Walker paintings behind me. After a short pause, he turns his attention back to me, clears his throat, and reads, "I give and bequeath twenty million dollars of my estate to Mr. Derek Alexander Reed."

Rocco digs nails into my leg, overzealous by Mr. Lusick's news.

Tanner Blue whispers, "Dear Jesus, that's a lot of money."

I'm numb all over, confused and derailed. What did Mr. Lusick just say? What's going on? Is this some kind of joke?

Rocco pats me on my back, and whispers into my ear, "Twenty mill isn't so shabby, is it? Congratulations."

"I have a few pages for you to sign, Mr. Reed. I'm sure Mr. Blue would like to review the information first, of course. Following your signatures, our meeting is adjourned." Mr. Lusick pushes forms across the desk, in front of me, ready to discuss.

I feel Rocco's arm around my back. One of his palms squeezes my shoulder. He leans into me and gives me a kiss on my cheek.

Tears bubble up in my eyes; I can't hold them back anymore. I ask Mr. Lusick, "Did you say twenty million dollars?"

"Minus taxes, of course," he responds.

I tremble, attempting to hold my composure together. I begin to cry because Felicia loved me and was willing to give me her entire fortune because of our friendship. The tears aren't about the twenty million, though – honestly. They are a reflection of love for the woman, and her love for me, only.

Rocco whispers into my right ear, "Are you okay?"

I wipe tears away from my eyes and cheeks, and whisper, "Thank you, Felicia. I love you, too." I place my head on Rocco's shoulder for support, completely in love with him, and continue to cry, happy as I'll ever be.

Later this night, following our celebratory dinner at a Greek restaurant called Apollo's, Rocco strips out of his clothes in the foyer at the beach house and requests, "I'll give you a blowjob for a million dollars. What do you think?"

"I don't think so." I kiss his neck, caressing the firming goods between his athletic legs. His shaft immediately swells, coming to attention and wanting to play.

"I'm not worth it?"

"I didn't say that."

We share a long kiss, which is blissful and feels right. Once the kiss ends, I pull away and add, "Rocco, if you really want to know, I'll pay you the twenty million for your heart."

"That's awful bloody," he jokes.

"I mean your emotions. Your love for me." I pull away and walk toward the stairs leading to his bedroom.

"You already have that," he whispers, stopping me from my escape. He leashes his arms around me, pulls me toward his stiff cock, nuzzles his lips against my neck, and chants, "How about the blowjob now?"

I spin around and watch him drop to his knees, next to the stairs, obviously delighted to have me back in his life and inside his mouth.

Chapter 25 – Three Months Later

December is a bit cold and windy. Of course there is no snow. Christmas is just two weeks away, and I bubble with joy and excitement. Rocco is going to love his holiday gift from me: a Beretta 967 Inox semiautomatic pistol with a Hogue rubber grip and a stainless finish.

I wonder what he intends to give me.

A short period of time has passed since the events on Paragon Island. Things have indisputably changed in our lives, though.

Fisk has a limp in his right leg; an impairment that will always be there, thanks to that fuckhead Mr. Drago on Paragon Island. To my surprise, he obtains a scholarship to Flamingo Cove College in pharmaceuticals. He starts classes in January. When he graduates, he'll still be dealing drugs, but legally this time.

I've given him a few hundred grand from my massive fortune to buy a bungalow on the beach, pay for his college expenses, and have a comfortable life. Something tells me Felicia would want it this way, to find some love in my heart, and not to be greedy with the cash. Keeping the twenty million all for myself seems absurd, but spreading a portion of it around feels right.

Fisk and I turn out to be best buds. We see each other every few days, hang on the beach, drink a few margaritas, and use each other as therapists to gain a little normalcy in our heads regarding our very brutal days in cages on Paragon Island.

Regularly, he admits that Walter is his true love, falling head over heels for the writer. He claims he likes to take care of the older queen, incapable of enjoying any other man's skin. Fisk is excited about his future, getting on his feet for good, and happy to be alive.

Walter Landing and Fisk are a permanent couple now. They sometimes fly to Florence, Italy because Walter is currently working on a new mystery series starring his Italian sleuth, Fredrico Manbolli. The two are inseparable, completely in love.

Fisk says the duo will be hitched in the spring. "You'd better be planning to attend another commitment ceremony."

223

"I wouldn't dream of missing it," I confess during an evening of chick flicks, popcorn and appletinis with him.

"Even after the last one you attended?" He drums up a memory of my abduction at Gulf Bay Stables.

"I try not to think about it."

"Good boy," he says, and we toast to a happy future for the lovebirds, and many more evenings watching chick flicks together.

Quinn and I are no longer roommates. Shortly after my return from Paragon Island, he left Flamingo Cove and moved to Daytona. He lives with his Aunt Marsha along the Atlantic, and works in a gym called Spanky's. Quinn is not currently dating anyone in particular and attempts to save up enough money to open his own gym.

Sometimes he'll send me an e-mail regarding his life. The e-mails are short and vague, simple notes just to keep in touch: working on my tan; staying fit; eating more vegetables; lifting more these days; fucking around with a different guy every night.

One e-mail stands apart from the rest: Quinn sees Tank in the Barret Bay Penitentiary, paying him conjugal visits. Honestly, this is no surprise to me. Quinn has always liked the bad boys, including convicts. He writes that he has a soft spot for Tank and always will. Quinn raves about Tank and his muscles. He mentions that once Tank gets out of jail, he'll help him out, and Tank can work at his future gym as a trainer. And maybe the two will become monogamous lovers in the near future, eventually marrying.

Tank is in the clink for twenty years for attempted murder. He sends a few letters to me, which I never read and throw away. Truth is I really want nothing to do with him after how he treated me. Sometimes you have enemies, and I feel that Tank is one in my life. Bottom line: My life is better without Tank running amuck in it.

Hurricane Brass now models for Undergear. Following his gunshot wound on Turtle Island, retiring from Mr. Malonni's regime, Hurricane has put aside his bodyguard days and is now into his looks. Glossy pages sport an arrangement of Lycra trunks, Jocko underwear, and Colt tees on his skin-tight body.

Hurricane accidentally bumps into me at Pallyo, spilling his festive Sea Breeze. Surprised to see me, he gives me a quick peck on my right cheek, and lathers me in compliments: you look great; I love your hair; I can tell you're working out more.

I'm introduced to his lover, Cole, who looks exactly like Dean Flynn, the XXX star. The three of us chat about Hurricane's success with Undergear, his future ambitions in modeling, and his retirement from bodyguarding.

As a local queer band called Cherub Boy sings live, Hurricane admits, "I'm the worst bodyguard in history. The Baskin guys took you right from under my nose."

I laugh and say, "I have to agree with that."

"Those days are over," he confesses.

"Thank Jesus." I take a chug of my beer, swallow, and ask, "How's the leg?"

Hurricane shows it off. It's perfectly muscular and flawless. "Plastic surgery does wonders. Cole's brother fixed me up. He is one of the best in Miami." Hurricane and Cole excuse themselves from my presence and end up on the dance floor, rocking to the live band.

Farrell MacCormick, Rocco's houseboy, adopts Princess Scampers. The two are a magical couple, finding bliss together. Farrell moves to Tampa Bay to be a houseboy for a new gentleman this time; a wealthy Russian named Vladimir Posnozvik. I give them three months to fall in love and become lost in each other. Farrell will change his name to Zoya, and no doubt carry out some awesome drag at all the gay clubs.

I learn through the grapevine that Miguel Sanchez, Rocco's head employee at Castlegate, turns a leaf of success. The Peruvian god has his own fitness show airing on Q in the spring, a book called *Latino Fitness*, and occasionally will make an appearance on *Ellen* as her fitness advisor.

Miguel, retired from Castlegate, sometimes visits the estate for a twilight dinner or weekend party. He stays in touch with Rocco, forever humble regarding the relationships with his previous employer and coworkers.

Tiempo and Carlos, the groundskeepers at Castlegate, gain my financial support to produce a line of male-on-male hygiene products, which include organic soaps, hair products, tempting lubes and herbal aphrodisiacs. Reed Incorporated will be a silent partner in their new enterprise. The products will be released next summer, sparking a mass-advertising campaign in *Out*, *Instinct*, and other various queer vehicles of support.

Tiempo already talks about creating gay and lesbian greeting cards, and beefcake calendars for the following year. Carlos wants to design leather handbags and belts for men. Reed Incorporated will be very busy in the years to come with their entrepreneuring minds.

After the incident on Paragon Island, the Baskin Fish Company was taken over by the DEA. Mr. Drago's cohorts, Luciano "Weasel" Spada and Tomas "Thumbs" Rineholt, were taken into custody, hearings pending. Following their arrests, the Baskin Fish Company in Flamingo Cove coincidentally burned to the ground – arson suspected.

Tank was mentioned in the local papers as one of the top affiliates of the Baskin bad boys; no surprise there. Rocco Malonni was pictured as a hero. Hurricane Brass was labeled the worst bodyguard in history. And Fisk and I were survivors, celebrities in Flamingo Cove for about fifteen minutes.

On a balmy evening in downtown Flamingo Cove while I'm Christmas shopping for Rocco, Mr. Chaz pushes me against the wall inside Qio's, a fabulous ultra-modern men's store specializing in underwear. Our faces almost collide. He smiles and says, "We meet again."

I hold a teal-colored Diesel thong in my right hand, intensely breathing. I think Mr. Chaz is going to kiss me, but he doesn't. Being polite, I chant, "I've seen your two movies. They're quite hot."

He pulls away from me, rubbing my chin with two fingers. "I fuck like a wild man. I was meant to do porn."

"You take a dildo like a master."

He laughs. "All fourteen inches of it. What did you think of my buddies?"

"The Manno twins are delicious. You eat them up like candy."

"I have three more movies to do in January: one with the twins; a spanking scene with Adrian Bradshaw of Pacific Sun; and a daddy scene with Francois Sagat. My schedule is completely full."

"I can't wait to watch them. Rocco and I will make a date out of it. I'm glad Worth Lewis is taking care of you."

"I'm a fucking star because of him. We're working on a mass-produced dildo right now. Hopefully it will be out by next Christmas. I hope you buy one."

"I just may do that."

Mr. Chaz pulls the teal-colored thong out of my right hand and asks, "For Rocco?"

I nod my head with pleasure and respond, "The love of my life."

"A very good choice, even if he's in the mob."

"Rocco is exceptionally nice to me with his heart. It's serious."

"That's good to know. Men need men, if you know what I mean."

"I do," I respond, taking the thong back from him.

Corey Chaz steps up to his father and tells him, "Dad, we have to go." He vanishes as quickly as he arrives at our twosome.

Mr. Chaz leans into my face, breathes me in, and asks, "Can I kiss you for old time's sake?"

"I can't do that," I whisper, shaking my head. "Our game is finally over."

"Too bad," he whispers. "I would have liked to kiss you."

I smile, dab his chin with a fingertip, and think: I have Rocco, happy with life, no more games.

Antonio "Boss" Malonni has not abducted me since the last fiasco at Gulf Bay Stables. Following my return to Flamingo Cove, he politely fetches me by limo and has one of his men drive me to his private plane where I am flown to his mansion in Miami.

We share dinner on the patio, next to the Atlantic. A soothing wind blows against my face and shoulders. The night is temperate and refreshing.

Over fillet of swordfish, curried rice and white wine, Boss informs, "You will become my son-in-law."

"Something tells me you're guaranteeing this." I eat a morsel of fish and take a sip of the wine. The dinner is excellent. The wine is even better. It's top-of-the-line service; the best of the best.

"People do not tell me no."

"I never assumed they did, Mr. Malonni."

Mika, the servant from Turtle Island, enters the patio area from the house. He removes dirty and used dishes from the table. Mr. Malonni bows his head and says, "Thank you, Mika." The servant vanishes, leaving the two of us alone again.

"Thank you for having me this evening," I share, sipping my glass of wine. "It's a shame Rocco couldn't make it."

"Business is business. Rocco will be available for many dinners in the future." Boss raises his drink and toasts, "To your promising marriage with my son. May both of you be very happy together."

"But only if he asks me to marry him."

Boss smiles and says, "He will. Remember, Rocco's my difficult child. Give him time."

We clink glasses together, consuming the wine. Following the toast, we share some light conversation, eat and drink.

Once our meals are complete, Rocco's father lights a Cuban cigar, blowing smoke upwards, away from me. He politely asks, "Would you care for more wine, Derek?"

I shouldn't, but accept. "Thank you," I whisper, on my best behavior.

He refills our glasses, sits back in his whicker chair, and admits, "I was very impressed with your survival skills on Paragon Island. I understand you were strong-willed and fought like the devil."

"Rocco saved Fisk and me. I can only take some of the credit."

He waves his cigar in my direction and supplies, "Never downplay yourself. Be bold and go for the gusto. Trust me you were a hero in your own way."

"Honestly," I whisper, "I'm just glad to be alive. I can think of better things to do with my life instead of being in a cage on Paragon Island."

Boss chortles at my statement, which causes me to feel uncomfortable. "Which brings me to my next question, Derek. Besides your current financial endeavors, what do you see in your life ... let's say in the next month or two?"

"I haven't thought about it," I gush. "Life has been so crazy lately. I think a vacation is in order."

"Have you ever visited South Africa?" Boss crosses one leg over the other, inhales on his cigar, exhales and blows a puff of smoke to his right.

"I haven't."

"And what do you know about diamonds?"

I shake my head. "Nothing really."

He reaches for a covered tray to his right, finds the lid, lifts it with his free hand, exposes a marquis diamond the size of the Liberty Bell, and a .9mm pistol.

Jesus, Mary and Jo Jo. What's going on? I quickly consume my entire glass of wine, impolitely wipe the back of my right palm across my mouth, and ask in the most serious tone, "Mr. Malonni, what are your plans for me?"

"Do you miss Rocco?"

"I do."

He pulls out two airline tickets from his white jacket and places them next to the diamond and .9mm. "Rocco needs a companion in Springbok, South Africa. The flight leaves in three days. He has all the details you need for this adventure. I do hope you join him."

"Again, you don't take no for an answer, do you?" I whisper.

"Of course not, Mr. Reed." He passes the .9mm and airline tickets to me. Once they're in my possession, agreeing to his mobster gig, he suggests, "We should have another toast to a safe trip with positive results."

"And to family," I add.

"Yes," he beams a smile, sharing a lift in his voice, "to family."

Spent, cuddled in Rocco's bare arms, breathing in his skin, I whisper, "I love you, Rocco. You're the man of my dreams."

"I knew that since the drive-by on Pilsner. I could see it in your eyes."

"What else did you see?"

"That you liked my cock," he laughs, toying with one my nipples.

"You're probably right about that. And by the way ... that was amazing sex we just shared."

"We should thank Tiempo and Carlos for breaking in this bed," Rocco whispers.

Together we lie in the underground bedroom at Castlegate. Candlelight illuminates our naked bodies.

"Your father's sending us to South Africa to buy diamonds."

Rocco laughs. "Is that what he told you?"

I nuzzle my nose against his firm chest, consume his sticky sweet aroma, and reply, "I was reading into it. What kind of mission will we be on?"

"We're stealing four million dollars worth of diamonds back."

He cradles me in his hulking arms. My lips press against one of his nipples. I think about licking his firm pec again, just for kicks, but decide two doses of hot sex in the bedroom are enough for one evening. Instead, I whisper, "He left that minor detail out."

"Don't worry. I'll take care of you while we're over there."

"You always take care of me. What would I do without you?"

"Love me," he whispers. "That's all I want from you."

"I think I can manage that."

Thunder rolls over the outside bedroom, welcoming a Florida storm. Wind slowly spirals down the rock staircase and teases the candlelight. The breeze caresses our bodies like a fine blanket.

"It's a dangerous mission in Springbok," Rocco murmurs. "Are you sure you want to go?"

"And be without you? I wouldn't dream of it."

Rain blows down from the heavens and thunder shakes the confines. Rocco presses me against his skin, kisses my neck with heavy passion, and asks, "Shall we go for round three?"

"Three?" I question, stunned and excited, already getting hard between my legs. "That's a lot of sex."

"Let's do it."

"Because you love me," I chant.

"Yes. Because I love you, Derek Reed," he whispers, rolls himself on top of me, buries his face against my chest, kisses one of my pecs, licks a firm nipple, and takes the skin tour of my body, again.

About the Author

R. W. Clinger lives between Pittsburgh and Tarpon Springs, Florida. He enjoys hockey, photography and John Patrick stories. His work has appeared in various STARbooks Press anthologies. The novels *The Pool Boy* and *Soft on the Eyes* were also published by STARbooks Press. R.W. is currently at work on a sequel to *The Skin Tour*.

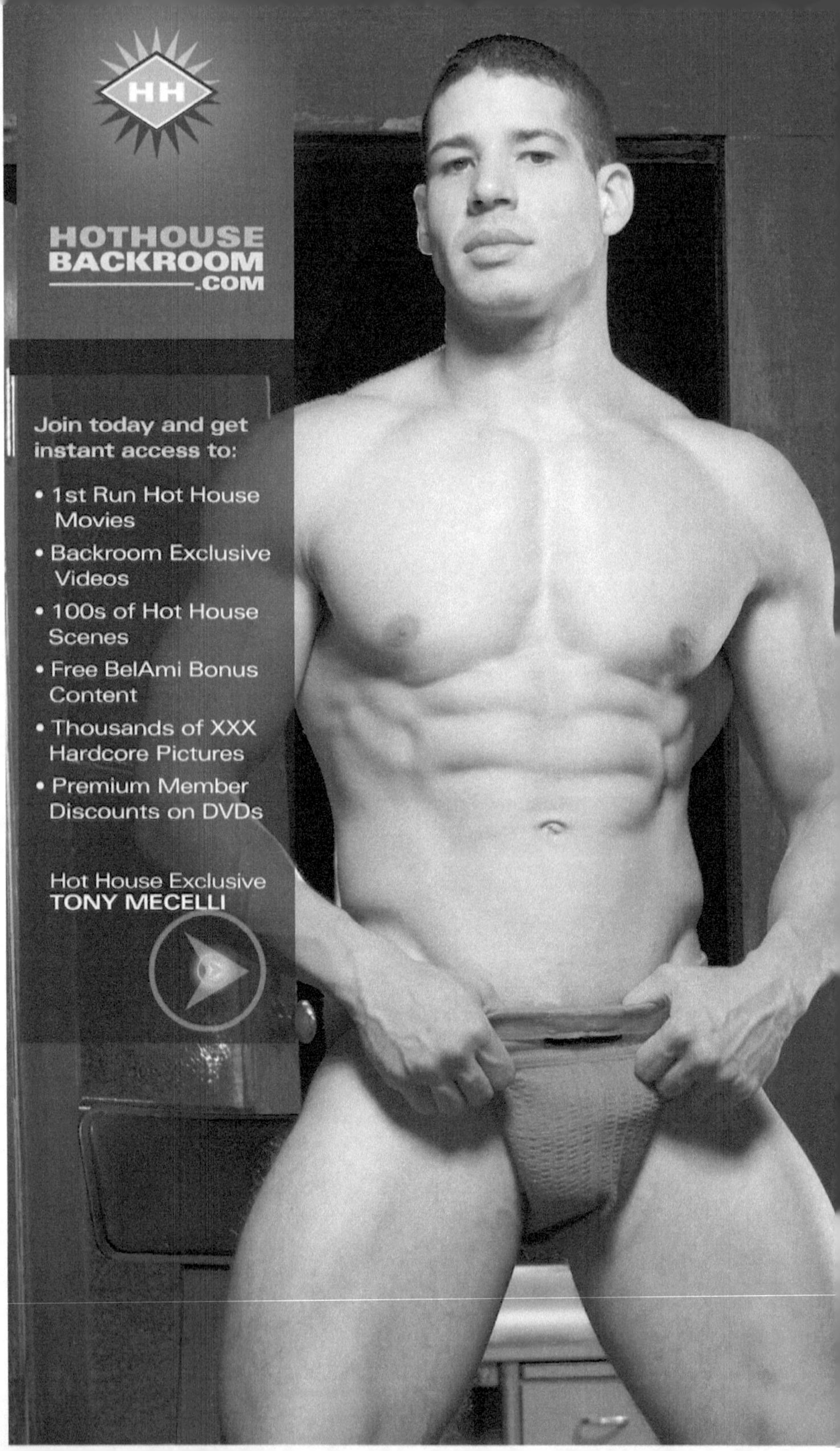
HH
HOTHOUSE
BACKROOM
.COM
Join today and get instant access to:
• 1st Run Hot House Movies
• Backroom Exclusive Videos
• 100s of Hot House Scenes
• Free BelAmi Bonus Content
• Thousands of XXX Hardcore Pictures
• Premium Member Discounts on DVDs
Hot House Exclusive
TONY MECELLI

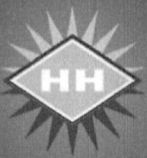